SHATTERED PROMISES

TAINTED LOVE SERIES - BOOK THREE

MONTANA FYRE

SHATTERED PROMISES

A DARK SECOND CHANCE ROMANCE

TAINTED LOVE
BOOK THREE

MONTANA FYRE

ISBN (Paperback) : 978-0-6459052-5-0

First edition, 2024.

Front cover and book design by Montana Fyre.

Edited by My Brother's Editor.

www.montanafyre.com

Acknowledgments

There was a long time that I didn't think this book would ever see the light of day.

Mia's story is dark and it was incredibly hard to write. Every piece of her trauma that I uncovered, made it more difficult for me to see how she could overcome it. And so I stepped away. I took some time, finished two other books, and then one day I decided to read back on what I'd written. At that point, 60% of the book was finished, and the more I read, the more I realized I was finally in the right place to finish their story.

So without further ado, I have some people to thank for getting us here, and for helping Ace and Mia finally have their story told.

To my wonderful husband, my rock, my safe place, the reason I can do what I do. There's no way Montana Fyre would exist without your continued love and support.

To Ellie, my editor, who has edited all my book babies and is still fixing all my Australianisms after all this time.

To Kiki, Megan and Anna at The Next Step PR, for always being my sounding board and rearranging my schedule every time I change my mind about what I'm writing next.

To my friends and family for putting up with my 3-5 business day response time because I'm deep in the cave with my imaginary friends…I mean characters.

And to my readers, the people that allow me to do what I love all day everyday. I'm endlessly grateful for everything you've helped me accomplish, and for loving the characters that live rent free in my mind.

I couldn't do it without you all x

TRIGGER WARNING

This book contains dark themes that some readers may find distressing, including, but not limited to:

Violence

Elements of BDSM

Kidnapping

Degradation

Domestic Violence

Sexual Assault

Human Trafficking

Rape

Torture

Child Abuse

PTSD

Disordered Eating

Dub Con / Non Con

Thoughts of Suicide

I urge you to please consider your mental health before continuing with this book. Mia's story is one of survival and strength, but it should not come at the expense of your own mental health.

For survivors and those who help them heal

I won't let pain turn my heart into something ugly. I will show you that surviving can be beautiful.

- CHRISTY ANN MARTINE

PROLOGUE

EIGHT YEARS AGO

Today is the day.

It feels like I've been waiting for this day my entire life, when in reality it's only been two years.

Two years of constant worry.

Two years of surveillance to make sure she's safe.

Two years of protecting her from afar wherever possible.

But today is the day we rescue her from the hellhole we once called home.

Tommy itches restlessly beside me, his blade dragging up and down his arm in rough strokes, but not hard enough to draw blood. I can always tell my foster brother's level of agitation by whether there's crimson dripping over the scars and tattoos that litter his arms.

Neither of us has been the same since the first time we stepped foot inside The Factory. Our lives up until that point were horrific on their own, but seeing so much evil at a young age is enough to destroy the humanity in just about anyone.

Tommy always protected me where he could. Took punishments that were meant for me, cut me off before I could say something I would come to regret, and he got me out when I was sure I would die in that house. Everything in the run-down bungalow was rotting, including the people inside it, and all I ever wanted was to escape it from the moment I stepped through the front door when I was seven.

But we couldn't take her with us when we got out. She was too young. Too vulnerable to live through what we were going to have to in order to build a life for ourselves. So we left. We fled in the middle of the night with the promise that we would come back for her, and that's exactly what we're doing.

Despite Mia only being a year younger than me, she's always been fragile. I guess that's what happens when you lose both of your parents in a car accident at the age of six and are thrust into the most unimaginable hell possible. She went from a loving family with people who cherished her to a house where she was regularly starved for not tucking her sheets in properly when she made her bed.

We were just a few of the ten children they had shoved in the three-bedroom house, only fostering us in order to collect the check each month, but they didn't like how close the three of us were, especially Mia and me. They did everything they could to separate us, to keep us away from one another, but we always found a way, and spending the last two years away from her has been like living without one of my limbs.

Mia wouldn't have survived on the streets, and even though being away from her has made it hard to breathe, I knew this was our best bet. Run. Get our lives together. Find somewhere to live. Rescue her. It just took longer than I would have liked.

Tommy started working for a Mafia family, and I became the youngest dark web hacker in the market at the age of fifteen. Not that anyone knew how old I was, and Tommy has stayed away to make sure of that.

The Saint James family has treated him right, better than either of us deserve after the things we allowed to happen at The Factory, but rationally I know we couldn't have stopped it even if we wanted to. The first time we stepped into the cesspool, I was nine and Tommy was twelve. Neither of us had any power to shut it down, and after we escaped, they moved the operation. It was too risky for them to keep training girls in that building because we knew everything, and even though we were young, they knew better than to underestimate us.

We became ghosts they knew were out there, but they couldn't find us, and that's exactly the way we wanted it to be, especially when it came time to rescue Mia.

My eyes flicker over the dark street again. We're a block away from our last foster house, and even this proximity has unease pooling in my gut. The memories that flood me each time we're nearby are enough to make nausea roll over me, but I can't let it get the best of me right now. We have one purpose, and she's all that matters.

"Something doesn't feel right," Tommy murmurs, his blade pressing harder into his flesh until his skin parts and blood pools around the knife.

"What do you mean?" I ask. He's always had a keen eye for this kind of thing, and it's the exact reason he's found such a solid role within the organization over at Frost Industries, despite his age. If he says something's off, I'm more than happy to believe him because he's almost always right.

He looks over his shoulder at the street behind us before returning his gaze to the front of the car. It's a beat-up old shitbox we picked up especially for tonight, but it will do the job. Even if the windows are kind of blurry and the faint stench of body odor lingers on the fabric. "This street. It's never this quiet at this time of night."

I look around at the sidewalk and the houses surrounding us and frown. He's right. It's just before midnight, which is usually the opportune time for the filth of Chicago to crawl out from the holes they live in during the day. This particular street has three drug dealers and a pawn shop, so this is basically rush hour. Except for tonight. Tonight it's dead, and now that I think about it, I don't think I've seen one person in the two hours we've been parked here.

In all the years I lived with the Bridge family, I never saw this street this quiet, and a new wave of unease crashes over me.

Do they know? I don't know how they could. Mia knew tonight was the night. It hasn't always been easy to get a message to her, but because we're close in age, I've been able to get into her school a few times to give her messages and reassure her that we are coming for her. But there's no possible way they could know. Not unless she told them.

I look back at Tommy, his face is completely passive, but the crimson tracks down his arms are the evidence of how he's really feeling. "What do we do?"

"We're going in now." He shoves the door open before he can finish his sentence.

I follow his lead, and the heavy door groans at the sudden movement. This car really is a piece of shit.

Tommy draws his gun from his waistband and trains it ahead of us as I cover our backs. The night air is crisp and quiet. Too fucking quiet.

Every step toward the house we spent too many years in, and saw too many horrors, has dread washing over me in heavy waves, and nausea pools in my belly.

What if we're too late? What if she's gone? The thoughts are anything but rational. There's no possible way they could know we've chosen an unsuspecting Tuesday night to rescue Mia from a life she never deserved.

Tires squealing behind us drag our attention away from the street ahead, and I swear everything happens in slow motion.

A van and two SUVs speed toward us, and before I can think to move, Tommy tackles me to the ground, his large body landing on top of me and knocking the air from my lungs.

A moment later, gunfire fills the air. "We need to get out of here," Tommy barks.

"We can't. We can't leave Mia." I'm frantic. Panic eats its way through my body until dragging in a breath feels impossible. We can't leave her here anymore. It's already been too long. She's been unprotected for so long that it keeps me up at night to think about the horrors she must have endured since we left her.

"We'll come back for her," he promises. "But we're no good to her if we're dead."

Before I can respond, Tommy drags me back toward the car, using the old hunk of junk as a shield from the bullets, but I realize too late only the SUVs have stopped. The van kept driving.

It could just be that they didn't need any more firepower against two teenage kids. I rationalize with myself, but even as the thought crosses my mind, I know it's wishful thinking.

This feels too planned. Too coincidental.

"In the car," Tommy barks, and I comply immediately. I tug the door open and throw myself across the seats, hissing out a breath when broken glass digs into my arms. Tommy gets in after me, quickly starting the engine and taking off without a second thought.

I riffle around in the backpack I left in the car, desperately looking for the burner phone I keep to communicate with Mia, identical to the one that she keeps hidden under one of the loose floorboards in her bedroom. My stomach drops when I see a voicemail from her, and even before her sweet voice fills the line, I realize it's too late.

"Ace," she sobs into the phone. "They know you're coming. I don't know how. I swear I didn't tell them. There's no way they could know, but they do." She chokes on her words, and my heart clenches for her. I've always hated seeing and hearing her cry, but right now I'm struggling to breathe. The line goes silent for a few seconds and then she's screaming, the sound slicing into me deeper than any knife ever could. "No, please no. Please don't take me. I don't want to go."

6

Every word cuts deeper, until her long wails are all that filter down the line.

"Shut up, you little whore," my foster father growls, and just the sound of his voice makes my skin crawl. "If you think you have something to cry about now, wait until you get where you're going."

"No!" she shouts. "I don't want to go. Please don't make me go."

A loud slap fills the line, and my stomach sinks. But it's her final cry that shatters my heart into a million pieces.

"Ace!" she screams, and then the line goes dead.

I failed her.

I promised I would get her out.

I promised I would never let them hurt her.

And I failed.

ONE

I wasn't always like this.

Once upon a time, I had dreams and motivations, things that pushed me through the hard days, thoughts of a future I knew I could have if I could just hold on a little longer.

But those dreams died a long time ago. They died with the girl that was stolen from her future, the innocent girl who never had a chance to grow into the woman she knew she could be.

I've been in survival mode for so long, I don't know what it means to be happy, to be complete, to be safe, because I can't see myself ever being anything other than broken. Not after the things I've seen and the things they've done to me.

I blink back tears at the thought, my stomach heavy with bile I refuse to let rise. Not while there are so many people around. Strangers.

Every stranger I've ever met has hurt me in some way. My foster parents. The people who bought me. Those who used me for entertainment and my body as if it weren't attached to a human being. Ace and Tommy when they promised they would keep me safe.

I curl further into myself, keeping my eyes low and my body as small as I can. I don't know these people, and at least one of them is linked to human trafficking, so I can't allow myself to breathe even if I have just been rescued from the most notorious crime family in the country. The Lombardi family will be pissed that Clara and I have been taken. Especially because Clara shot the two heirs to get us out safely. I doubt they're going to forget a thing like that.

I chance a look around the back of the van. Storm Saint James is driving. To escape, I had to climb over an eight-foot stone wall, and he was the one that caught me on the other side. The hands of men usually make my skin crawl, but he was gentle, and only touched me where absolutely necessary. His gray eyes were kind as he placed me down and walked me to stand beside the van.

Rayne Saint James is sitting in the passenger seat, and he's every bit as imposing as he looked in the newspaper articles I've seen. My second owner had a kind housekeeper who would occasionally bring me something to read, and sometimes that was something as simple as the paper. His hair and eyes are the same shade of black, and it's almost overwhelming to look at him, which is why when he helped me over the wall, I avoided his gaze at all costs.

Elijah Russo is the one I want to avoid like the plague, because on the off chance they're not already planning to sell me to the highest bidder, I'm not risking being a target of him or his family. His uncle Angelo used to come to The Factory with girls to sell, and they were always beat-up and broken before they even got through the doors. Elijah's green eyes have been mostly locked on his phone, but occasionally they flicker up to survey the van. His dirty blond hair is messy from running his hands through it so many times, and I wonder how long they've been looking for Clara. It must be nice to have people willing to drop everything to find you.

A pang of hurt fills my chest. The other two men in the van were meant to be that for me. They were meant to rescue me. In fact, they promised they would. They swore they wouldn't let me rot in that house. But they lied. Just like everyone else in my life.

Tommy holds Clara close. His messy, dark-blond hair is a little longer than it was when I knew him, but his blue eyes are shining with something akin to relief. The way his arms are wrapped around her, his face buried in her neck, it makes me long for that kind of connection. She's holding on just as tight, and if I were capable of feeling happiness, perhaps I would feel it for Clara. I've only known her for a short time, but the idea of having someone by my side in that house was enough to make me breathe easier as soon as we met. Her dark brown hair is still piled in a messy ponytail on the top of her head, and her deep-brown eyes are closed as she breathes Tommy in.

I have to admit, I never really thought he would settle down. Never seemed the type. But the way they cling to one another is proof of just how wrong I was.

And then there's Ace. The boy I loved before I understood what love was. The one who held me the first night I arrived at the foster home at six years old, having just lost both my parents, and even though he was only a year older than me, he seemed to know all I needed was for someone to hold me. He protected me from our foster parents, took the blame for things so I wouldn't be hurt or starved, helped me with my homework when I was struggling, and camped outside the girls' bedroom door to make sure none of our foster father's friends came in at night. He was always my hero. Until he didn't save me.

His blond hair is shorter than I remember, but still wild like the boy I knew. His green eyes still have butterflies fluttering around my belly like a silly schoolgirl, even if I'm far from that now. I'm nothing more than a broken shell of the girl he once knew.

The van comes to a stop, and my stomach drops. They're probably dropping me off somewhere, ready to sell me to the next sick fuck who has more money than God and can make my life a living hell. But when I glance out the front window, I notice a large jet. I've been on a few flights before, but I'm normally blindfolded and bound when I get on and off the plane. Apart from the trip to Disneyland my parents took me on when I was five, this is the first time I'll step onto one with my own two feet.

"Come on, sugar, let's get you on the plane and settled," Ace says softly. His voice is deeper than it was the last time we spoke, but there's something heartbreakingly familiar about the way he uses my nickname.

I squeeze my eyes shut as I force a memory down. The first time I asked why he called me that was from the very first day we met.

"Because as soon as I saw you, I knew you were the sweetest

girl I'd ever meet."

But I can't allow myself to enjoy hearing the term of endearment again, no matter how my heart flutters uncomfortably in my chest.

"Mia?" he presses, and I shake myself from my daze. I'm not used to people being so gentle with me. I've spent so many years being told what to do in harsh orders, and perhaps that's all I can respond to now.

"Sorry," I whisper and hesitantly link my hand with his. It's warm and gentle, despite how hard he looks now. The easy-going boy I remember is long gone, and in his place is a tattooed man with too many ghosts behind his eyes.

He gives me a weak smile and pulls me toward the back door before gently lifting me down to the tarmac. His hands on my hips send equal parts panic and comfort through me. The two are such contrasting feelings, but somehow they're warring inside me.

He guides me to the jet and helps me up the steps without hesitation, his hand pressed to the small of my back in a caring gesture, but all it does is remind me of all the men who have touched me since the last time we saw one another. The skin beneath his hand crawls at the thought, but I breathe through it just the same way I always do. Every time a man has touched me in the last eight years, I have compartmentalized it. I go to another place within my mind and stay there until it's over. My safe place.

I stop dead at the entrance to the cabin, my breath stuck in my throat. Holy shit, this thing is huge. Dark gray leather lines the seats that look both luxurious and comfortable as hell, and although I likely won't be able to close my eyes for long enough to sleep, exhaustion tugs at the edge of my consciousness.

Ace leads me to the middle of the cabin and into one of the oversized seats, quickly clipping the seat belt around my waist. His hard body is tense, but the tenderness he's showing me has butterflies erupting in my belly.

Tommy argues with the flight attendant about something, but I can't tear my eyes off Ace for long enough to work out what's going on.

I've found myself lost in his eyes a lot in the past, but it's never felt quite as meaningful as the connection I'm not brave enough to break.

It feels like coming home, and that terrifies me.

Shattered Promises

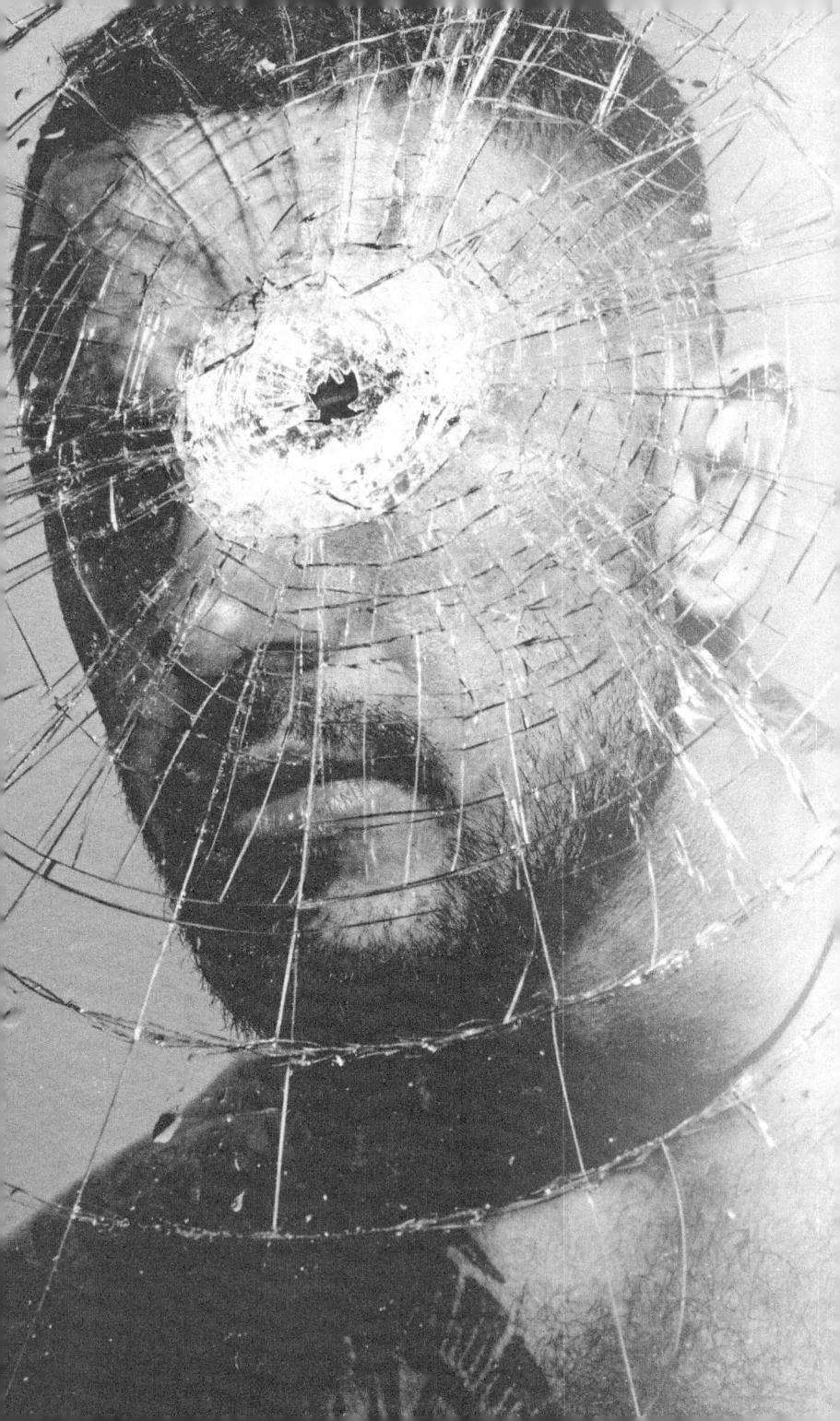

TWO

ACE

The ocean blue I'm staring into has always had the power to bring me to my knees. When we were kids, I had no idea what the feeling was, and it wasn't until I lost her that I realized.

Mia was my everything from the first time I saw her, and having her within my reach again is almost overwhelming. She looks so fucking broken. The spark I remember is gone, and even though her eyes are still the unreal color they always were, the life has been drained from them, and the emptiness left behind makes me want to tear my own heart from my chest and hand it to her as an offering, as penance for letting her go through whatever the fuck she's had to endure since she was taken from me.

Her blonde locks are long and unkempt, even in the messy ponytail on top of her head, it's clear it hasn't been cut in years.

And yet it's her body that has bile climbing up the back of my throat. Not because she's too fat or too thin, I don't give a shit what my woman looks like as long as she's healthy, but that right there is the problem. Mia is anything but healthy, and her body is the ultimate proof of that.

I noticed it when I had my hand pressed to her lower back, the way her spine protruded unnaturally into my palm. And then again as I wrapped the belt around her waist and my knuckles brushed over her hip bones that are far too prominent. I can't begin to fathom what she's been through in the last eight years, but at the very least she hasn't been fed well, and that's about to change, even if I have to force-feed her every bite of food for the rest of her fucking life.

"Do you need anything?" I rumble, the words burning my throat as I force them out past the bile. I've hated myself for every single second of the last eight years for letting them take her, but never more than I do right now. At least before we found her, I could surmise she was dead and no longer in pain or scared. But this is so much worse than death.

She shakes her head and diverts her gaze to the window. She's barely said a word since we found her and Clara, and every moment of silence makes me a little more uneasy.

I settle into my own seat across from her and clip the belt over my hips, never tearing my eyes off the woman in front of me. Although she's skin and bones, there are womanly curves that even starvation couldn't steal from her, and as fucked up as it is, I want to explore every fucking one.

Before she was taken, I had all these grand notions of whisking her away and giving her a life she rarely allowed herself to dream of growing up. I wanted to give her the puppy she always wanted but was never brave enough to ask for, the kids she never dared hope for, and the happiness she deserved more than any other human on this planet. But most of all, I dreamed of giving her love. An endless amount so she would never spend a day without a beautiful smile stretching across her full lips.

But I fear she doesn't know how to smile anymore, that they took it from her, and no matter how much I try, no matter how I burn the world down around her as penance for all she's been through, I may never see those rosy lips turn up at the corners and the blue of her eyes sparkle like the ocean on a sunny day.

I meet Storm's eyes across the aisle, his brows pinched together with concern. I don't particularly like the guy, but that may have more to do with the fact he stole the only family I have in the world while simultaneously taking out my business. But it's been years since he took down the key players of the Chicago dark web and left me without work. Thankfully, most of my clients are out of state and abroad, but still, I don't have to like the guy.

His eyes flicker from me to Mia and back again, like he's trying to figure out what's going on between us. We've barely said a word to one another. She's too frightened, and I'm afraid the anger beating in my veins will come out in the words I speak and scare her more. She's known too much fear in her life, and I refuse to add to that.

The pretty blonde flight attendant comes to tell us we'll be taking off in a few minutes, but I don't look away from Mia as she pulls her legs up underneath her. I wish I could hold her, and if I thought she would let me, I'd have her on my lap right now, but every time I touch her, she flinches.

The jet rolls forward a few minutes later, and I don't miss the way Mia curls in on herself further. Is she afraid of flying? Or is it something else that has her knuckles turning white around her knees? But she just watches out the window as the plane takes flight and we're finally on our way back to Chicago.

Mentally, I start a list of things I need to do when we get back. I need to find a new apartment because there's no way in hell I'm allowing Mia to live in the dank one I've been living in the last eight years. At one point, it almost became a punishment for myself. If she couldn't live a happy life, neither could I. If she couldn't have a nice home, neither could I. Everything I've done for the last eight years has been to punish myself for letting them take her, but now there's something that matters more than my own self-pity.

"I'm surprised she could fall asleep," Storm whispers, his words dragging me out of my mental to-do list. Mia's eyes are closed, her head resting against the window and her arms still wrapped tightly around her knees, but her breaths are steady and even, and the faintest snore fills the cabin. "She doesn't trust any of us."

"Would you?"

He shakes his head. "No."

I rub my hand over my face. None of us have slept in days. Not since Tommy called to tell us Clara had been taken. Everyone on this jet jumped into action to try to bring her home, but for me, it felt especially personal, like somehow bringing her home might extinguish some of the guilt that I could never bring Mia back.

"You should sleep," he says, dragging me back to the present.

I chuckle and shake my head. "*You* should sleep too."

He sighs and nods to his phone sitting on the tray beside him. "I have to get ahead of the Lombardi thing. We did just storm his compound, take the two women he thought would provide him grandchildren, and then shot his sons for good measure."

"Sounds bad when you put it like that."

He chokes on a laugh, but his cold gray eyes show all the exhaustion sitting heavy on his chest. He flickers his attention to Mia again before returning to me. "I know we haven't always seen eye to eye, but if she needs anything, let me know and I'll arrange it." I open my mouth to argue, but he lifts a hand and continues. "Last year, my fiancée was taken. It was only a few days, but the impact it had on her was challenging for the both of us. She didn't want to burden me with the scars the days left on her soul, and all I wanted to do was give her the world to apologize for allowing anyone to harm her. I obviously don't know your situation, but sometimes we're too close to look at what they need objectively. Rayne's wife is about to finish her master's in counseling, and she helped Ayvah get through those first few weeks when I was too deep in my own guilt to be objective."

I consider him for long seconds. Storm Saint James is not a man who ever allows himself to be vulnerable, so why is he telling me this? Why would he lay out what I can only assume was one of the worst times in his life to help me?

"We've saved a lot of girls from trafficking over the years, and we do what we can to set them up and help them move past what they've been through. You have no reason to trust me, but if you need anything, if Mia needs anything, just give me a call."

"Thank you. I'll keep it in mind."

He gives me a short nod before picking up his phone and turning his attention back to business.

I look back to Mia's sleeping form across from me, her eyes flutter as she dreams restlessly.

The wild part of my heart that has always beat for her settles. I have her. She's here. And nothing else matters, as long as she's safe.

Shattered Promises

THREE

MIA

The feel of unfamiliar hands on my body wakes me with a start, my heart beating so hard in my chest I'm sure it's going to leap out from behind my ribs. You'd think after eight years I would be able to accept strange men using my body for their own pleasure, not stopping to consider my comfort or consent, but if anything, it's getting worse.

"No, please," I cry out, my eyes flying open and taking in my unfamiliar surroundings. Where the hell am I?

"Mia, it's just me. It's Ace." His worried tone drags me back from the brink of panic, and I allow myself to relax just enough that my muscles no longer scream at me for release from the tension.

"We've just landed in Chicago."

I look around and find everyone standing from their seats, paying us no mind. Tommy and Clara are at the back of the jet, his arm wrapped tightly around her body as if letting go would be as painful as losing her in the first place. And not for the first time since they rescued us, I long for that. For connection. For love. For belonging. Things I haven't felt in years, so long I've almost forgotten what it feels like.

I meet Ace's worried gaze and let out the breath I didn't realize I was holding. I'm safe. For now. I must know that instinctively because, in the last eight years, sleep has always been restless and broken. Every sound wakes me because it could be someone coming to hurt me. In fact, it usually is. But I don't think Ace will hurt me like that, even if I'm not entirely sure what he's going to do with me now that we're back in Chicago.

He holds his hand out to me, and I find myself taking it without thought. His warm skin on mine makes my palm tingle as he helps me to my feet.

Clara appears beside him, her eyes full of relief and worry as she looks me over before turning her attention to Ace. "Would you like us to take her back to Tommy's apartment?" she asks softly.

"No," he snaps.

Her eyes widen, but she doesn't recoil at his harsh tone. "Ace, I've seen your apartment. Don't take this the wrong way, but it's not exactly suitable for house guests."

He turns his hard eyes on her, but she doesn't stand down. I wish I could be that strong, but after being beaten down and trodden on by men my entire life, I've been known to startle at my own shadow.

I quietly think to myself that it can't be worse than some of the places I've lived but decide to keep that piece of information to myself.

"I'm taking her to a hotel until I can find a suitable apartment for the two of us," he tells her matter of factly, like he spent the entire flight rearranging his life to accommodate me.

"You don't have to do that," I whisper, wrapping my arms around myself as if it will do anything to protect me. "I don't want to put you out at all. You can just drop me in the city and I'll work it out from there."

Every set of eyes in the cabin turns to me, and I can't help but drop my chin and hold myself closer. After so many years of the only attention I've been given being to harm me, I tend to shrink in on myself anytime anyone looks my way.

"Absolutely not," Ace snaps, and instinctively I flinch, taking a step back from him. I've been around too many angry men not to do everything I can to protect myself, even if my attempts have almost always been pointless.

"I don't want to inconvenience you," I say quietly, keeping my eyes on the carpet below my feet.

Ace sighs, and his heavy boots appear in my eyeline. A second later, a single finger presses to the underside of my chin and pulls my face up until I'm looking into his mesmerizing green eyes. "I didn't spend the last eight years looking for you, just so I could drop you into downtown Chicago and let you get away again."

My breath stutters in my chest, and although every muscle in my body screams at me to look away from the intensity in his eyes, I can't tear them away.

He was looking for me.

For how long?

Did The Factory know?

Is that why they always moved me in the middle of the night?

For fear that Ace would intercept the transfer.

"Come on, sugar." He tugs me forward, effectively cutting off any further questions or complaints. He wraps his arm around my waist, and the skin beneath his palm tingles with both comfort and panic. His touch is somehow familiar and foreign all at once, just the same way his gentleness is.

He leads me toward the exit behind Tommy and Clara, the former talking to the latter in hushed whispers. She doesn't seem impressed by whatever he's saying, but relents and takes his hand to let him help her down the steps to the tarmac.

The cold Chicago breeze whips around me, the sun sitting low on the horizon. I've been a lot of places in the last eight years, but Chicago holds all the memories I wish I could forget.

EIGHT YEARS AGO

The thin nightgown does nothing to protect me from the brutal wind whipping around my body, and my bare feet ache from the freezing concrete below them.

My asshole of a foster father didn't give me a chance to change before he dragged me from my bed in the middle of the night and dumped me in the trunk of his car.

I should have known this was coming. The signs were there, but I thought I had more time. He started looking at me

28

differently a few months ago, like he was the lion and I was the prey. Then there were the hushed conversations between my foster parents and how they suddenly tightened the reins, but only for me. They never really cared where we were or how late we came home, so long as we put on a pretty smile when the agency worker came to make sure we weren't being mistreated.

When the trunk opened, I was too disoriented to fight, but that didn't stop the man from hurting me. Not too bad. No worse than I'm used to after living with Colin and Jan for so many years, but still a shock to the system in the middle of the night.

"Move, bitch," the man growls at me. He's the one who dragged me from the trunk and threw me to the ground before pulling me up with a harsh yank I'll be feeling for days.

I glance up at him under my dark lashes, careful not to look him in the eye. If there's anything I've learned in foster care, it's that dominant men only want submissive women, and challenging that can land you in the hospital…or worse.

I try to shove down thoughts of one of the little girls they fostered last year. Sadie was a wild spirit, even after losing her entire family in a house fire, but Colin and Jan beat that out of her. Locked her in the closet for days at a time without food or water, beat her until she could barely breathe, and one day took it too far. They told the foster agency she ran away, and because every other kid in the house was more afraid of the devil they didn't know, we all kept our mouths shut.

I still hear her screams when I close my eyes at night.

The guilt hits me the same way it always does, right in the gut, knocking the air right from my lungs and forcing me to look away from the man before I can take in any of his features. Maybe this is my karma for not protecting her. Maybe I deserve all that awaits me behind the heavy warehouse doors.

We're near the docks. That much I knew before the trunk even opened. The familiar scent of Lake Michigan mingles with the stench of fish permeating the air. But I don't need anyone to tell me where I am or what I'm doing here, because I already know. My foster brothers tried desperately to protect me from where Colin would take them at night, but neither of them were the same after the first time, and although I can only guess what happens here, I can assume it's sinister enough to change the only two people I've trusted since my parents died.

I step forward, and a hiss drags its way up my throat. The cold concrete makes my bones ache, and each step is excruciating, but the alternative will be worse, so I keep moving, not bothering to look at the man standing beside the door or the one on the other side of the room whose eyes peruse my body, leaving nothing but filth in their wake.

It's not until I'm shoved into a small room and my body slams into another that I finally look up. It's a woman, her hair shaved and chopped in places, her skin black and blue, and dried blood drips from her nose.

She's huddled in the corner of the small concrete space, her fear-filled eyes stealing the breath from my lungs.

"Better be good if you don't want to wind up looking like this slut." He chuckles and slams the heavy metal door behind me, locking me into a fate that's worse than even my nightmares could conjure.

Ace and Tommy were meant to save me tonight. But they

were too late, and now I'm beyond salvation.

FOUR

ACE

Tommy and Clara help us check into the hotel and to get Mia settled. She doesn't seem uncomfortable with me by any stretch, but I'd be an idiot not to notice how the tension falls from her shoulders when Clara is around.

Does that mean I'm going to let her go home with them? Not a chance in hell. But I'll accept their help when they offer it if it's the best thing for her.

The penthouse suite at the Marriott is a world away from the shitty apartment I've had for almost a decade. Spending money on nice shit always had guilt washing over me in nauseating waves. I didn't deserve to have anything more than I needed to survive, and that shitty apartment and the mattress on the floor were exactly that.

The way Mia's eyes tracked over every expensive inch of this place makes my stomach clench, but I needed to give her the best of everything. She has no reason to forgive me, but that doesn't mean I'm not going to fight tooth and nail to get that forgiveness, and if that means spending an ungodly amount of money to book this place out for the next month while I find a suitable apartment and have an adequate amount of security installed to ensure her safety, that's exactly what I'm going to do.

Clara ushers Mia into the main bedroom in the suite while Tommy stays behind. He looks almost as out of place in this hotel room as I feel, but he doesn't let his discomfort show. He has a little more experience around the finer things in life than I do, having worked for the Saint James family for almost ten years. But people like us don't forget our roots or where we came from. Once a dirtbag, always a dirtbag.

"Are you sure it's a good idea for her to stay here with you?" he asks quietly.

"Why wouldn't it be?" I snap, the exhaustion from the last few days finally settling over me. I need a shower because I stink to high heaven, and then I need to close my eyes for a few hours.

My phone hasn't stopped blowing up with work shit, and I have to get to my apartment and pack up the key pieces of equipment I need. A hotel isn't the most ideal place to be hacking, but it's just going to have to work in the interim.

He sighs and drags me further from the door the girls disappeared through. "We have no idea what she's been through, Ace, but I'm more than comfortable making some assumptions. I know what she means to you, and I know you don't want her out of your sight, but what about what she needs? Do you think she's going to be okay waking up in the middle of the night in a strange place with a guy she hasn't seen for the better part of a decade?" he challenges.

I open my mouth to respond, but I snap it shut immediately because he's right. Mia would be better off with someone else, someone who can be gentle with her as she gets used to a world she hasn't lived in for so long, but I can't let her go. I can't allow her out of my sight, much less out of the building.

"That's what I thought," he says smugly.

I sigh and rub a hand over my face. It's been too fucking long since I slept to make a case for why exactly she needs to stay here, especially when he's not exactly wrong.

"Look, Ace. I'm not going to push you on this. I get it. Believe me, I do. But I'm going to leave Mia with a phone and my number, as well as the Saint James family." I open my mouth to argue, but he holds his hand up to silence me. "I know you don't like it, and again, I get it, but they're good people who will go to the ends of the earth for the people they think are worth it, and I can tell you as soon as they realized Mia was helping Clara, she became one of those people." He claps his hand on my shoulder, a rare touch from the man who has always despised it. "All I'm asking is that if she wants to leave, if it's too much for her and she asks you for space, you give that to her."

I glare at him for a few seconds, but no matter how badly I want to argue, I know I can't because he's right. It would be selfish of me to keep her here if she doesn't want to be here, if she doesn't want to be with me. The idea burns my chest, but I can't be selfish with her, not after the horrors she must have seen in the years since I knew her.

I give him a sharp nod as Clara appears in the doorway, worry etched into her features. I'm glad Tommy found her. The tortured boy who had seen more than anyone deserves to see

35

in their life, found a light so bright she can guide him through his own darkness, just the same way Mia always has for me. Even when she was gone, she was the guiding light I needed to keep going, and now that I have her back, there's nothing I won't do to keep her safe, to protect her from the cruel world that has already hurt her so much.

She glances over her shoulder before closing the distance between her and Tommy. He immediately pulls her into his arms once she's within range, and I don't miss the way the tension melts from his shoulders as soon as she's in his arms.

"How is she?" I ask.

Clara sighs, her eyes closing for the briefest of moments before meeting mine. "I think she's okay. I…" She hesitates. "I don't know what she went through before she found herself with Lombardi, but I get the impression it was pretty horrific." She draws her bottom lip between her teeth and lets out a breath. "I asked her if she was comfortable staying here with you. Not because I think you'll hurt her, I just…I want to make sure she feels safe. She said she was fine, that she didn't want to be a bother to any of us."

I flinch. She doesn't want to be a bother to us? She doesn't want to interrupt our lives? Doesn't she realize my life has been on hold for the last eight years? That every spare second of every day has been spent looking for her? Searching in the darkest parts of the web, looking in every corner of the world for any sign of her? The only thing that would be a *bother* is if I lost her again.

"I'm sorry, Ace, I didn't want to undermine you or anything. I know you care for her, I just…she helped me, so I want to make sure she feels safe." Clara rushes to defend herself, not realizing it's not her I'm upset with. It's me.

"It's fine, Clara." I scrub my hand over my face, my heavy eyes burning with each second they're open. I'm no stranger to fatigue. I've often worked days on end without sleep, but the tiredness has set into my bones and it's only a matter of time before I crash. "I know you're only doing what's best for her."

"Ace is a little shortsighted when it comes to Mia," Tommy admits.

I glare at him, but he just shrugs. "It's true, you always have been. It's not necessarily a bad thing. I'm the same with Clara."

A small smile tugs at the corners of her lips, and she burrows her face into his chest. The moment is too intimate for someone to watch from the outside, and yet I can't bring myself to move. It's everything I've deprived myself of—the life I never allowed myself to live because I let Mia down.

I made her a promise once and broke it, there's no way I'll make that mistake again.

FIVE

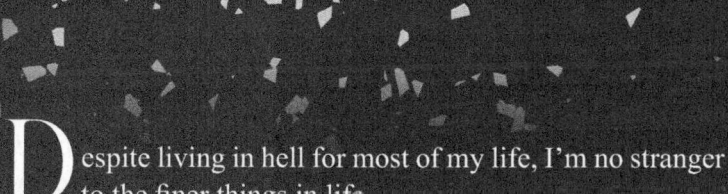

D espite living in hell for most of my life, I'm no stranger to the finer things in life.

The men who have owned me in the past all had money. Too fucking much of it. They say money is the root of all evil, and in my experience, that couldn't be closer to the truth. It makes people cold and greedy, makes them think they can own other humans as if they're a piece of property.

Hotel rooms like this were a "treat." That's what Craig used to call them. When he brought me to places like this, it was a reward. I always wanted to scoff when he said that word. Like I was being rewarded for being his own personal punching bag, for allowing him to violate me whenever he chose. None of the things he was rewarding me for were my choice, but that was irrelevant to him. His money and upbringing made him think it was okay to buy another human being for his sick games.

Voices in the living area carry into the room Clara has set me up in. There are bags of clothes sitting on the end of the bed, all from designer labels I recognize but was never allowed to wear. Except with Lombardi. Although marrying a Mafia prince who would likely treat me as nothing more than a baby farm isn't how I foresaw my life going as a child, it's a better alternative to some of the futures life could have dealt me.

Craig could have killed me any number of times. He wasn't exactly a gentle man, and his proclivities made me question how long I would live with him as my master. But he was killed before he could end my life, and once again I was on the market.

I peek into one of the bags that I recognize as a pajama brand and a small smile tips up the corners of my mouth. The bag is full to the brim of items I only could have dreamed of sleeping in just a few months ago, but the reality of the situation quickly has me stepping back. I can't wear any of them. I can't owe the Saint James family more than I already do. They helped to save me, and although they say they don't want payment for their generosity, I don't want to push it. I know there's a fine line with people like them, where generosity turns to taking advantage, and that's how you get yourself killed…or worse.

A violent shudder quakes through my bones. No. I can't do it. I can't do any of this.

I look over the room again. The luxurious-looking king-size bed. The view of the Chicago skyline. The marble peeking out from the connecting bathroom. I don't belong here.

I don't belong anywhere.

A soft knock at the door drags my attention away from the bags, and I find Clara and Tommy standing in the doorway with tentative smiles playing on their lips.

"Hey," I say quietly. I wonder if they noticed how freaked out I am by the clothes and the way sweat beads at my hairline as panic descends upon me.

"We're going to get going." Clara looks up at Tommy with uncertainty. "We just wanted to double check you're okay here and that you have everything you need."

"I'm fine. Thank you for...everything." A simple thank you doesn't seem like enough considering the gravity of what they've done for me, but what else can I say?

Tommy takes a step forward, and I force myself to keep my feet planted and my body still. This was the first thing I learned when I was in training. Don't flinch. Don't show fear. Men will always exploit weakness. It doesn't matter if Tommy kept me safe through my childhood and did everything in his power to keep me away from the shit our foster parents were into, my fight-or-flight instinct doesn't know the difference between him and every man who has hurt me in the last eight years.

He pauses a few feet away, as if he knows I can't handle him being any closer. He holds a phone out to me, but I don't immediately reach for it. I've never been allowed to have one. The only phone I've ever had was a shitty burner Ace gave me after he and Tommy escaped so he could check in with me, but this iPhone is the newest model. I saw an ad for it when I first arrived at the Lombardi compound and I was locked in my room for the first few days. It was the first time I'd been allowed to watch television in years, aside from the odd news program my owner was watching and I was in the room for.

"This is for you. It has mine and Clara's numbers programmed in already, as well as Ace's and all the Saint James family. If you need anything, I want you to call one of us. Doesn't matter what it is, doesn't matter what time it is, we'll be here, okay?"

I open my mouth to respond, but I can't conjure any words to say. People only ever do nice things for you when they have an ulterior motive. That's something I learned long ago, but usually I can see the wolf dressed in sheep's clothing a mile away.

Clara appears at his side, her hand reaching out to squeeze my shoulder. "Promise us you'll call if you need anything?"

I nod, words still lost to me, but it's enough to grant me a bright smile.

Some of the tension releases from Tommy's shoulders when I take the phone from him, but he still seems uncertain about leaving me here with Ace.

"I'll be fine, Tommy."

He sighs and brushes his fingers along the stubble on his jaw. "We're only a phone call away."

Clara moves to the bags on the bed and frowns when she finds them untouched. "Snow did what she could on short notice, but if there's anything you don't like or if you want something else, we can have it here in a few hours."

I shake my head. "They've already done too much," I whisper. "I don't want to owe anyone anything more than I already do."

She closes her eyes for a long second, gathering her composure before turning back to me with pity shining in her eyes. I hate that look. I hate when people feel bad for me because of my circumstances, but it's worse coming from her because she saved me. Doesn't she realize that she's already given me everything? That she gave me freedom? Something I stopped allowing myself to hope for years ago. "Mia, I can't even begin to understand the things you've been through and how that must have affected your ability to trust when people are doing things out of kindness rather than their own benefit, but I promise you that the Saint James family is not expecting any kind of payment, and they would be devastated if they knew you were thinking that way. Please use the things they've bought you, and please reach out to one of us if there's anything else you need."

An unfamiliar tightness in my throat forces me to nod rather than speak. I don't cry anymore. I haven't in a long time. Because to cry is to show weakness, and weakness only shows people where to hit you for the hardest impact. But this lump in my throat is exactly what I remember it feeling like to be on the brink of tears, and no matter how hard I try to swallow past it, it only seems to grow.

Hesitantly, she and Tommy turn to leave the room, clearly sensing that I'm not at a point where I can be touched, and I'm grateful for that. Truthfully, I'm not sure I'll ever not shy away from human touch again.

I lean back against the wall behind me and let out a choked sob, but no tears fall against my cheeks. I may be safe on paper, but I'm not sure my old habits will ever die.

SIX

ACE

Despite the way my eyes droop and my body relaxes as I let myself sink into the overly soft mattress, sleep doesn't come.

Hours pass, the moonlight moving across the room as it rises and falls in the sky, making way for the dim sunrise I should sleep through, but instead I'm hyperaware of every sound in the hotel room. The mini fridge clicks and whirs, doors down the hallway open and close, nothing that's a legitimate threat to the woman sleeping in the room beside mine, and yet it's all I can focus on.

I lost her once, and I refuse to do it again. Even if it means watching over her, guarding her with every beat of my fucking heart, I'll do it to keep her safe.

Perhaps sleep never comes because a part of me is afraid this is all a dream. I spent so many years searching for her, looking under every rock I could think of, hacking into criminal organizations, trying to find any trace of the girl I promised

I would save, but there was nothing for me to find. What if I close my eyes and wake up to the helplessness I've felt for the last eight years?

The thought is cut off by a soft whimper from the room beside mine, and I'm moving before I'm conscious of the decision to climb out of bed. I tug my shirt over my bare chest and slip into her dark room. The blinds are pulled, the sliver of light from the living area behind me illuminating the small body curled up on the edge of the king-size bed.

The covers are pulled up around her neck, her fists tight at the edge as if she thinks the blankets can protect her from the threat in her dream. But it's the terror etched into her perfect features that forces my heart into my throat.

Tommy was right. I have no concept of what she's been through. I have no idea the horrors she's been through in the last eight years, and even though *I* know I would do anything to keep her safe, it's unfair for me to expect her to know that.

I approach the bed hesitantly, aware that if she wakes up to me towering over her, it will terrify her. How the hell do I wake her without scaring her?

"Please," she cries out. "Not again. Please."

The lump in my throat grows impossibly, and I squeeze my eyes shut to calm the thundering of my heart. I want to tear the hearts from every person who has ever hurt her. I want to do every one of the fucked-up things they did to her, to them. To make them feel the pain they caused the precious girl I couldn't save. It's not rational. But there isn't a fiber of my being that doesn't itch to destroy them.

"Mia," I whisper into the quiet room, her name rolling from my lips, but she must be too caught up in her nightmare to hear me. I try again, a little louder, and this time her head moves to the other side as she brings the blankets up higher around her neck.

I sigh, looking behind me at the suite. Maybe I should have asked Tommy and Clara to stay. Or one of the Saint James siblings. Storm mentioned that his sister-in-law is a counselor, maybe she would be better suited to be here with Mia.

A soft yelp forces my attention back to Mia's sleeping form, and I take a step toward her instinctively, like I can protect her from the demons that haunt her at night.

I kneel a few feet from the bed, hoping that when she does open her eyes, I won't seem so imposing if I'm not standing over her.

"Mia, can you wake up for me?" I say a little louder, and she finally opens her eyes with a start, the brilliant blue shining with terror in the dim light. As soon as her eyes focus on me, a loud scream tears through the room, and I flinch at the sound.

She's not afraid of you. You have no idea what she's been through, I remind myself, but it doesn't make it any easier to swallow the idea of the girl I've loved since before I knew what the word meant being afraid of me.

"It's just me, sugar." The nickname falls from my lips like it has so many times in the past. It comes naturally, even after all this time.

The panic remains etched into her features for a few torturous seconds before she finally relaxes ever so slightly. Her grip on the edge of the blanket remains so tight her knuckles have long turned white, but it's a start.

"You were having a nightmare," I explain, as if she wouldn't be aware of it. Idiot. I have no idea how to care for someone with trauma. Hell, I haven't even dealt with my own. What makes me think I can help someone else through theirs?

"Oh," she croaks, her voice laced with sleep.

"Do you need anything? Water maybe?"

She shakes her head, her eyes darting over the dark space surrounding us looking for danger. I wish I could tell her that she won't find any. That I'll protect her from anything that dares look at her the wrong way. But she wouldn't believe me. Not when I already let her down in the worst way.

I let out a steadying breath, but it does nothing to calm my racing heart.

"I'm sorry for waking you," she whispers, her eyes fluttering closed for a moment before they flick back open and settle on me.

"I was awake anyway," I tell her truthfully.

We stare at one another in an uncomfortable silence for long seconds. What do you say to the girl you've dedicated your life to saving when she's finally in front of you?

"You should eat something." I say the first thing that comes to my mind. We found her and Clara twenty-four hours ago, but she never touched any of the food we gave her. Not on the flight, not when Tommy and Clara left and I ordered every single room service item in the hope she would eat something.

Nothing.

She shakes her head slowly, panic flashing in the unreal blue before her mask slips back into place. I hate how good she is at hiding. "I'm not hungry."

I rub my hand over my face, the fatigue weighing down on me. But it doesn't matter how tired I am, not when the idea of not being able to protect Mia will stop me from sleeping. "Mia—" I start, but she interrupts.

"You can go back to bed, Ace. I'm fine." And before I can even process her words, she turns over and tugs the covers higher until she's nothing but a small lump in the center of the bed.

I watch her for another few seconds, but in the end, I turn on my heel and close the door gently behind me. I'm not sure what I was expecting when I finally brought her home, but it wasn't this.

SEVEN

MIA

I linger in my room for as long as I can, but after being locked away for years, being in one room for too long leaves me antsy and anxious.

There were voices a couple of hours ago—Ace and another man speaking in low whispers for a few minutes before the door to the suite clicked shut quietly behind whoever it was—but there's been no sound since.

After the worried looks he was giving me in the early hours of this morning, I half expected to wake up to Ace sitting in the chair in the corner watching over me, but when I opened my eyes, he was nowhere to be seen, and I hate to admit to myself that I'm disappointed by that.

Why would he be here after the way I handled things after my nightmare? I've been nothing but cold toward him since the moment he came back into my life, which is unfair considering what he saved me from. He could have dumped me on the street as soon as we set down in Chicago, but instead he booked this extravagant room and has seen to my every need, even the ones I haven't admitted to having.

I peek through the crack in the door to find Ace at the small table beside the kitchenette, surrounded by computer screens and laptops. The soft whir of the motors fills the otherwise quiet room, and the scowl on Ace's face tells me there's something on one of the screens he's not pleased about.

The door creaks and his eyes shoot up to meet mine, his features softening as he looks me over as if I may have hurt myself overnight. It's hard to reconcile the boy I knew before with the man who sits in front of me. He's harder now. His baby face has changed into sharp lines with a dusting of stubble. His hair is just as unruly as it always was, except now it makes him seem unpolished in the most delicious of ways. And his eyes are haunted, just the way mine are when I look in the mirror.

"You're up," he says, standing from his seat. "I was about to come check on you."

"Where did all this come from?" I ask.

He drags his eyes away from me to the screens set out in front of him. "I had a friend bring it over from my apartment. I have a whole lot of pissed-off customers who are waiting for things to be done."

"Oh." I look down at my feet, warmth spreading across my cheeks. I'm in the way. Of course I am.

"Do you want some breakfast? I can order you something?" He reaches for the phone balancing on the corner of the table, every other inch of surface covered with equipment.

I shake my head, my stomach squeezing painfully at the thought of food. He seems to have a fixation on my eating habits, and I'm not sure how long I'm going to be able to keep denying him before he starts asking questions. "No, thank you. I should get going. You're busy."

I turn and quickly slip my feet into the tennis shoes I left by the door. They're the same muddy pair from when we escaped, but they're all I have apart from the things the Saint James family bought me, and I want to owe them as little as I can. I had to take a pair of leggings, a long-sleeve shirt, and a jacket, but the rest are still sitting in their bags with the tags attached.

By the time I turn back around, Ace is standing a few feet away, his eyes wild and panicked. A pair of sweatpants hang low on his hips and a tight gray T-shirt wraps around his bulging biceps. Tattoos wrap around his forearm, mingling with the veins that protrude from his skin. Jesus, did he grow up. If I were capable of being attracted to another human being after everything I've been through, I'm sure I would fall to my knees for the boy I always looked up to, who I thought would save me.

"Please stop trying to leave," Ace says as calmly as he can manage, but the tension in his jaw gives him away. I've been around enough men over the years to know when they're on edge, and Ace is as close to the precipice as anyone I've ever seen, and I instinctively take a step back.

Move away from anyone who can hurt me.

Do it quietly.

Don't make them angrier than they already are.

It didn't take me long to learn these rules, but I have a feeling it will take the rest of my life to break them.

His eyes widen at my movement, and he too takes a step back. The agony etched into his features is almost enough for me to step toward him, to reassure him that he hasn't done anything wrong. The years since I last saw him have been worse than he could possibly imagine, and it's left me scarred and broken, both mentally and physically. But I remain rooted in place.

"Emerson is going to come over this morning if you feel like talking to someone. She's a qualified counselor and I thought you might feel more comfortable talking to her."

"I don't want to bother her," I rush out. Fuck. It doesn't seem to matter what I do, I'm racking up my debt to one of the most notorious crime families in the country, and that's the last thing I need when I finally have my freedom.

Ace rubs his face, and I finally notice the dark smudges beneath his eyes. Did he sleep at all last night? Guilt slams into me and knocks the air right from my lungs. Was he awake because of my nightmares? I don't think I make much noise during them anymore, not after how they would beat me at The Factory if I caused a scene at night and made the guards' jobs hard. It was irrelevant to them that I was a teenage girl who was being trained how to be the perfect pet, my entire life stolen from me, my future, my friends, my hope, and my happiness. All that mattered was pleasing the men who now owned me.

"Mia, I won't even pretend to know what you've been through, but I want to make something very clear so there is no room for misunderstanding. You're not bothering anyone. Everyone who has offered to help, have done so because they want to, because they're grateful to you for helping Clara, and because they know you're important to Tommy and me. I promise you that when all is said and done, you won't owe anyone. Not me, not Tommy, and not any of the Saint James family." He takes a hesitant step forward, and this time I force my body to remain rooted to the floor. Ace won't hurt me. I'm almost positive of it. "I asked Emerson to come speak to you because, although I want nothing more than to give you everything you need and to hide you away from the rest of the world where I can keep you safe and give you everything you've missed out on, I know that's selfish of me, and I would be an asshole to not give you every chance I can at getting to live your life."

I only hesitate for a moment before I nod, but for once, it's different. I'm not agreeing because I have to or because if I don't, Ace will hurt me. No. I'm agreeing because I can see how desperately he wants to help me, and although I should tell him I'm beyond help, too broken to cobble together the pieces that remain, somewhere deep down, I'm still that teenage girl desperate to see one of Ace's rare smiles.

And I'm not disappointed by the one that tugs at the corners of his lips.

I fidget with my hands in my lap as Emerson lowers herself into the armchair across from me, her hands immediately resting on her growing belly. Her auburn hair is styled into a neat ponytail, and her emerald eyes meet mine across the small table that separates us.

Ace and Rayne have made themselves scarce, although I'm pretty sure they're standing outside in the hallway, considering Ace didn't take anything but a room key with him when he left. They both seemed hesitant to give us any space, given the way Rayne's eyes hovered on Emerson, worry causing his brows to pull together.

"Sorry about Rayne." She shakes her head with an overexaggerated eye roll. "Ever since we found out I was pregnant, he has trouble letting me out of his sight for more than a few minutes. I'm surprised the man didn't spontaneously combust being away from me for twenty-four hours."

A small laugh fills the space between us, and it takes me a second to realize it came from me. It's been such a long time since I've been able to show emotion of any kind, and although I was able to fake some while I was at the Lombardi compound, this is the first time it's come naturally. "It's sweet," I say quietly.

She smiles and glances at the door, as if she knows they're standing on the other side of it waiting for us to be done. "It is. The start of my pregnancy was a little rough, and he really struggled to see me so unwell. He had a lot of guilt because he was the one that did this to me." She laughs, but the obvious love in her eyes and the way she rubs her stomach absentmindedly show me just how much that baby and her husband mean to her. "Anyway, we're not here to talk about my overbearing husband." She turns her full attention to me, and I tighten the hold on my hands, as if my own grip will be enough to hold me together. "I'm just about to finish my master's in counseling, and I promise anything you tell me will stay between us. I won't tell Ace, or Rayne, or anyone else. This is a safe space, and I want to assure you that I will not break that trust."

I nod slowly. I'm used to finding the lies people are telling me, but there aren't any here. Emerson is telling the truth, and some of the tension in my shoulders releases.

"Is there anything you need? I know Snow bought you some things and Tommy gave you a phone, but is there anything else that might make you more comfortable during this transition?"

"No, you've all already done too much."

Her brows pull together. "Why do you say that?"

I sigh and lean back into the plush couch. It's strange enough to speak freely after only being able to speak when spoken to, but to add my own feelings into the mix has anxiety bubbling low in my belly. "I guess I'm used to nice deeds being followed by owing someone something," I tell her truthfully. "The men who owned me over the years would occasionally do nice things for me. Let me watch television, give me books to read, some chocolate, that kind of thing, but it always came with conditions. Things I had to do for them, and usually those ulterior motives only came after the fact. I guess I'm waiting for the other shoe to drop."

Emerson does her best to school her features, but I don't miss how she flinches or how she takes an extra split second each time she blinks to gather herself. "I see. It's only normal when you've been conditioned to feel a certain way that it can be hard to accept when things change. However, I can assure you that none of us—not me, not Ace, not Tommy or Clara—feel like we're doing enough to help you. It must be scary knowing what our family is involved in, but the Saint James family has spent their lives taking down trafficking rings. Are they criminals? Yes. But are they bad people? Would they ever be involved in the kinds of things you've seen and been through?

Absolutely not. If there is anything you need, I want you to promise me you'll ask for it. You can call me, and I'll make it happen. Tommy let us know you have all our numbers so honestly, night or day."

"Thank you." I choke out the words I've been forced to say so many times, but for once I don't feel like they're enough.

"Now, one thing I did want to talk to you about is whether you've seen a doctor recently."

I shake my head. "No, not for…" I close my eyes and take a deep breath. "Not for a long time."

Emerson swallows heavily as she struggles to train her emotions. "We have a doctor, his name is Doc, and he has treated all of us, as well as many women that have been saved from trafficking. Would you be comfortable if I organized for him to come see you?"

Panic slams into me. The idea of a man touching me, of him seeing me naked, has a cold sweat breaking out across my brow. Can I do that? Logically, I know I should see a doctor. Even growing up in foster care, I saw one somewhat regularly. But I'm not sure I'm ready to be that vulnerable in front of a stranger.

Emerson notices my obvious panic and gives me a reassuring smile. "Have a think about it. I can be there if you want, or I'm sure we could organize for Clara to come sit with you. Whatever you want to do. I think it would be wise for a doctor to look you over, check your vitamin levels and those kinds of things." But it's what she doesn't say that rings loudest in my mind. I need to be tested for diseases, and maybe that's what terrifies me most.

Shattered Promises

EIGHT

ACE

Rayne and I stare at the door the entire time Mia and Emerson are talking. We don't have much in common, but the one thing we do share is how protective we are of the women on the other side of the wall. We've both let them down in the past, but his mistakes didn't result in Emerson being tortured for years. Being sold from one rich asshole to the next and used like a piece of meat. The thought makes my stomach churn painfully, and the bacon and eggs in my gut threaten to make a reappearance.

I failed her. There's no two ways about it. But I won't do it again. I'll keep her safe. I'll give her everything she needs. I'll do anything to give her the life I so desperately wanted to give her eight years ago.

"Storm wanted me to let you know that he's dealt with Lombardi. They won't be coming after Clara or Mia and have agreed not to retaliate." Rayne breaks the silence we fell into as soon as Emerson shooed us out of the suite.

I nod. "How'd he swing that?"

Rayne chuckles and leans his broad shoulders back against the wall. "There's a reason he's in the position he is. If I ran the family as I technically should, being the oldest, we'd be at war every other day."

I crack a smile, but my eyes stray back to the door almost as soon as they left it. "Thank you for all you've done for Mia."

"She's innocent in all this. She never asked for what they did to her. She didn't ask to have her early adult years stolen from her. Our family has been touched by trafficking more than we will ever admit publicly. Storm's fiancée, Ayvah, was almost sold by her family. Everett and Elijah were forced to see a lot of shit from a young age, and Emerson was taken by the Russos. We'll do everything we can for the people we can save."

I'm surprised he's speaking so candidly considering we're far from friends, but I suppose we have a common goal now. Help Mia.

Rayne lets out a breath before meeting my eyes. The darkness staring back at me is solemn, and my stomach does another painful flip. "There's something you should know though. We've saved a lot of women and children from trafficking, some of which have been in the life for a long time, and sometimes they can't be saved. The things they've seen and the things they've been through, it's enough to drive even the strongest of people to insanity."

"Why are you telling me this?" I snap.

"Because you need to go into this with your eyes wide open.

We have no idea what Mia has been through. We don't know who she's been with, what they've done to her, what she's seen. We have no idea if, after all is said and done, whether she can live with all of that. I think Mia will pull through, but we've thought that before and have been wrong, so I want to give you the heads up."

"She'll pull through." She has to.

Silence falls over us again, and I make no attempt to break it. I don't want to discuss the possibility that my girl is beyond saving. That the woman I spent years searching for may be too far gone. It's not a possibility I'm willing to entertain.

The door opens a little while later, Emerson standing on the other side with an amused smirk. "Did you two stand here the whole time?" She doesn't try to hide the amusement in her voice. She's clearly used to Rayne's overprotective nature.

"You know we did, sweet girl." He tugs her into his arms and his hand splays across her growing belly. If you told me a year ago that the most ruthless Mafia enforcer to ever call Chicago home would be so whipped, I would have laughed in your face, but I guess we all change under the right circumstances.

I slip past them, desperate to get Mia back into my line of sight, and the restless part of me settles when I see her perched on the edge of the couch with a glass of water nestled between her palms. "How are you doing, sugar?" I ask quietly, trying not to startle her.

She looks over her shoulder at me, but her face is passive as if there's no emotion behind the unreal blue. Except I know her better than that. I know when she's hiding from me. I just wish I understood what she's holding so close to her chest.

"I'm okay." Her eyes dart toward her bedroom door. "I'm a little tired though. I might take a nap." Lie.

"Do you want to have something to eat first?" I already know the answer will be the same as every other time I've offered in the last thirty-six hours, but I have to try.

"No, thank you," she says quietly as she skirts around me, desperate to avoid my touch. I shouldn't take it personally, not after the hell we suspect she's lived through, but it's hard not to compare the woman standing in front of me to the girl who came to me for comfort when we were children. She pauses by the door and gives Emerson a small smile. "Thank you for coming to speak to me."

"My pleasure, Mia. Please think about having Doc come check you over and don't forget you can call anytime."

She nods and disappears behind the door, quietly closing the door.

I turn to Emerson, and her brow furrows as she stares after Mia. "She's not eating?"

"No. She hasn't eaten anything since we rescued her."

She lets out a heavy sigh and looks up at Rayne, as if her husband has all the answers, but he looks just as worried as the rest of us. "I'm going to come back tomorrow. She's holding on to a lot, which is not uncommon in these situations. Survivors often think their captors will come back for them and that if they haven't disclosed too much of their time with them, that it may save them some pain. I'm not saying that's what's happening here, but I wouldn't be surprised."

"No one is getting near her," I growl, the sound deep and

unnatural to my own ears.

Emerson nods. "I know. And she likely knows that too. But it's the way survivors subconsciously protect themselves. I've recommended she see a doctor and think Doc would be the best bet. He has had a lot of exposure to women who have been trafficked and knows what to look for in terms of trauma. I also think she should speak to someone more qualified than myself. While I'm more than happy to walk this journey with her, I think she may need to speak with a psychiatrist who can medicate her if need be."

I nod. I've met Doc a few times, and the idea of that tattooed giant asshole anywhere near my woman makes my skin crawl, but she's not wrong. He is best placed to help her, and I can't deny Mia anything. "Can you recommend anyone?"

"I'll flick through a few, and if you have any trouble getting her in, let me know, I'll pull some strings."

"How's the apartment search going?" Rayne asks.

I sigh and rub my hand across my face. "It's not. I have so much shit to catch up on after the impromptu few days off, and everyone's up my ass for the shit they're waiting on."

"I'll ask Wynter to have a look for you. She's bored out of her mind at home with the baby, and Everett barely lets her leave bed so she could use a project." Emerson rolls her eyes, but the affection for her family is written all over her face.

"I can do it."

She reaches out and squeezes my bicep. "I understand you've been on your own a long time and you don't like leaning on people for support, and you don't particularly trust us, but let us help. We only want what's best for Mia."

I watch her for another beat before nodding in defeat. Like I said, there's nothing I could deny Mia, even if it means working with the people who almost ended my career before it could begin.

Shattered Promises

NINE

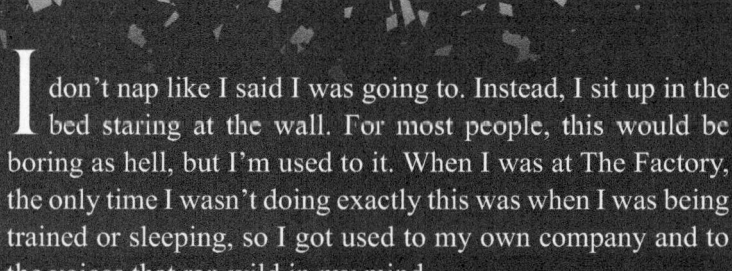

I don't nap like I said I was going to. Instead, I sit up in the bed staring at the wall. For most people, this would be boring as hell, but I'm used to it. When I was at The Factory, the only time I wasn't doing exactly this was when I was being trained or sleeping, so I got used to my own company and to the voices that ran wild in my mind.

At first they were hopeful, like a little mascot who was by my side through some of the worst days of my existence, but it didn't take long for them to get as mean as the people who hurt me. The voices morphed into the men who took what I never offered them, the women who could allow such heinous things to happen and treat me like I deserved it, and occasionally, my foster father's voice would creep in just when I thought I had already hit rock bottom.

But there was always one voice that dragged me back from the edge. When I was ready to give up, to take my own life just to make the pain stop, it was Ace's deep voice that convinced me to keep going. So why can I barely speak to him now that he's right in front of me? When he's trying so fucking hard to take care of me? Why can't I let him?

I press my eyes closed, emotions threatening to spill over in a way I haven't allowed them to in so long, but I force it down and bring my knees up to my chest, holding them close as if it will do anything to make me feel secure.

The phone on the bedside table lights up, and I reach for it reluctantly. This morning when I was avoiding leaving my room, I took some time to learn how to use it. It's been a long time since I've been allowed to even touch a cell phone, and iPhones have come a long way in the last eight years.

Emerson: I hope you don't mind, I spoke to Doc and he's happy to come past and see you anytime.

Mia: Thank you. I think you're right, I do need to be checked over.

Emerson: There's no rush. Just when you're ready. Ask Ace to organize it with Rayne when you decide.

Emerson: Would it be okay if I came to see you again tomorrow? Snow would like to come as well if you're okay with that?

I hesitate for a moment. Snow Saint James is one of the most beautiful women I've ever seen, and although I've only seen photos in the gossip columns of grainy newspapers, I'm sure she's incredible in real life.

Mia: Only if you both want to. I don't want to put you out.

Emerson: We'll bring some lunch.

70

Fuck.

Did Ace tell her I'm refusing food each time it's offered? Have I been that obvious about my aversion to food? I thought I was doing it subtly enough that he would pass it off as me not being hungry. But that's not the case.

No. I'm always *starving*. But I learned early on that food is a privilege and to only eat when I have to. If I allow myself to eat more now, what happens when I get dragged back? When someone inevitably comes for me, and I have to go back to a life of starvation?

It's better this way.

The acceptable time for a nap comes and goes, and eventually I have to leave the safety of the bedroom. I'm not sure what to do when I'm in the living area with Ace. I don't want to turn the television on when he's working, but it's also weird for me to just sit staring at the wall in his presence. At least I'm self-aware enough to know that's not normal behavior.

Ace's eyes meet mine the second the door swings open, and he gives me a small smile as he lets out a relieved breath. He seems to think I'm going to disappear if he doesn't always have eyes on me. Probably not an unreasonable concern considering it's happened before.

"Hey," I say quietly.

"How was your nap?" He pushes his chair back from the table and stretches. I can't help but stare when his fitted black shirt creeps up, revealing his toned stomach.

I force myself to look away because if I stare for another second, he's going to catch me, and I don't need that kind of mortification right now. "It was okay."

He rummages around on his desk before he stands and walks over to me. "I had these delivered for you while you were asleep." He thrusts a laptop box and Kindle into my unready hands, and I stare at them blankly. The MacBook looks like the newest model, and I wouldn't even know where to start with an eReader.

"You didn't have to get me these," I whisper, my eyes darting up to meet his.

"I know, but I thought you might want to do something other than watch TV and nap." He shrugs. "Wynter is going to help us find an apartment, and then we can get you a space of your own all set up."

I stare at him for long seconds as I process his words, and once they sink in, guilt slams into me like it has so many times since they rescued Clara and me. Everyone is doing so much for me. They're buying me clothes and going out of their way to arrange for doctors and counselors to come see me, but no one is more inconvenienced by my return than Ace is. He's shelling out for this ridiculously over-the-top penthouse, he's moved his computers to a tiny dining table, and the chair he's using looks anything but comfortable, and now he's uprooting his entire life for me? Moving out of his apartment just so I can be comfortable?

"What's wrong?" he asks, taking a step toward me, and for the first time since he's been back in my orbit, I don't step out of his reach. In fact, when his arm extends and his palm gently cups my cheek, I find myself leaning into his warmth and the safety he provides me.

My eyes press closed of their own accord, and for one blissful moment, I allow myself to feel safe. I allow my fight-or-flight instincts to take a break, and I just be. And it's the most beautiful few seconds of the last eight years. I wish it could last forever.

But I know better than to hope for that, and almost as if the universe senses the calm I've allowed to wash over me, a loud explosion in the hallway propels me forward into Ace's hard body.

I should have known better than to allow myself to hope for anything other than a life of misery.

TEN

I see the moment she lets her guard down, and it's beautiful.

She leans her cheek into my palm and her eyes flutter closed, her long, dark lashes whispering across her high cheekbones, and the tension she holds so close releases ever so slightly. It's the first time she hasn't flinched when I've touched her, and the significance of that isn't lost on me.

I brush my thumb across the soft freckles she hated as a child, relishing in the softness beneath my rough hand.

A quiet click drags my attention from Mia a split second before the door explodes, the power of it shaking the floor beneath our feet. Before I'm aware of the decision, I push Mia to the ground and roll my body over hers, shielding her from whatever is coming through the door.

What the fuck is going on?

I reach for my phone on the table above us, quickly shooting an SOS message to the Saint James family. I wouldn't normally ask for help from anyone, but this is different. It's for Mia.

"Stay down," I command, leaving no room for argument. I roll toward the couch and slip my hand between the cushions, letting out a breath of relief when my fingers wrap around the handle of my Glock. Normally I have the thing laying around, ready to use if someone strolls into my apartment unannounced, but I didn't want to frighten Mia, so I hid it nearby.

Almost as soon as I've left her, I'm back with my body shielding hers. No one has come through the door yet, but it's only a matter of time.

"Ace," she whimpers, her hands gripping the back of my shirt like an anchor.

"It's going to be okay, sugar. Just do exactly as I tell you and we'll be fine." The promise rolls off my tongue, even though I have no right promising such a thing when we're bound to be outnumbered, and there's no way Frost can deploy backup that quickly.

She nods frantically, but her attention is focused on the doorway, waiting for someone to walk through it.

I train my gun right in the center of where the door used to be and let out a deep, steadying breath. "I want you to run for your room and lock yourself in the bathroom, do you understand?"

"I can't leave you," she whispers.

"Mia," I snap. "Go now. I'll be fine."

She hesitates for another beat before crawling across the carpet until she disappears through the door, and I'm equally relieved as I am anxious about having her out of my sight.

I pull my attention back to the hole in the wall just in time for three men dressed head to toe in black tactical gear to breach the entrance. The first one through is dead before he can even see me as the bullet hits him in the center of his forehead.

The other two dive out of the way before I can aim at them, and I quickly move behind the oversized couch.

It won't protect me from being shot, but it will slow the bullets down enough that they shouldn't kill me.

"We just want the girl," one of the men calls out. "Hand her over and we'll be out of your hair."

"Does that line ever work?" I ask.

"You'd be surprised how many men are willing to throw their women to the sharks to save themselves."

I close my eyes and map out the hotel room, trying to place where the voice is coming from. He's not near the doorway anymore, but he's also not on the same side of the suite as Mia's room.

"Sounds like you deal with a lot of assholes."

The other one chuckles, and I quickly look to my other side. They're surrounding me. "You have no idea."

"So where is she, Ace?" I'm not surprised they know my name, especially because I've probably worked with these idiots at some point, but I hate that he thinks I'm going to hand her over.

Everyone I've met in the last ten years thinks I have no

attachments. A true loner. And that perception has worked for me. Anyone who works with the underbelly of society knows having attachments only makes you seem weak. But that also means these two dipshits think I'm going to hand over the woman I've been obsessed with for almost my whole life.

"Not likely," I mumble, focusing on each of their footsteps as they approach from each side. They're close. Too fucking close.

Just as they come into view, their guns trained on me, two loud shots fill the suite, and my heart leaps into my throat for the split second it takes me to watch the two men fall to the ground.

I peek over the couch and find Elijah Russo standing in the doorway, his gun raised, but his face is a calm mask as it always is.

"Friends of yours?" he quips, looking around to make sure there's no one else before slipping his gun into his waistband.

I roll my eyes and crawl to the guy closest to me. I slip his balaclava up, and my brows pull together in confusion. "I know this guy. He's a contractor. You can hire him to do just about anything. Kidnap someone. Kill them. Whatever."

Elijah crouches beside the guy on the other side of the couch and follows my lead. "This guy used to do odd jobs for Angelo."

"They wanted Mia," I whisper, and he meets my eyes.

"We need to get you two somewhere safe."

Shattered Promises

Eleven

I tried not to let myself get used to being safe. But I guess it's not an easy thing to deny yourself after being in danger for so long.

Perhaps I should have expected something like this, but they assured me it would be okay. But nothing is okay. All I've managed to do is drag my shit into their laps, and I can't be responsible for them being in danger. I won't.

It's irrelevant that I barely know any of the Saint James family, or that the only reason I crossed paths with Clara is because we both found ourselves in the possession of a notorious crime boss, or that Tommy and Ace failed me in the past. I won't be the reason they're hurt…or worse.

I huddle between the wall and the end of the clawfoot bathtub, the cold porcelain digging painfully into my skin, but I allow the pain to push down the panic. If they're here for me, I'll walk out with my head held high. The taste of freedom isn't nearly enough, but it's something.

Gunshots slice through the otherwise quiet suite, and each one makes me flinch. What if Ace gets hurt trying to protect me? What if they kill him? The thought has dread pooling in my belly. None of this would be happening if I never came back into his life. Or if he just dropped me off at a bus station and sent me on my way.

A loud knock on the door drags a yelp from my throat, and I quickly slap my hand over my mouth. *So much for showing no fear,* I admonish myself.

"It's me, sugar. Can you let me in?" Ace's voice is soft but strained. He's trying to sound calm, but I know him well enough to know he's anything but right now. "It's safe, I promise."

I let out a shaky breath and shuffle out from my hiding place.

Ace is okay.

I'm okay.

Everything is okay.

The words replay in my mind as my trembling hand reaches for the lock, but I don't get a chance to touch the handle because as soon as it's unlocked, Ace barrels in, his eyes wide and frantic.

As soon as the stunning green brushes over me, he lets out a breath before tugging me into his arms. My first instinct is to panic. I don't like to be touched. Not anymore. But there's something about Ace's touch that's different. It doesn't elicit the same terror as almost every other human being.

His hand finds its way to the back of my head, and he presses my face further into his chest. Ace has always been the calm one. Tommy had already been through so much by the time we met him, so his demons were always lurking, but Ace was nothing but calm, and that's what makes the way his body trembles as he holds me that much stranger. "You're okay," he whispers, more to himself than to me.

"We need to go," someone announces from the doorway. "I called Snow. She's meeting us at her apartment. It's been empty for months, and the security system is top-notch."

Ace tenses but lets out a breath and nods. "Thanks, man." He manages to pry his body from mine just enough that he can look down at me, but I find myself back in his arms a second later. My heart beats heavily in my chest. Was Ace really this worried about me? "Let's pack up, and I'll get you somewhere safe."

He stalks out of the room before I can respond, and I find myself staring into Elijah Russo's moss-green gaze. He seems just as confused as I am by what he just witnessed.

T wo hours and three random bodyguards' help later, and we're set up in one of the most elegant penthouses I've ever seen in my life, and strangely I've found myself in quite a few.

The high ceilings give the space an expansive feel, the floor-to-ceiling windows that surround us bring in so much natural light even on a cool Chicago afternoon, and the white and gold accents make me wish for a space like this of my own.

Too often rich people use their money to buy the most expensive of everything, and it normally makes everything gaudy and has the opposite effect. But although I'm certain everything in this apartment costs more than I can comprehend, it's tasteful.

Ace relaxed as soon as he saw the extra security Elijah had organized, and the extensive protocols that have been put in place seem to have dragged some of the tension from his shoulders.

A huge desk appeared beneath one of the windows twenty minutes ago, and he's busied himself setting up his computers again. I'm not sure who packed them up as we were hustled out of the hotel suite, careful not to get in the way of the two men in hazmat suits that Elijah called "cleaners."

It's been a weird day, and that feels like a strange thought to have for someone who has lived the life I have. Nothing about my life has ever been normal, but today has been extra odd.

Elijah is by the door, barking orders at some poor guys that have been tasked with guarding me. He got extra grouchy when Ace informed him Doc would be coming to check me over after what happened at the suite. I didn't have the heart to remind him that apart from the explosion, I wasn't actually in the room for any of it.

I messaged Emerson to ask if she could come sit with me during the examination because if he's going to be here anyway, I might as well have him do all the other checks too. Ace hasn't stopped moving for long enough for me to tell him, but we'll cross that bridge when we come to it.

His eyes flick up to make sure I'm still where he left me on the cloud of a couch. It's without a doubt the most comfortable surface I've ever sat on, and I'll be happy to sleep here if it comes down to it. He can't keep his eyes off me for more than a few minutes at a time, and each time our eyes clash, it makes my heart skip a beat because I know he's worried about me. Because he lost me once, and he can't bear the thought of losing me again.

Commotion drags both our attention from the other, and I find Emerson standing in the doorway with Rayne on her heels. He surveys the area closely, including each of the guards as if he's vetting them for whether they should be close to his wife or not.

"I wasn't sure we'd beat Doc here," Emerson admits as she crosses the apartment to the couch I'm perched on. She's changed into a pair of yoga pants and an oversized sweater, but she looks just as beautiful as she did when she came to see me earlier.

Ace's brows pull together in confusion, and guilt hits me. I should have told him. "I asked Emerson to come sit with me during the examination. She suggested that perhaps I should have some tests given…" But I can't finish the sentence. I don't want to tell this room full of people that I was used and abused for years. That my body and my choices stopped belonging to me the moment my foster father shoved me into the trunk of a car and sold me into trafficking.

It takes a few seconds for the pieces to fall into place, but it's the flash of disgust that crosses his eyes that makes my stomach drop.

Here I am with my stomach flipping when he's worried about me, but it's nothing more than pity. He feels responsible for the things that happened eight years ago, and now I'm a burden. Just like I've always been.

Twelve

Something changed when she told me she was going to have Doc run some checks, but I can't quite put my finger on what it is. I thought we were finally making progress. She hasn't looked ready to do a runner since I settled her on the couch when we got here, and she's welcomed my touch on several occasions.

So what changed?

She disappeared into the bedroom with Emerson and the tattooed giant twenty minutes ago, and I'm having a hard time distracting myself.

I should be in there with her.

"Can you sit down? You're even making me anxious," Elijah grumbles from where he's perched on a barstool. I'm surprised he's still here. I thought he would have left as soon as we were settled to get back to Snow, but he seems content barking orders at the security team and helping me set up my shit.

"They've been in there for hours."

Rayne chuckles and shakes his head from where he's leaning against the counter in the kitchen. "It's been twenty minutes."

I glare at him before finally relenting, taking up the stool beside Elijah. I don't know why these assholes are here, but they're getting on my nerves.

"Does it get easier?" I ask before I realize the words have left my mouth.

"Letting them out of your sight?" Rayne asks.

I nod, and they both shake their heads.

"No. After Snow was taken, I couldn't even let her pee without having the door cracked open so I could keep an eye on her," Elijah admits.

Rayne brushes his fingers along the stubble on his jaw. "As you can see, I'm still not able to let Emerson out of the house without me or without a substantial security presence. And even then, I obsessively watch her tracker to make sure she gets where she's meant to be going."

I sigh and drop my head into my hands.

"But they get used to it. Emerson still gets frustrated, but she understands that I'm only doing it because I'm terrified of losing her again."

That makes me pop my head up to look at him. Rayne Saint James, the most ruthless enforcer in the city, just admitted to what scares him the most. I've spent all this time resenting their entire family for shutting down my operations all those years ago, but all they've done since we rescued Mia and Clara is help us, admit their vulnerabilities, and use their expansive resources to keep us both safe.

"Snow's the same." Elijah nods. "We've always had an… unconventional relationship anyway, but after I almost lost her, it got a lot worse."

"Unconventional?" Rayne scoffs. "Is that short for stalking and kidnapping?"

Elijah glares at his brother-in-law. "Yes."

Before Rayne has a chance to respond, the door to the bedroom opens and Doc strolls out, his tattered medical bag looking more than a little worse for wear. The handle is worn and discolored, and I wouldn't be surprised if the thing disintegrated before it makes it to the front door.

I'm out of my seat before I make the decision to approach him. His tattooed arms are covered to his wrist by a tight black shirt, and even at my very respectable six foot two, he towers over me. How tall is this motherfucker?

"How is she?" I ask.

He gives me a once-over, the same way he did when he walked in and immediately started fussing over Emerson and Mia. Rayne told me not to take it personally, that he hates people, with the exception of a few select people. "She's not hurt from the explosion, apart from a bruise on one of her knees. I've taken some blood and I will have the results to you in the next twenty-four hours. Mia has granted permission for you to receive these results. I would like to get her in for some X-rays and perhaps an MRI. There seems to be a few old injuries that were not treated at the time, and it will help with a treatment plan if I can gauge how bad these injuries were."

Each word out of his mouth has bile climbing up my throat. Unhealed injuries? Test results? All things I can't fix for her. Pain I can't take away. And I fucking hate it.

"Thank you for coming on such short notice."

"I'm used to it. This asshole calls me every second night with questions about Emerson's pregnancy." He gestures to Rayne, but there's a small smirk playing on his lips. He obviously finds his antics amusing despite the surly exterior he shows them.

"Does he call more or less than Everett when Wynter was pregnant?" Elijah cajoles.

Doc turns his intense eyes on him and smirks. "I'm sure neither will be anything compared to when Snow finds out she's pregnant."

"Oh Jesus." Emerson rolls her eyes as she strolls back into the room with Mia on her heels. "You're never going to sleep again if the Saint James and Russo families keep procreating."

"Don't remind me. I'm thinking it might be time to fake my own death and disappear off the face of the earth." He chuckles, and I'm so stunned by the display that I don't know what to say. I've met Doc a few times, and each time he's been more distant than the last. Perhaps all the times he's had to tend to the women of that family are softening him.

"It might be time. What happens if all four of them knock us up at the same time?" Her eyes widen in mock horror.

"Sweet girl," Rayne warns.

She smirks and walks into his arms, wrapping herself around her husband. "You know I'm teasing. We're Doc's favorite patients."

"Only because you always shower, and I can't say the same for the assholes I normally have to dig bullets out of."

Mia watches the exchange like she's watching a tennis match, her eyes flitting from one person to the other, but she doesn't seem afraid. No, if anything she's amused by the bickering. I've tried not to think too much about the company she's kept since she was taken from me, but I can't imagine it was anything like this.

She wraps her arms around her middle, but it's not a defensive gesture like it has been the last few days, it's just a place to put her arms, and I'm relieved by it. Maybe this is what she needs. She needs people. She needs to laugh. She needs to feel normal.

And I'm going to give her everything she needs, no matter what.

THIRTEEN

MIA

I yawn and snuggle deeper into the cushion I'm wrapped around on the couch. Jesus, this thing is comfortable.

Ace types furiously on his computer, the steady clicking lulling me in and out of sleep. After everyone left, I curled up on the couch, and I haven't moved since. It's probably the small amount of soup I allowed my stomach to sustain me for another few days. The cramps I was rewarded with were less than pleasant, but I managed to keep them to myself and avoid Ace fussing over me.

He's seemed more settled since Doc checked me over. As if having a doctor confirm I'm not about to drop dead has allowed him some semblance of peace.

And if I'm honest, it had the same effect on me. Even if Doc did comment on my need to put on weight. I suspect the blood tests will return the same conclusion, but that's a bridge I'll have to cross when I come to it.

A phone ringing breaks through the quiet apartment, and Ace

quickly silences it. "Everett," he answers coldly and listens for the response before cursing under his breath.

"Are you sure?"

Another beat of silence before he sighs.

"Thanks. Let me know if you find anything else."

He ends the call as quickly as he answered it before looking over his shoulder at me with his brows pulled together.

"What's wrong?" I ask.

He hesitates for a few seconds, weighing up whether to tell me whatever it is, but he stands from his seat and closes the distance between us. He sits on the chaise across from me, resting his elbows on his knees to bring his eyes down to meet mine. "That was Everett Masters. He's done some digging, and he's figured out who hired those contractors to come for you."

My breath hitches in my throat. I'm no one. Just some girl they stole and who was sold from one man to the next when they grew bored. I'm not worth this kind of hassle.

"Do you remember much from your time at The Factory?"

I shake my head. It all feels like a blur. There are bits and pieces I remember so vividly I swear they happened yesterday, but mostly it seems like a life someone else lived. Not that I would wish that on my worst enemy.

He nods and scrubs his hand over his face. "Can you think of any reason Kyle Clark would go to such extremes to get you back?"

The mere sound of his name has bile climbing the back of my throat. The Factory has many faces, many men who parade the patriarchy in front of the women they hold captive and sell. But he's the one my nightmares will never be free of.

Ace's eyes widen, and I realize I've stopped breathing. I quickly draw in a ragged breath and hold the cushion in my lap tighter.

"I...I...I don't know," I whisper.

He takes a deep, steadying breath, but the way his hands clench into fists proves how close to the edge he is. "That's who put the ad up on the noticeboard. And it was an open call."

"Which means there will probably be more coming?"

He nods, barely schooling his features from showing the rage that shines in his eyes. "I'm not going to let them take you, Mia. I lost you once, and I have no intention of ever losing you again."

I let out a shaky breath, the words poised on the tip of my tongue, but I struggle to force them out. "You should hand me over."

The anger he was trying to hide from me contorts his face, and a second later, his fingers curl around my chin, his face so close his breath whispers across my cheeks. His masculine scent is overwhelming, but I don't try to escape his hold. I don't want to. "Never."

I open my mouth to respond, but the heavy set of his face leaves no room for argument. This isn't a fight I can win, at least not yet.

Ace's thumb gently brushes across my cheek as his eyes follow the path with reverence before flicking down to my lips. The move has my breath stuttering in my chest, but I still don't pull away.

He only hesitates for another beat before his lips crash down on mine and steal the air right from my lungs. His lips are as soft as I remember them being when he took my first kiss the night he and Tommy ran away, but there's more to it now. Years of pent-up sadness, longing, and fear pour into the gentle caress of his lips on mine, and when his tongue demands entrance, I'm powerless to deny him.

He consumes me, taking exactly what he wants, and I give it freely. Because this is the first time I've been kissed in the last eight years and the other person's touch hasn't made me want to tear my own skin from my body. It's the first time I've craved touch in so long I almost forgot what it meant to be desperate for it.

He tears his lips from mine all too soon, pressing them to my forehead before pushing back to look me over. "Never again, Mia."

I nod, even though I know ultimately it won't be his decision to make. When Kyle Clark wants someone, there's nothing he won't do to get to them, and that includes going up against Frost Industries.

Shattered Promises

Fourteen

I glance over my shoulder at Mia sleeping on the couch behind me. She hasn't moved since I told her there's an open bounty out for her, and I don't blame her. As if she hasn't been through enough. As if her life hasn't been riddled with enough terror, she still has to look over her shoulder, looking for the next asshole who wants to hurt her.

But I won't let them.

I meant it when I said I'd never hand her over. She's mine. She was mine when we were kids, and I didn't understand what it meant to need someone with every beat of your heart. She was mine when I built a life for us that she never got to lead, and she was mine every single day she was missing. Mia will always be mine, and I will always protect her.

I cast my eyes over the ad Everett sent me and sigh. We've been trying to get the thing down for hours, but almost as quickly as we manage to get it off a noticeboard, it appears on another one. Everett and I make up the two best hackers in the country, so I'm not sure how they're outplaying us like this.

I look at my other screen as it refreshes, a new batch of contractors who have viewed the ad appearing. For fuck's sake. Between the constant refreshes and the amount they're willing to part with to get her back, it's going to be open season around here.

Everett has been working on figuring out where she's been all these years. Who bought her from The Factory, how many assholes dared to hurt my woman, but it's slow going, and I'm so fucking snowed under, I'm not sure I'll ever catch up. That'll teach me for constantly taking enough clients that I'm too busy to wallow in my own self-pity.

Mia's whimpers drag my attention back to her sleeping form, and I run my hand down my face. I'm so fucking tired, so tired that my bones ache with exhaustion, but I doubt I'll be able to sleep. How could I possibly close my eyes and relax when she's in danger?

I shove myself to my feet and cross to where she's sleeping. I know better than to touch her while she's asleep, but I'm drawn to her the same way a moth is to a flame. She's always had the power to destroy me, I just wonder how long it will take her to realize it.

I drop into the seat above her head and gently brush my fingers through the blonde strands. Our foster mother was obsessed with her hair. She said there was no way she wouldn't grow out of the white-blonde locks, but she never did.

There's so much about the last eight years I don't know, so many chapters of her book that I haven't read, so many things that don't quite add up, and I can't ask her without trudging up the hell she's lived through.

She leans into my touch, her head lolling to the side until she's resting on my palm. There's some part of her that still finds solace with me the way she did as a child, but she's fighting it. She doesn't know how to trust anymore, and she certainly doesn't know how to love or be loved.

I've spent a lot of time since she disappeared feeling helpless, but as I stare down at the broken shell of the woman I've obsessed over most of my life, I realize I didn't know the meaning of the word until right now. I can't let them take her. I can't allow her to be hurt again. It's not an option.

I drift off to sleep in the armchair across from where Mia sleeps, unable to drag myself away from her even when I should. This isn't sustainable, even if the men of Frost Industries have reassured me it's normal for men like us. Men who are used to being in control of everything. But I also can't see it changing anytime soon.

Mia was stolen from me for eight years. She lived through hell, to an extent I'm too afraid to ask her, but I'm not willing to risk that again, even if I know it's unhealthy to be attached to someone at the hip the way I am her.

My neck is stiff when consciousness returns to me. How long did I sleep like that for? I've never been much of a sleeper. When I was in foster care, it was more of a safety measure. You can never allow your guard to fall too low when the people around you are almost always fucked in the head.

And then when we got out, it was the worry for Mia that

stopped me from closing my eyes at night. After that, it's obvious what made me choose a life of permanent exhaustion.

I flick my eyes open and notice there's a soft blanket wrapped around me. Confusion quickly turns to panic when I realize Mia isn't asleep on the couch across from me anymore.

Where the hell is she?

And how the fuck could I allow myself to sleep so soundly? Ordinarily, every bump in the night is enough to wake me up.

"Mia?" I call through the penthouse as I drop the blanket onto the armchair.

I look around for any signs of where she might be, but everything is where I left it last night. The kitchen is untouched, the desk Elijah set up for her still has the chair neatly tucked under it, so where could she be?

I move through the penthouse, calling her name, but each step I take has dread washing over me. Please tell me she didn't run. Please tell me she wouldn't be so stupid as to put her life in danger.

Every room I check is empty until I come to the master bedroom. The bed is still neatly made, the bathroom untouched.

She's gone.

She fucking ran.

Movement on the balcony catches my eye, and a small figure curled up on the outdoor couch allows me to breathe.

I push the door open and step into the cool morning air. I didn't bother to check the time in my panic, but from the sun's position in the sky, it can't be any later than seven.

Mia's tiny frame is folded in on itself with a blanket wrapped around her shoulders. She doesn't look up when the door clicks open, her eyes glued to the city beneath us.

"Hey," I say on a hushed sigh. I don't know how this woman so easily sends me into a blind panic when nothing else has ever been able to do the same. "You should have woken me."

"You haven't slept since you found me," she whispers. "You needed the sleep."

"And you don't?"

She looks up at me, a sad smile tugging at the corners of her lips. "I don't sleep well. Sleep was always risky, so I got good at surviving on very little."

I nod and drop into the seat next to her. "It's cold out here."

She shrugs and pulls the blanket tighter around herself. "I didn't get to sit outside much. All the places I was kept had intense security, but I guess the outdoors were harder to ensure I wasn't a danger to myself, so I was mostly confined. It's just nice getting some fresh air." Her haunted eyes flit back to me. "Would you prefer I stay inside?"

The question isn't posed as anything other than that, but it cuts me to my fucking core. She thinks I want to cage her the same way every other man in her life has.

But all I've ever wanted is to set her free.

FIFTEEN

MIA

T he brisk air settles on my skin, the Chicago skyline the same as I remember it.

I've stayed in places like this before, but I was never allowed out on the balcony. I guess my owners were too afraid I'd jump. Don't get me wrong, the thought occurred to me on more than a few occasions, but I was never brave enough to end it.

The idea that I could fail and that I'd be punished was enough to bring me back from any ledge I ever thought about leaping from.

And although I'm free now and I have my whole life ahead of me, I barely caught those intrusive thoughts when they crossed my mind before Ace materialized in all his rumpled glory.

Everyone would be better off if I wasn't here.

Ace would be able to get work done.

Emerson would be able to focus on her growing family.

The rest of the Saint James family would have one less person to watch over.

But most importantly, I'd be at peace.

I used to think about what it would be like to be free. I thought I'd be able to go on living as if nothing ever happened, but unfortunately, that's not the reality I'm living right now.

At least before, I knew what to expect and what others expected of me.

I had a purpose, and while it was one I hated with a fiery passion, at least I knew what to do to keep myself safe.

But now? Now I have no idea what I'm doing. I have no idea what's around the corner or who might come for me.

The idea that Kyle, the man who broke me into a million pieces just so he could mold me into the perfect whore, is looking for me, has ice-cold dread seeping into my every muscle.

I've been racking my brain for hours trying to work it out, trying to think of any reason he would want me back so desperately, but I keep coming up empty, and that only adds to my fear.

Whenever my owners wanted an upgrade, Kyle was the one to facilitate it, but I can't see why he would care if I escaped. I presume he's been paid each time, so what the fuck could be the reason he's going to such an expense to get me back?

"No, sugar. You can come outside anytime you want." Ace forces his voice to soften, but the edge in his tone would be enough to slice even the strongest of men.

I nod and drag my attention off his haunted green eyes. I've been known to lose myself in them since the first time I saw him. A lot of that time in my life is a blur of sadness, but Ace is the one thing I remember as clear as day. The way he took my hand and showed me my room. How he checked in on me in the early days to make sure I was coping with the change okay. How he protected me and took the fall for things I did so I wouldn't be starved or beaten by our foster parents. It may as well have happened yesterday, the memories are so vivid.

But I can't let myself fall into those beautiful eyes anymore, because I'm not sure I'll survive being torn from him again.

The kiss from last night plays in my mind, the softness of his lips on mine and how badly I wanted him to give me everything, to replace all the bad memories with nothing but him. Except that's unrealistic.

If Ace had taken things any further, if he'd touched me the wrong way or trapped me beneath his body, I would have been thrown into memories I would rather not remember during my time with him.

It's for the best we never take things any further, no matter how badly I want to.

"Do you want me to make you some breakfast?" he asks.

"No, thank you."

He sighs, but he doesn't argue with me. I almost wish he would. I wish he would stop treating me like I'm broken, because that's never how I want him to see me.

I want him to look at me and see the girl he loved before he even understood the meaning of the four-letter word. But not even I see her when I look in the mirror anymore.

We fall into a comfortable silence, the sounds of the city below the only background noise as we stare out at the horizon.

My days here are numbered. That's the only truth I can bring myself to accept right now. If Kyle has set his sights on me, there's no way he's going to drop it, even if it means he has to go up against the Saint James and Russo families to get me.

Ace's phone buzzes in his pocket, and he quickly checks the caller ID before sighing. "Storm," he greets and waits for the other man's response.

He's been nothing but kind to me, but Storm Saint James is as intimidating as hell, and just the sound of his name makes me shift in my seat. I believe Emerson when she says that their family has been involved in freeing a lot of women and children from trafficking, but that doesn't make their leader any less terrifying.

Ace pinches the bridge of his nose at whatever Storm says on the other end of the phone, but he's trying to keep his cool at whatever he's being told, I'm assuming for my benefit. "Have you found anything else?"

The rest of the call goes in the same fashion. Storm says something, Ace gives a brief response, usually with a question that gives nothing away, before finally he gives a curt thank you and hangs up.

His grip on the phone is so tight his knuckles turn white, and for a moment I wonder if it's possible for a human to crush a phone in their bare hands. "I need to ask you some questions."

"Okay…"

"About where you've been the last eight years. We need to try to understand why Kyle is going to such lengths to get you back when we know you're not the only girl that's escaped." He rubs his face with both hands. "Everett has found six girls who have escaped in the last twelve months, and as far as we can tell, there's been no attempt to get them back."

I suck in a breath and hold the blanket closer to myself. "I don't know why I would be any different," I whisper.

"Which is why we need to trace back since you met him to see if we can find any hint as to why he's willing to put so much into getting you back."

Bile rises in my throat. I've spent a lot of time mastering the art of shoving the horrors into a tiny box in the back of my mind. The thought of opening that box, of unleashing those memories, makes me want to throw up, even if there's nothing in my stomach to expel.

"I hate that I have to ask this of you, Mia. I can't fucking stand the idea of making you relive any of it, but it's the only way to keep you safe, and right now that's my main priority." He turns to me, his eyes pleading with me to understand. And I do. I get it. But once I tell him everything he wants to know, he'll never look at me the way he did that sixteen-year-old version of me, the one whose first kiss he stole. I'll always be the broken woman he didn't save from a lifetime of terror.

SIXTEEN

ACE

I've spent years loathing my own existence for ever letting Mia be taken, but right now is the lowest point I think I could possibly hit.

She's not ready for this.

I'm not sure she ever will be, and yet here I am asking her to divulge all the things she would rather forget, like the fucking asshole I am.

While Storm was telling me about all the dead ends they've hit, I was trying to work out how to broach this with Mia. How I was going to ask her to reveal her darkest moments to me, and I considered asking Emerson to come speak to her. She's better placed than I am, has more experience with trauma survivors than I do, but I realized that was more to protect myself than it was Mia.

I need to hear this because I need to be forced to deal with the fact I let her down, and no matter which way you look at it, everything that happened to her was my fault.

She takes a steadying breath and nods. She pulls the blanket tighter and stares out at the cityscape in front of us. "Kyle's the one who organizes buyers. He vets them, makes sure they're not buying women to set them free. He doesn't care if people buy girls to kill or hunt, just as long as they're not giving them freedom." She chokes on a laugh, but there's no humor in the sound, just sadness.

"How do you know all this?"

"He used to get chatty during training sessions. I guess it didn't matter what he divulged to us girls because we were never getting away. Our lives were set out for us, and no one would ever care what we had to say, so he had nothing to lose by telling us his secrets."

I force my body to remain relaxed despite the nausea that rolls through me at the idea of Mia being "trained." I don't know what that means, but my imagination is more than enough to make me homicidal. "Is there anything you can think of that he may have told you but not the other girls?"

She shakes her head. "I don't think so. We weren't really allowed to talk to one another though. Our job was to stay quiet and do as we were told, and part of our training was to learn our place. We were there to serve, not to speak. Anytime we weren't serving, we were to be in silence waiting for our next chance to serve." Her voice is so robotic, like she's reading straight from a script, and it's clear she heard that bullshit enough for it to be embedded in her mind.

I tighten my fists until my knuckles ache, but it's not enough. It's taking every ounce of control not to lose my shit right now, not to tear this whole fucking penthouse apart with the rage bubbling in my chest, but I remain in place, waiting for whatever else is going to come out of Mia's mouth that will throw fuel on the fire.

A soft sob fills my ears, and when I look over at Mia, she's wiping her cheeks.

"If this is too much we can stop." We can't. I need this information, but I won't push her, I refuse to subject her to any more pain than she's already been through. We can find another way. It's not worth dragging all of this to the surface if all it brings her is pain.

She shakes her head and brings her deep blue eyes up to meet mine. There will never be a day, in this life or the next, where I don't lose myself every time I look into the unreal pools. "I'm okay." She sucks in a breath before continuing. "He didn't train me like most of the girls because I was a virgin. He knew he would get more for me if I was intact, but that didn't make the things he did to me any less horrific. Toward the end, I started to wonder if he was going to sacrifice the whole thing and take a lesser amount for me."

"Did you ever…" I pause, not wanting to ask the question as soon as the beginning falls from my lips, but this is important. "Did you ever see Kyle again after you left The Factory?"

"A few times, but he never had the chance to make up for lost time if that's what you're asking."

I nod and brush my fingers over the stubble on my chin. I wonder if that's it. The one who got away? "Did he spend more time with you than the other girls? Give you any kind of special treatment?"

She thinks on that for a moment, and I take the time to calm myself, to focus on anything other than the conversation I'm having with the only woman I've ever loved about how she was sold into sex trafficking. "Yeah. He spent a lot more time with me than the others. I don't think I noticed it or, I guess, thought much of it because I assumed it was because I was inexperienced. But…he used to have a nickname for me." Her brows tug together as she tries to think back. "I can't remember what it was. But when I saw him interacting with other girls, I never heard anything like it. He also didn't beat me like he did the others. When I broke the rules or didn't please him the way I was taught, my punishments were different."

"Different how?"

"His torment of me was more psychological than it was physical, but I guess I put it down to me being sold as a perfect blonde virgin with big blue eyes. I thought he didn't want to mark me in case it brought down my value."

"Who were you sold to first?"

"A man named Douglas Finch. He wasn't as mean as the others, but he had a thing for innocence. He grew sick of me in a little over a year. Kyle facilitated my next sale on behalf of Douglas to a man named Craig Lewis, who had me for maybe two years…" She thinks about it for a second, her eyes squeezing shut as if it will help the memories come easier. "He died. A heart attack while he was…while he was on top of me. And then I was sold on to a man named Cyrus Kemp." Her body trembles as the name falls from between her lips, and I already know I'm not going to like whatever comes out of her mouth next. "He was…violent. He got off on causing others pain, both physical and mental. He would starve me for days, and then when I was almost to the point of no return, he'd force-feed me until I threw up. He'd string me up and beat me until I passed out, and then when I woke up, he'd be using my body. He would drug me regularly, getting me hooked on God knows what, so I relied on him, so I wouldn't try to end it because I needed my next fix." Tears fall against her soft cheeks, and each word brings bile further and further up my throat. He tortured her. He fucking tortured my girl. He better fucking hope he's not still breathing because the death I'm planning for him in the back of my mind is worse than any even a sick fuck like him can imagine.

I reach over and brush my thumb across her cheek, wiping away the tears as they fall. "We can stop, sugar. If this is too much, we can stop."

"I'm okay," Mia whispers, leaning into my hand to give herself the strength to keep going. "Cyrus grew bored after a couple of years. My responses to his torture became predictable, and I really thought he was going to kill me, but then one day everything stopped. He stopped torturing me, he stopped using me, it just stopped, and it wasn't until a few weeks later when Kyle arrived that I realized they were getting me back to baseline so I could be sold on again."

I close my eyes and take what feels like my fiftieth steadying breath since I asked her to go through the worst years of her life. I don't know how much more I can handle listening to.

"I was relieved, but also afraid. Some of my injuries from Cyrus weren't quite healed yet so I wasn't ready for sale. Kyle took me to a house in the middle of the woods, and he left me there with some of his guards with strict instructions not to hurt me, but they didn't listen. They saw it as an excuse to use a free whore as much as they could like they did the girls at

The Factory."

I shove myself to my feet and move away from Mia as the rage I've been desperately trying to push down boils over the edge. I need to get her out of the firing line, because right now I'm ready to tear the head from every man who even thought about touching my woman. It's irrelevant if they did or whether they were just a bystander, they all need to be wiped from the face of this planet, and I will not rest until I lay the heart of every one of them at Mia's feet like a sacrifice to a deity.

My deity.

SHATTERED PROMISES

Seventeen

MIA

Ace paces up and down the balcony, his hands fisted at his sides as he tries desperately to reign in his emotions. The muscles in his neck and shoulders are tense with the pressure of his anger, and he won't look at me.

I don't know if he realizes it or not, but his eyes are looking anywhere but at me.

I knew this was a possibility.

I knew there was a very good chance he would look at me differently once he knew even a fraction of what I'd been through, but I wasn't ready for it.

He can't even look at me.

He's disgusted by me.

The tears falling against my cheeks come harder and faster as choked sobs escape my throat. I spent so long repressing my emotions that now I have no idea how to control them once

I've set them free.

I dart my gaze to the door. Maybe I can sneak back into the apartment. I just need to put some warmer clothes on and then I'll be able to leave. I'll work everything else out afterward, but I need to get out of here. I won't be able to handle the disgust when he finally forces himself to look at me.

It's not like this is my first rodeo. Everyone I've met in the last eight years has looked at me like I'm the scum of the earth, because to them that's exactly what I am. I'm just a piece of meat, a warm body for men to use when they need a stress reliever. But I can't handle Ace looking at me like that, not when the memory of him was the only thing that got me through some days.

As quietly as I can manage, I slip from the outdoor couch, heading for the door. Each step is planned in my head, but going through the motions won't be as easy as it seems in my mind.

I only make it three tentative steps before a strong, tattooed arm wraps around my middle and tugs me back into a body so hard it may as well be made from stone.

"Where do you think you're going, sugar?" he murmurs against the shell of my ear.

It occurs to me that I should be panicking right now. That being restrained like this should have me spiraling into an anxiety attack or at the very least fighting like hell, but even without being able to see who has me wrapped in their arms, I know it's Ace, and my body relaxes into his on its own accord.

"I was going to go," I whisper.

"Go where?"

"I don't know. I just—" I choke on the words before they can make it to my lips.

"You just what, Mia?"

"I can't see you look at me with disgust." The words are so quiet I barely hear them myself, but the tension in his body tells me he heard every last one.

He moves so quickly I barely catch myself when he spins me around and presses my back against the railing. The hum of the city below should frighten me, but Ace would never let me fall, and when you've been through the shit I have, you learn what should be feared on this earth. And heights? It ain't it.

The intensity of his eyes makes me want to look away, to look anywhere but into the fire, but I couldn't even if I wanted to. His body traps mine, holding me exactly where he wants me, and I won't be able to move until he decides I can.

"Do you see disgust, sugar?" he drawls in a low growl that sets my belly alight. It's funny, I assumed I would always be broken, that there's no way I would ever feel arousal, or want to touch a man again, but it's like my body remembers Ace. It remembers our first kiss and the way I used to wonder what our first time would be like. And it's not afraid, it's not repulsed by the idea of being touched. It craves Ace just like the rest of me does.

I shake my head slowly, keeping my eyes locked with his.

"Words, Mia. I always want your words."

"No."

"What do you see?"

I open my mouth to respond, but words fail me because the things I see in Ace, they're nothing like anything I've ever seen in another man, or woman, for that matter. The way he looks at me is wild and unhinged, but also so fucking beautiful.

He rests one of his palms on my cheek and carefully cradles my face while the other remains locked on my hip, keeping me exactly where he wants me. "I don't need to look in the mirror for me to tell you the answer to that question. It's adoration, and obsession, and a whole lot of anger that I missed so many years with you by my side. It's guilt that I let that happen to you, that I couldn't find you no matter how fucking hard I tried. It's frustration that I'll never be able to take away all the pain those assholes inflicted on you. I'll never be able to take those memories away. But most of all, sugar, all you should see when you look into my eyes is how fucking much I love you and how I've loved you since the moment I realized what that word meant."

The air leaves my lungs in a sudden whoosh, and I can't breathe. Love? That's an emotion I never imagined I'd get to feel. I thought eventually, maybe with Damon Lombardi, the man I was supposed to marry before Clara and I were rescued, I might be able to convince myself he loved me, but I never thought in a million years someone would be able to look at the broken shell of a woman and feel so strongly.

His thumb brushes over my cheek, wiping away tears I didn't realize I was crying. "You gotta stop trying to leave, sugar. I know this is a lot for you. I know you've been through hell and your perception of the world is fucked up, but if there's one thing you need to know, it's that I will hunt you to the edge of the fucking earth if you run from me. I spent eight years searching for you. I spent endless nights scouring every fucking noticeboard I could find. I used favors to try to figure out where the fuck you were, and now that I have you, I can't let you go. I fucking can't, Mia."

The reverence in his voice, the way he holds me so tight, just shy of the point of pain, like he knows where that line is and he's not willing to cross it, makes me believe everything that's come out of his mouth.

"Okay." I nod. "I'll stop trying to leave."

A small smile tips up the corners of his lips. "Thank you, sugar."

Eighteen

I t didn't take as long as I thought it would to track down Kyle's men.

The man himself is a different story, but the assholes that work for him, the ones who thought no one would ever care enough about their low-level asses to go after them, were almost too fucking easy.

Part of me wanted the chase. I wanted to use all the skills I've amassed over the years and dig and dig and dig until I uncovered all there was to know about these assholes.

But it was too easy.

Five men who violated my woman. Five men who will soon find their way to the bottom of Lake Michigan for their sins.

Because it was so fucking easy to find them, I dug around in their lives a little. None of them are married, surprise, surprise, but a few of them are deadbeat dads. From what I can tell from social media, they only see their kids on holidays and the occasional birthday, so I'll be doing them a favor by wiping their pathetic sperm donors off the planet.

Three of the five still live in Chicago, so they'll be my first targets. I'm not ready to go far from Mia just yet, and I'm not sure how on board she'll be about taking a weekend trip to murder people, even if they did hurt her.

I look up from my computer to where she's on her laptop at the desk Elijah set up for her. She hadn't used any kind of device since high school, so I took some time this morning to show her the basics, but every now and then she lets out a frustrated sigh when she can't remember how to do something.

Emerson is going to help her enroll to get her GED, but aside from that, she hasn't given any indication about what her next steps might be, and I don't think she knows.

Right now, Mia is trying to survive. She's trying to wade through the pool of her new normal, one so vastly different from all the ones she's lived through the last eight years.

She must feel my eyes on her because she looks up and her gaze clashes with mine right before a blush creeps up her neck and onto her cheeks.

This morning was heavy. And I threw the L bomb onto the fire without giving it much thought, but it made her stop trying to leave, and if I'm honest, she's been more at ease since. Those words have been sitting heavy on my cold, dead heart for years, and there's something liberating about having finally set them free.

She tilts her head to the side, waiting patiently for me to say something.

"Do you want some lunch?" I know I'm beating a dead horse at this point, that her issues with food stem much further than just since she came home, but I'll keep trying, because eventually she'll say yes.

She opens her mouth to say no but pauses and swallows heavily. "Maybe just some soup if that's okay?"

I smile and shove my chair back. I don't give a shit what she eats. She could ask for lobster for three square meals a day and I'd make it happen as long as she's eating something.

I pull open the fridge and spot the soups I had delivered this morning while she was showering. It's the only thing I've been able to get her to eat since she came home, so I bought every type I could from the local health food store. I don't normally buy into that bullshit, but Doc said she needs to be eating nutrient-dense foods, and I'm following his advice to the goddamn letter.

I tip a chicken noodle soup container into a saucepan and light the stove to warm it, all the while aware of Mia's eyes on me.

"Do you want some toast?" I ask without looking at her.

There's a long pause again, but I give her the time to think it through. It's more than a little encouraging that she's thinking about it at all considering she's answered before I've even finished my sentence on every other occasion.

"Yes, please."

I let out a relieved breath but don't turn to her. I have limited experience dealing with people in general, but I know this is something Mia would be self-conscious about, and I don't want to scare her off.

I put a piece of sourdough bread into the toaster and stir the soup until both are ready. I serve them up and carry them over to where Mia's still sitting at her desk, chewing her bottom lip nervously.

Her eyes widen when she sees how big the bowl of soup is and swallows heavily.

I place them down in front of her and crouch down, placing both hands on her bare knees. "You don't have to eat it all. Just eat what you can, okay?"

Her eyes dart to mine and holds them for long seconds before nodding. "Thank you."

I force myself back to my desk and stare at the screen in front of me without turning back. If I watch her, she won't eat at all. I have to give her space, even if every instinct in my body urges me to feed her myself to make sure she eats enough.

A notification pops up that drags my attention from the clinking of the spoon on porcelain, and the sight of Everett's name makes me sigh. I've always been a lone wolf, always preferring to work alone because dealing with other people is my idea of a fucking nightmare, but I need his help. The rate at which Kyle is replacing the ads we take down is too much for just one person to manage, and I'm grateful for the help.

Everett: Three more ads went up this morning. I got them down at the point of nine viewers.

Ace: Thanks, man.

Everett: I've been digging around in Kyle's past and found some interesting shit. I'll send it to you now.

A second later, an email pops up with a file attached. I scan the document, the photos of the cunt who stole my woman from me, who took her innocence even if it was indirectly. Most of it is shit I already knew from my own searches, but as I scroll, my eyes focus on a photo that makes me pause.

It's a woman, a blonde with blue eyes and a sad smile. A woman that looks so much like Mia that I do a double take.

Angela Thompson

10.28.1990–06.10.2014

Married to Kyle Clark for two years.

Prior to this, owned by Angelo Russo and Cyrus Kemp.

Died by suicide.

Each word etches its way under my skin, and suddenly things start making sense.

Another image on the next page makes me suck in a breath. Another woman who looks too much like the one sitting across the room from me.

Denise Potts

02.10.1991–04.29.2011

Married to Kyle Clark for eighteen months.

Prior to this, owned by Cyrus Kemp and Robert Langley.

Died by suicide.

The images of blonde women and stories that are too similar to one another blur together. He has a type, and Mia fits the bill to a tee. He sells them, makes his commission each time they change owners, and then when they're broken beyond repair and too used to be sold again, he marries them, sentencing them to a life that none of them asked for.

The marriages date back to the late nineties, normally just a few months between one wife's death and the next wedding, except for the last eight years.

He hasn't replaced a woman since he met Mia, which can only mean one thing.

She's special to him somehow. And we've just made this the greatest game of cat and mouse for a man like him.

Shattered Promises

Nineteen

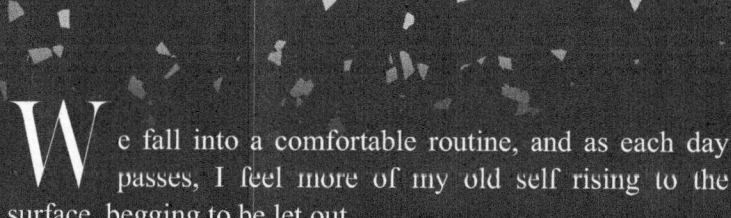

W e fall into a comfortable routine, and as each day passes, I feel more of my old self rising to the surface, begging to be let out.

Ace treats me like I'm made of glass, but if I'm honest, I don't hate it. It's nice to have someone who cares for me, someone who I know will never hurt me.

I've managed to choke down at least one meal a day for the last week, and although I see Ace's disappointment each time I say no when he offers me food, the relief in his eyes when I say yes always brings a smile to my face and makes eating a little more bearable.

Emerson comes by most days to chat, and I find I enjoy her company more and more each day. The concept of friends is strange to me now. I spent so many years alone with my own thoughts, usually my only contact was with a man who saw me as nothing more than a toy for him to use, but things have changed so much.

Every morning when I wake up, it's not dread that washes over me, it's relief. Relief that I'm free. Relief that I get to see Ace as soon as I step out of this room. And relief, that at least for now, I'm safe.

I pull on a pair of soft gray sweatpants and the matching sweatshirt before slipping on a pair of slippers Snow brought around for me a couple of days ago. It still doesn't come naturally to accept things, but I'm getting a little better at it.

I step out from the primary bedroom and head down the stairs to where Ace is banging around in the kitchen. I get the impression he doesn't usually cook much, mainly from how many pans he's ruined in the last few days, but it always makes me smile because he's doing it for me.

When was the last time anyone did anything just for me?

His eyes flick up to meet mine, and a bright smile crosses his face. "You're up."

The corners of my lips tug up. "What are you cooking?"

He looks behind him at the stove, and his brows tug together as he stirs something. "I was making you some oats, but the back of the packet lied to me."

I raise a brow as I approach him, careful to remain out of his reach. I'm not sure that it's a conscious choice, more so a habit I'm yet to break. I peer into the pot and a giggle that I can't quite swallow bubbles in my throat.

His intense green eyes turn on me, a smirk crossing his face. "What's so funny, sugar?"

"Your lack of cooking skills." The words are out of my mouth before I can think them through, but I don't get the chance to reprimand myself before Ace has me perched on the edge of the counter, wedging himself between my legs.

I gasp at the contact, but his touch doesn't make my skin crawl. If anything, it sets me on fire.

"Are you laughing at me, sugar?" Ace rumbles, his face so close I can almost taste him. He hasn't kissed me again, although sometimes I wish he would. He's doing his best not to trigger me, and I appreciate that more than he could ever know.

I nod, tucking my bottom lip between my teeth to try to squash the smile that still feels so unnatural. I've faked a lot of them over the years, but it's strange having something to be genuinely happy about.

A low growl fills the kitchen as Ace slowly lifts his hand from where it was pressed to the counter. His slow movements are for my benefit, to make sure I know the hand that's approaching my face isn't doing so to harm me.

His thumb tugs my lip from between my teeth carefully, his eyes glued to my mouth in a way that makes me hold my breath in anticipation. I need him to kiss me again. It doesn't make any sense, but it's all I can think about.

"You keep biting this lip and I'm going to be tempted to bite it too," he murmurs, his eyes flicking from my lips to my eyes and back again. The fire in the depths of his gaze should frighten me, but more and more I'm remembering the boy who protected me and reconciling him with the brutal man who saved me from a life of horrors.

I take a steadying breath and drag it back between my teeth. My heart thumps wildly in my chest, but it's not fear that makes it race, it's excitement. This moment with Ace, it feels normal, something I never thought I'd get to feel again.

Lust flashes through his eyes as he carefully tugs the battered pillow from its prison again and leans forward. He flicks his gaze to mine one last time, searching my eyes for hesitation, but he won't find any, and then he does exactly as he said he would.

His teeth sink into my lower lip, eliciting a soft moan from my throat. The bite of pain sends shock waves straight to my core. His tongue moves in a soothing motion, only heightening my need for him.

I lean forward, intent on capturing his lips with mine. In deepening the moment I feel like I've been waiting for my entire life, but the soft buzzing of a phone drags us both away from the moment.

Ace curses as he reaches into his pocket. He rolls his eyes and plants one hand on my thigh, holding me in place while he answers the phone. "This better be good, Tommy," he all but growls, and I can't help but smile at the annoyance in his tone.

The faint sound of our foster brother's voice carries between us, but I can't quite make out what he's saying.

Ace's eyebrows rise, and he blinks a few times. "Today?"

Tommy replies something, and Ace runs an irritated hand through his hair. "You're getting married today?"

The unmistakable sound of Tommy's laugh fills the line, and the corners of my mouth tip up of their own accord. I've missed that sound, just like I've missed so much about the only two people I could ever rely on.

Ace's gaze catches mine, worry filling the green pools. "I'll text you and let you know."

He ends the call without another word and blows out a breath. "So, Tommy and Clara are getting married this afternoon."

"I got that much." I giggle.

"They want us to go."

I nod slowly. I don't want to miss their wedding, not when I've already missed so much of his and Ace's lives, but the thought of stepping foot outside of this penthouse has a cold sweat breaking out across my brow. The safety of this apartment has given me the chance to adjust to freedom, even if I am still locked up, I'm as free as I've been in years, and leaving risks that.

"We don't have to if you don't want to, Mia." His palm cups my cheek, cradling my face in his calloused hand.

I open my mouth to respond but drop it closed again a second later. I don't know if I *can* leave the only place I've felt safe in the better part of a decade. It's not even a question whether I want to at this point, because I do want to.

Clara gave me the strength to be brave. She's the reason I escaped an endless cycle of men using me and brought me back to the family I fell into all those years ago. And Tommy was always right there with Ace, protecting the both of us, keeping us safe, making sure none of the older boys touched me, and beating up the kids at school that would pick on me for being an orphan.

The two of them have given me more than I can ever put into words, and I won't let them down by missing their big day.

"I want to go." I whisper the shaky words.

Shattered Promises

TWENTY

ACE

T his is a bad fucking idea.

In fact, it's not just a bad idea. It's the worst fucking idea I think I've ever allowed to go ahead.

But Mia was confident in her decision, and I couldn't fault her for it. I didn't want to miss Tommy's big day either.

After Mia was taken, we grew apart, more because of me than him. He tried to keep in touch, but I felt like I didn't deserve to have anyone to lean on while I went through the hardest time in my life. I was destined to be alone because I let the only girl I'd ever loved down. I allowed her to be taken from me. I allowed her to be sold into trafficking, and not only that, I couldn't fucking find her. Every rock I turned over was another failure, and I didn't deserve to have anyone in my life if all I was going to do was fail them.

I tap my desk impatiently, waiting for Mia to get ready. I had to get a suit couriered over, seeing as it's not something I would ordinarily wear in my hermit lifestyle, but Mia said she found something in the shit Snow bought her, so I've left her to her own devices for the last hour.

It took everything in me to not try to talk her out of the decision she made, but I'm all too aware of the fact that if I don't let her make her own choices, if I insist on keeping her here, I'm no better than the men that kept her caged for all those years.

The door upstairs cracks open, and my attention is dragged to the stairs immediately. I don't know when I'll be able to breathe when she's out of my sight again, but I have a feeling it won't be anytime soon. Especially with Kyle lurking in the shadows, waiting for his chance to take her away again.

After I realized his pattern, it became easier to track his next moves based on what we could find on what he's done before. He's never had to cover his tracks before because the women he forced to marry him had no one. An unfortunate reality for most who are sold into trafficking.

Mia appears in a mid-length green satin dress with a slight split up one leg. The spaghetti straps over her slender shoulders force me to follow the neckline that gives me the slightest view of her perky tits. The shiny black pumps she's paired with it have filthy thoughts flicking through my mind.

The urge to bend her over the nearest surface, shove the soft fabric up her thighs and slam home is almost too much for me to push down. But that's not a fantasy I can live out, nor is it one we may ever be able to.

But that's okay.

If it means I can have Mia by my side, I can live with stolen touches and kisses that set my body alight. It's not like I went out of my way to fuck before, only when I couldn't stand another shower with my own hand did I find a willing body to sink myself into, and never could I look them in the eye. It always felt like I was betraying Mia somehow, and now that I have her back, I'll never even think of touching another woman.

"Is this okay?" she asks as she descends the steps, holding the railing in one hand and a black coat in the other.

"You look breathtaking, sugar." I can barely get the words out past the lump in my throat.

A smile touches her ruby-red lips as she meets me at the bottom, and I tug her into me, needing to feel the contact and remind myself this moment is real.

Her body relaxes into mine instead of tensing the way it would have a few days ago. Progress might be slow, but we're getting there.

"You ready to go?"

I've never seen Tommy smile like he is right now, staring down at his new wife.

Men like Tommy and I rarely get happily ever afters because our souls are black. There's nothing redeemable about us, and therefore we're cursed to walk this earth alone.

But somehow, by some fucking miracle, he's found the woman who completes him, who softens some of his hard edges.

I look down at Mia, who hasn't moved from my side since

we left the penthouse. I considered reading her the riot act, but apparently it wasn't necessary because she seems content watching the people around us celebrate, a soft smile on her lips.

The Saint James family has embraced not just her, but me as well, despite our differences in the past. They may have shut me down all those years ago, but they haven't held a grudge, and maybe I shouldn't have either.

Despite having never met the eldest daughter of the Saint James family, Mia took to Wynter immediately, and Wynter to her. After the ceremony, while Tommy and Clara signed their marriage certificate, Emerson, Ayvah, Wynter, and Snow chattered animatedly to Mia like they'd been friends all their lives, and when Mia cooed at Summer, Wynter and Everett's one-month-old daughter, the baby was promptly thrust into her arms.

I never imagined having kids, thought there was no way someone with a childhood as fucked up as mine was had any right being a parent. But as I stare at Mia with a tiny baby in her arms, her blue eyes lit up as she looks down at the little bundle of pink blankets, it's all I can imagine.

The thoughts come down on me like a ton of bricks until I can barely breathe through the need.

A chuckle beside me drags my attention from my woman and the tiny baby she's staring down at. Everett smirks beside me, his shit-eating grin matches Elijah's, and I can't help but glare at both fuckers.

"I know that look." Everett chuckles.

"You don't know shit," I snap.

"We've all been there, bro. The moment you realize you *need* to knock your woman up as soon as humanly possible." Elijah glances at Snow before turning his attention back to us. The security presence at the courthouse rivals that of the Pentagon, but that doesn't stop every man in attendance from keeping a close eye on their woman.

"You don't know what you're talking about."

"Still in denial." Everett nods. "Noted."

I sigh and run my hand through my messy hair before turning my full attention to them. "I'm not in denial about shit. I'm realistic about the trauma Mia has been through and how that may or may not limit our future."

I don't think it comes as a surprise to either of them that I'm thinking about the future and what will be possible for us, but neither of them gets a chance to respond before Emerson joins us with both hands resting on her swollen belly. I'm not sure how close she is to popping, but she seems to be growing every time I see her.

She glances over her shoulder at Mia, and a smile tugs at the corners of her lips. "She looks like she's doing well."

I nod. "The last few days, it's been leaps and bounds. Even when we were leaving the apartment, she was okay. Nervous but okay."

"And you said she was eating better?"

"One meal a day," I confirm.

"Better than the first few days." She shrugs. Her gaze falls back to Mia as she bounces Summer gently with a soft smile on her lips. "That's a good sign. Sometimes women who have been through trauma the way she has won't have anything to do with children. Even women who have children themselves before they go through it will reject their own kids, not because they don't love them but because they think the child is better off without them because they're broken. The fact Mia has taken to Summer like that is a very positive sign for her recovery."

I let out a breath but try to keep my face neutral. It's still in the early days, but any good sign is worth its weight in gold right now.

"I think Tommy is going to steal his bride away any minute now. I was wondering if I could take Mia to the youth center. I think she might get a lot out of it."

I open my mouth to say an emphatic no. There's no way I'm letting her out of my sight yet, I can't. Neither of us is ready.

"You're welcome to come," Emerson rushes to add. "But if you have to get back to work, Rayne will be around—and my eighteen security guards I have attached to me anytime I'm out of the house."

"They're around the apartment building when you're home too," Everett informs her, and she whips her head around to where Rayne is talking to Storm across the room.

"Are they now?"

I meet Elijah's eyes, and he gives me a small nod. "It's a good idea."

I sigh and shove my hand through my hair. Not for the first time in our lives, I realize I could never deny Mia anything. Except maybe orgasms, but that's a thought for another day.

TWENTY-ONE

I thought I'd be more panicked being out in the open. I thought I'd be craving the safety of the penthouse as soon as I stepped out the front door. But this is the first time I've felt truly free in almost a decade.

I'm still having trouble reconciling the boy I knew as a kid with the ruthless killer Tommy has turned into, but the way he looks at Clara gives *me* butterflies, I can't imagine how she feels being on the other end of those looks.

When Emerson suggested we take a trip to the youth center she runs with her father, I was hesitant. I'd already been out of the house for a few hours, and while I've enjoyed every single second, I've basically been alone with my own thoughts every minute of every day for so many years that being surrounded by conversation has been a little overwhelming. But there's something in the back of my head that urges me to go.

So I say yes.

The drive from the courthouse to downtown Chicago isn't

particularly long, but I can't help but fidget the whole way.

Ace keeps his hand on my thigh, his eyes scanning the streets as he navigates them. I've never been that interested in cars, but Cyrus was into them. He used to go on and on about his collection for hours while he tortured me. The classic Chevy looks to be in original condition, but it's immaculate. When he first helped me slip into the soft leather seats, I was afraid I somehow had crumbs on me that I would leave behind. Maybe that's my trauma speaking—the memory of all the times a perceived mess was used as an excuse to hurt me.

The closer we get, the more tense Ace seems to become, and my stomach rolls uncomfortably. "We can go back to the apartment if you need to get some work done," I tell him.

His eyes flick to me, the green softening as soon as they clash with mine. "It's not that, Sugar. I just get nervous about having you out of the house."

I hesitantly drop my hand to his and squeeze. The contact sends a zap of electricity straight to my chest, and from the way the tension in his shoulders softens slightly, I know he feels it too. "I'm not going anywhere. And Emerson said there's a large security presence at the center now."

He nods, but it doesn't seem to make a difference as he brings the car to a stop across the road.

I don't know what I was expecting, but it wasn't this. The buildings that line the street are run-down, some so much so I would call them decrepit, but there's one that stands out from the rest.

The bricks have recently been cleaned, the sign above the

door is so clean I'd swear it was hung yesterday, and the connected basketball court is fitted with soft flooring rather than solid concrete. It's a haven for children like I was when I was in foster care, and I find myself reaching for the handle instinctively.

Ace stops me with a squeeze of my thigh, and I look up at him expectantly. "I want you at my side at all times, okay?"

I nod. "I know."

He lets out a breath and reaches for his own door.

I slip from the car and look down at the emerald dress I'm wearing. I'm not really dressed to be here, but when I see Emerson getting out of Rayne's black SUV in her fitted black dress and heels, I relax.

She beams at us as we cross the street. "What do you think? We were forced to do some remodeling recently because there was a fire here, but the changes we made have made all the difference!"

"It's incredible." I smile as she leads me through the front door and into what I assume is the heart of the center. There are a few seating areas with comfortable-looking couches and games strewn across the tables.

A couple of boys are engaged in what seems to be an intense game of chess, while three girls, probably around twelve, are huddled around the one gossip magazine, giggling between themselves.

I know from experience that this is as peaceful as their lives get. At home, it's a constant rat race. Even if they live in a home where their parents love them, this is their safe haven.

"This is incredible," I hear myself say as I look around the wide-open space. The carpet beneath our feet is brand new, the tables and chairs the same, but the space feels homely.

Emerson beams proudly, which drags a smile to Rayne's usually intense face. "It's been in our family for three generations. This is where I grew up and where I met Rayne." She leans into him, and he doesn't hesitate to wrap an arm around her shoulders and press a kiss to the top of her head.

Not for the first time, I long for that kind of closeness, but I'm not sure I'll ever be able to handle it. So far everything Ace and I have done has been met with no anxiety, but I'm certain there's a line we're rapidly approaching.

I look up at the man in question and catch him looking at them with the same longing I feel in my chest. The overwhelming need to leave hits me out of nowhere, sucking the air right from my lungs. It's not fair on him to stay. I'll never be able to give him what he wants.

But I promised I wouldn't try to leave again.

I swore I would stay.

And I won't break my promise to him, even if it would be for the best.

Ace pulls his phone from his pocket and curses before taking it a few steps away and answering the call as he glares at the blank wall in front of him.

One of the younger kids, a boy around twelve, runs to Rayne and starts talking animatedly with him like he's not the enforcer of a ruthless Mafia family, his eyes lit up with excitement as he tells him about his basketball carnival over the weekend.

Emerson steps toward me, her eyes watching the sweet display with a soft smile. "Rayne comes in a couple of times a week to play basketball with the kids, and they love him."

"Their parents aren't concerned?" I ask cautiously.

"Some were to begin with. Obviously, there's rumors about the family, but a lot of the people around here have worked in the underbelly of the city, so they know those rumors have some truth to them. But a lot of the kids that come here have been for a long time, and they know my father and I, they know we wouldn't let anyone hurt them." She looks around the space with a bright smile. "Plus, a lot of them saw how the whole family pitched in after the fire. Especially Wynter, she refused to have the doors shut for more than a weekend to make sure the kids had somewhere to go."

I open my mouth to respond but pause as Ace rejoins us with a frown. "I have to go."

"Oh, of course, we can get going whenever you want." I smile, trying not to let the disappointment show.

"You stay here with Rayne. I'll get him to drop you back at the apartment once you're done here."

I open my mouth to argue, but before I can, he's gone, only stopping to quickly talk to Rayne before disappearing the way we came.

What on earth was that about?

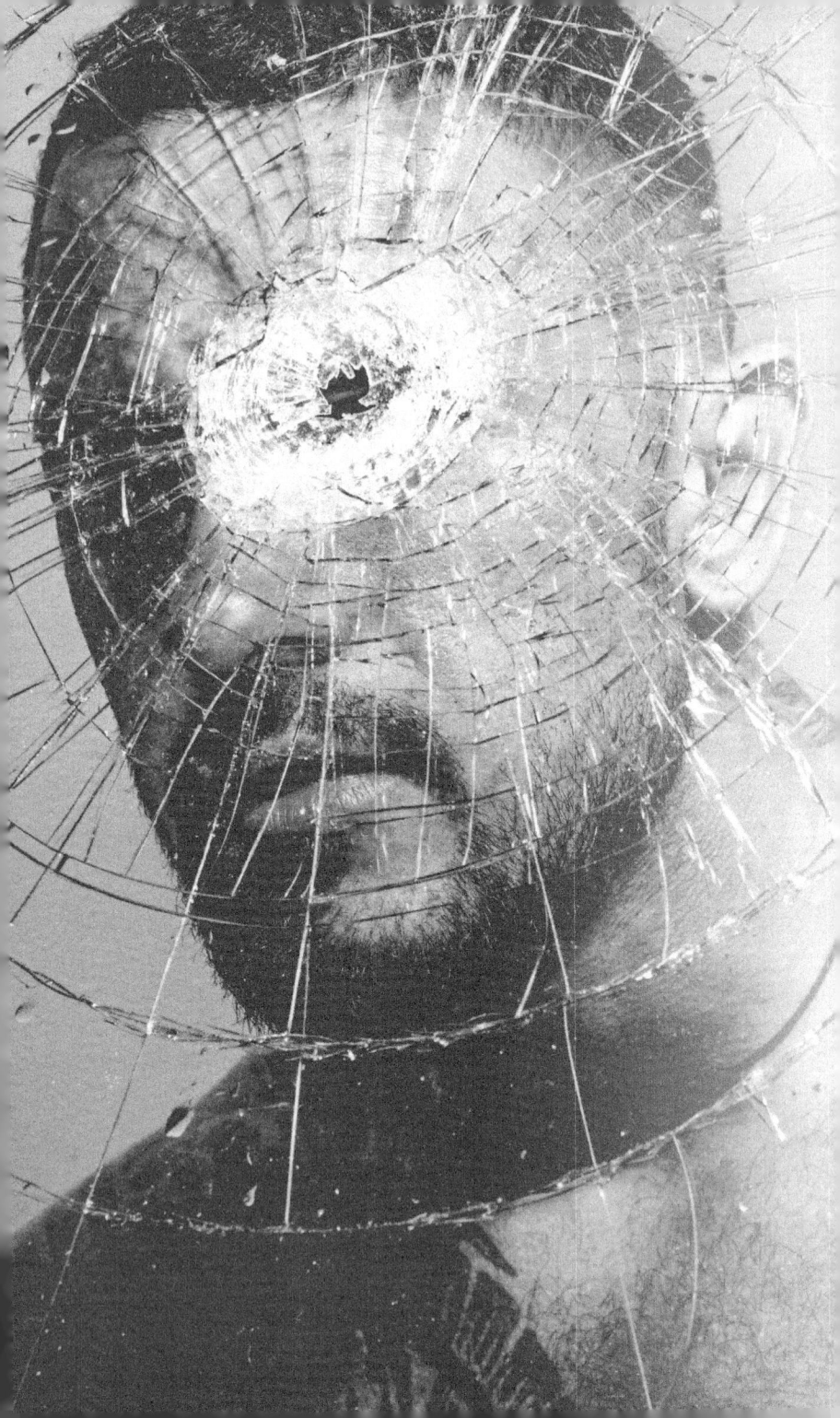

TWENTY-TWO

ACE

The last thing I expected when we got ready for the wedding earlier was that Elijah would be delivering two of the five men who hurt Mia in that cabin. Who used her when she was meant to be healing from the treatment she'd received from her last owner.

I have special plans for Cyrus when I can finally get my hands on him, but the fucker is a ghost. We haven't been able to get a lock on his country, never less his fucking location, and the idea of him continuing to walk this earth after the hell he put my woman through makes my skin crawl.

He needs to be wiped from existence. But only after I've tortured him extensively.

I navigate the tunnels beneath the city from muscle memory alone. Tommy and I lived down here for a time when we first escaped, when we thought our foster father might come for us, and Tommy has been thriving down here ever since, using the abandoned offshoots as his very own torture chambers.

I step into what I can only assume is his favorite cell, considering the table of knives laid out on the far wall and the chairs drilled into the rotting bricks. Two men are chained to the chairs, their eyes frantic as they watch me enter.

Elijah's men picked these two assholes up a few hours ago and left them to stew while we enjoyed the wedding, but as soon as I found out they were here, all I could think about was killing them. Hurting them like they hurt Mia.

Their wide eyes meet mine, confusion washing over them because they have no fucking idea who I am.

All the more fun.

Without a word, I tear the tape from their lips, giving no consideration for the skin I'm tearing from their bodies.

"Who the fuck are you?" David Walls demands. His balding head and rounded cheeks a dark shade of red with anger as his deep-brown eyes glare at me.

"Would it be cliché of me to say your worst nightmare?" I muse before nodding to myself. "It would be. So, let's just say I'm the guy who's going to make you repent for your sins."

I'm far from a priest, but fuck it sounds good.

The other man remains silent. He's a little younger than the others, in his midthirties, but there's a darkness behind his gaze that is all too familiar. There's no soul in the depths, just pitch-black nothingness. He's the kind of fucker you want to work for you, because he has no conscience, there's no line he won't cross. But he'll be wiped from existence long before he earns another paycheck.

There wasn't much to find on Luke Burch. He's been off the radar since he was seventeen. Not a trace of him unless you know where to look, which lucky for us, we did. After a while living among the scum of the earth, you get very fucking good at predicting their next move.

Everett has been tracking every visitor to the listings Kyle adds to noticeboards. These fuckers were fired after what they did to Mia, that much we were able to work out, but men like this wouldn't blame their boss. They blame the woman they brutalized.

Like I said, predictable.

Ideally, I would have had the five of them here at once. Watching them blame one another, try to barter for their lives with tidbits of information that's irrelevant and probably falsified. It would have made this whole ordeal a little more fun. But beggars can't be choosers and all that.

"What do you want?" David snaps, obviously not finding my cliché amusing.

I drag the metal chair from the corner—the only one not bolted to the ground—and swing a leg over it. I fold my arms over the back and use the cold metal that penetrates my shirt to steady myself.

I'll be the first to admit I have a temper, and it's got me in trouble more times than I can count, but I need to keep my cool. I don't want to end this too soon.

"Tell me what you remember about a girl Kyle Clark had you two and three other guys guard."

They stare at me for a few seconds before shooting looks at

one another. "This is about the reward for bringing her in?" David asks.

"You're a crazy fucker if you think we're going to help you steal that reward for yourself. We already know where the slut is, and we'll be the ones to deliver her on a silver fucking platter," Luke finally speaks, his deep voice low and menacing.

I chuckle and shake my head slowly. "Answer the question before I start using the knives over there to get the answers I want."

"She was just some whore getting ready to be sold. She was fucked up after her last owner. He had a thing for marking her, and she needed time for those marks to fade before Kyle could get a good price for her again," David tells me.

"Not that she was worth a dollar of it. The stupid slut should have been put out of her misery after the shit Cyrus did to her. She certainly wasn't worth whatever they sold her for." Luke stares me dead in the eye, and I hold his gaze. Hearing him talk about Mia like this makes my blood boil, but I force myself to remain seated.

The longer I stay put, the more they'll believe this is just a shakedown, a dirty tactic to get to the mark first. I want to lead them into a false sense of security, so when the time comes, slicing into their flesh will be even sweeter.

I do my best to keep my face neutral, but each word alluding to Mia makes rage drum through my veins.

"What if we share the payday?" David offers. "Split it three ways instead of two?"

Luke shoots his partner a glare but doesn't get a chance to

respond before a laugh claws its way up my throat. These motherfuckers have no fucking clue what they've stepped into.

I shove myself to my feet and approach Tommy's torture table, a chuckle clawing up my throat at the nickname. It's an apt name for the wooden table covered in knives, hammers, and a blowtorch, as well as a shit ton of other shit I wouldn't want to see my crazy foster brother wielding.

"What...what are you...you doing?" David stammers. He's the weaker link. I could have told you that from the research we did alone, but this just proves it.

"Do you know the girl's name?" I ask, running my fingers over a couple of the knives as I choose which I want to start with. The large hunting knife has some appeal, but it might do too much damage. I'm not trained in the art of keeping cunts alive during torture like Tommy is. All the killing I do is quick, but I want to drag this out for as long as possible. I want to make them suffer for what they did to Mia. I want to hand her their bloody hearts as penance and a reminder that I will always keep her safe.

"Mia," David answers immediately.

I nod as I pick a smaller knife. It's too easy to make mistakes with this kind of shit, it's better I take the less menacing knife to begin with. Maybe after the first few of these assholes I'll have the patience and skill to upgrade, but right now, it's all about patience. "What else do you know about her?" I turn and lean against the table, running the blade through my fingers, testing the sharpness to make sure it'll do what I need it to do.

I shouldn't be surprised it's sharp as fuck. Tommy takes killing and torture very fucking seriously.

"She was just some slut," Luke pipes up. "Went through The Factory young. Sold to some rich fuckers who got bored of her before Cyrus picked her up for his games. By the time she went to Lombardi, she was nothing but a brainless whore only good to be used and abused."

A chuckle claws its way up my throat despite every word out of his mouth being more vile than the last.

He's dying first. And painfully.

Shattered Promises

TWENTY-THREE

MIA

T his might be the most normal I've felt since I was in high
school.

These kids don't know me. They don't know what I've been
through. All they know is I'm a new face, and each of them
tries desperately to find something they have in common with
me.

A boy with black hair and dark eyes, I think around ten, shows
me his extensive *Pokémon* card collection, pointing out all his
favorites, while a girl of the same age with neat braids and
sparking blue eyes talks to me about her doll.

Before these two caught me, three boys in their early teens
were telling me about the basketball competition Rayne
helped them prepare for, and before that, a little girl, no older
than eight, confided in me about her first crush.

I never had much interest in children, even when I was one,
but there's something so innocent about them, even if I know
their lives outside these walls are anything but.

Two boys on the other side of the room drag my attention from the doll the girl handed me with a loud shout. My brows pull together, but their yelling doesn't make my stomach knot. Maybe because I know they're not a threat to me.

Emerson and Rayne quickly cross the room, neither of them seeming visibly annoyed by the outburst. I suppose this is their safe space and probably the only place they can let out their emotions, even the negative ones.

A hand touches my shoulder, and I startle, looking up at an older boy, probably around sixteen. His chocolate-brown curls are unruly, and his deep-brown eyes are almost void of emotion. I don't need him to tell me for me to know he's been through shit. I've come face-to-face with enough people with trauma in their past to recognize it from a mile away.

He hands me a piece of paper, his gaze flicking up to make sure Emerson and Rayne are still distracted, before saying, "A man asked me to give this to you."

I look down at the envelope in my hands, but by the time I look back up to ask the boy any questions, he's gone.

When my eyes land on the envelope again, my stomach rolls uncomfortably. Was this planned? The distraction to have Rayne and Emerson move away for long enough to get this to me? The paper between my fingers makes my skin crawl, but curiosity gets the best of me, and I slip the card out, the messy scrawl only bringing bile closer to the surface.

You were always meant to be mine, and anyone who gets in my way will pay dearly. Can you live with that on your conscience?

I don't need to recognize the handwriting to know who's responsible, I just can't understand why he would care this much. I was nothing more than another payday to him, so why go to all this effort?

I'm so distracted by the words in front of me that I don't notice the hulking presence that looms over me, and by the time I do, Rayne's dark eyes have already run over the note.

"Where did this come from?" he asks, the harshness in his tone causing me to flinch involuntarily. His eyes widen, horrified that he startled me. "I'm sorry, Mia. I didn't mean it to come out like that."

I release a breath, trying desperately to swallow the panic that threatens to overwhelm me. "A kid," I whisper. "He handed it to me and said a man told him to give it to me."

He flicks his gaze around the room, searching for a danger that's probably no longer lurking. "We should go."

Before I can argue, he takes off toward his wife, the tension in his shoulders obvious as he approaches her, only easing once his arm wraps around her protectively. He says something to her quietly, and her gaze darts to me, worry tugging at her brows. It's strange having people care about me, especially when I have nothing to offer them.

All I've done since I've been back in Chicago is cause everyone around me pain.

Emerson crosses the room quickly, careful not to let the worry become too obvious for the kids that look up to her like she's their own personal savior. Hell, she probably is for a lot of them.

"Are you okay?" she asks as soon as she's within range.

I nod as she carefully extracts the note from my hand and reads over its contents.

"Let's get you home." She places a comforting hand on my shoulder, but I'm too numb to feel it.

I can't stay. Not when the people who have done nothing but help me are in danger because of me. But I have nowhere else to go.

Nowhere, but back to Kyle.

Shattered Promises

Twenty-Four

T he first cut is always the most satisfying.

Tommy used to tell me that, and I thought it was just another one of his crazy musings, but he was right. I knew it the first time I ever picked up a knife and sliced through someone's flesh, and I'm reminded of it now as I slide the blade over Luke's forearm, careful not to nick any veins.

He screams despite himself. The big bad man who probably laughed when Mia begged him to stop, can't swallow his own pain, and that brings a smile to my lips.

"What the fuck?" he shouts. "You're fucking crazy."

I nod, stepping back to admire my own handy work. "If you think I'm crazy, you should meet my brother."

"Please." David's eyes lock with the seeping blood that gushes from his partner's arm. "Please don't do that to me. I'll help you. I'll help you, and you can take the money."

My head falls back on a laugh, the sound bouncing around the tunnels. He hasn't worked it out yet, but he will. He still thinks this is about money. Little does he know that he's hurt the woman who holds my heart, who's the reason the cold, dead organ in my chest still beats after all this time.

I turn my attention back to Luke and mirror the cut on his other arm, relishing in the sound of his screams as the blade glides through his flesh. Fuck. I can almost see why Tommy loves this shit so much.

Blood coats my hands, and I stare down at the crimson on his skin before using the fucker's shirt to wipe it off. Who fucking knows if this asshole has any diseases?

That thought has a fresh wave of rage beating down on me. He probably didn't use protection. He could have given Mia anything. It's a fucking miracle her blood work came back clear, not an STD in sight, but I'm sure he didn't know he was clean when he took her against her will.

I shove the anger down. I'm not ready for this to end yet.

"We won't take the job. We'll walk away and you can take it," David continues to bargain.

"You can't kill everyone who picks up the job. Kyle is fucking crazed to get the whore back," Luke spits.

"Watch me." A smile tugs at the corners of my lips, and I don't need to look in a mirror to know I look crazed. I feel it deep in my gut.

He keeps his eyes on me as I run the knife over his hand, not putting enough pressure to cut him, but making sure he remains still from fear I'll cut his fingers off. He can only hope that's all I'm going to remove from his scummy ass today.

I turn his palm over, roughly moving him into position despite how tight the ropes are around his wrists. The angry red marks the bindings have left bring me a sick amount of satisfaction.

I press the knife into his palm, slicing it toward his fingers. His screams only egg me on as I carefully cut my way up each finger.

The symphony of screams settles the part of me that wants to tear these men limb from fucking limb for how they hurt Mia.

I lean back on my haunches and admire my handiwork. Pun totally intended. Violent red runs down his arm, and when I meet his eyes, I see the emotion I crave.

Fear.

I want these assholes to be fucking terrified when they take their last breath.

I don't want them to know another second of peace in their miserable fucking lives.

"You're fucking sick," Luke snarls, but it's missing some of the bravado from before I started. He hasn't lost nearly enough blood to pass out, but it will be starting to weaken him, taking away some of his fight.

I nod, a smile pulling up the corners of my lips. "And what you did to Mia wasn't?" I ask with a raised brow.

David watches me for a moment as understanding dawns on him. "You're not doing this to remove us from the race to return her…"

I shake my head slowly. "No, I'm doing this because you deserve to die a slow, painful death for what you did to my woman."

I plunge the knife through David's hand, the first time I've touched him since I walked through the door, and his screams are so fucking sweet I can barely handle them.

Three hours and a whole lot of blood later, and I'm strolling back into the penthouse feeling more settled than I have since Mia told me what those assholes did to her. There's still a long list of people for me to kill, but it feels fucking good to cross off a couple of them.

I stopped off at my apartment to shower and change, not wanting to risk Mia seeing me covered in blood. Given all she's been through, I don't think she'd cope well with that.

As soon as I step foot out of the elevator, the atmosphere feels wrong. I rush into the open space and spot Emerson sitting on the couch with Mia's head in her lap, her fingers moving through her hair comfortingly.

Rayne is out on the balcony, shouting something into his phone. What the fuck happened?

I step toward Emerson, but when she catches sight of me, she shakes her head slowly and nods toward her husband. Mia's asleep, small whimpers filling the room, and my entire body screams at me to go to her, to pluck her out of Emerson's arms, and to protect her from whatever has upset her, but instead I step onto the balcony and close the door quietly behind me.

"About time you got back," he snaps.

"What the fuck happened?"

He shoves his phone into his pocket, and I'm not even certain he was finished on his call before he ended it. "Something happened at the youth center."

I look back into the apartment, my view of Mia obstructed by the couch, but surely someone would have called me if she was hurt…right?

"She's okay," he assures me. "Some kid was told to deliver this to Mia while Emerson and I were distracted."

He hands it to me, and I scan the words over and over again, my stomach plummeting. "She's going to try to leave again," I whisper.

Rayne nods. "Everett is searching through security tapes, trying to work out when that kid got the envelope, but so far he's coming up empty."

If it were anyone else, I would assume they're doing a shitty job, but Everett is the only person in the city, maybe even the goddamn country, that rivals my own skill, so I know that's not the case. Still, my hands twitch to look for myself, to hack into every camera within a mile of the center, to trawl through hours and hours of footage. And ordinarily, that's exactly what I would have done. I would have spent hours, if not days, searching, but that was before I had other priorities.

My gaze darts back into the apartment, where just the top of Emerson's head is visible over the back of the couch. "You should have called me."

Rayne nods. "I wanted to. But Mia asked me not to. She said you'd already done so much for her, and she didn't want to

173

drag you away from work."

I scoff. If only she knew.

"I didn't know if you were going to tell her what you were doing, so I did as she asked."

"Thanks for getting her home, man." I quietly step into the apartment and immediately make my way to where Mia is curled up with Emerson, who gives me a small smile.

She carefully shuffles out from under Mia, and I move into her place, feeling immediately at ease having her in my arms again.

Rayne drops the note on the cushion next to me on his way out, and as soon as my eyes move over the page, my stomach sinks again.

Kyle may not be able to get anywhere near her, but if he keeps this shit up, she'll walk right into his trap, and I can't let that happen.

If Mia thinks she'll be able to run from me, she'll quickly learn how much I love the chase.

TWENTY-FIVE

Rough fingers move through my hair, each stroke more calming than the last.

As soon as I started to come to, I knew it was no longer Emerson I was using as a pillow, but Ace. His cologne surrounds me, settling some of the anxiety running rampant through my mind.

He's always been my safe place. My home.

Pain moves through my chest, taking my breath away at the thought of losing him again after I just got him back. I spent years dreaming of the day we would be back together. Some days, when all I wanted to do was give up, the memory of him was what pulled me through. How am I meant to walk away?

But I don't have a choice. I can't allow the people who have given me so much to be hurt because of me.

"You awake, sugar?" Ace rumbles, his voice pulling me away from my thoughts.

The apartment is dark when I open my eyes. How long has he been sitting in the dark?

I stretch my sore muscles out, giving me the impression I've been lying in this position for a long time. "I'm sorry. You didn't have to sit here with me."

He brushes his fingers down my cheek with his eyes glued to my face like he's afraid I'll disappear if he closes his eyes for even a moment. Does he know I'm planning on leaving?

No. He can't know I'm going to break the promise I made him just a few days ago.

"Why didn't you let Rayne call me, sugar?"

"You were working."

He lets out a breath, and if I didn't know him so well, I would have missed how hard he's trying to keep the tension from the parts of his body that are touching me. His fingers wrap gently around my chin until I'm forced to look him in the eye. "There is *nothing* more important to me than you, Mia. If you needed me to tear my fucking heart from my chest to make you smile, I would do it. I don't give a fuck what I'm doing. I don't fucking care if I'm lying on my goddamn death bed, if you need me, I'm going to be there."

I open my mouth to respond but snap it closed again. What am I supposed to say to that?

His calloused fingers move over my cheek, and I commit the feeling to memory. The only thing that dragged me through those years were the times we spent together. I'm going to need that again because this time, when I'm taken to my fate, there will be no chance of coming back. The first time never would have happened if it wasn't for a twist of fate that found Clara and me in the same place.

"I'll keep you safe, Mia. I won't let him take you again."

My eyes flick closed of their own accord. I can't look him in the eye and tell him I believe him when I'm going to take the choice out of his hands.

"I might go to bed," I whisper. "It's late."

He sighs, and I hear his head hit the back of the couch. "I'll make you something to eat."

"I'm not hungry." I am, but I don't want him to know that. If I'm going to return to only having a meal here and there, I have to train my body again. It was nice eating more, and I've had more energy in the last week than I have in years, but Kyle won't feed me like this, and my next owner sure as hell won't either. They spend enough to buy us, our upkeep is at the bottom of their priority list.

Before Ace can think to respond, I slip from the couch and carefully stand. I may be eating more, and Doc came by to give me an iron infusion a few days ago, but I'm far from being strong, and getting up too fast will always put me on my ass.

Stars dance in my vision, but I manage to remain standing, smoothing down my dress so Ace doesn't notice the change in me.

When I meet his eyes again, they're frustrated, but he doesn't argue despite the fact I know it's all he wants to do. Ace is a dominant guy. He was when we were kids, always calling the shots, making sure I did as I was told when I was told, and I can't imagine much has changed in the last eight years, but he keeps it hidden around me.

"Good night," I say before scurrying upstairs.

But sleep doesn't come when my head hits the pillow, instead, regret eats me alive, gnawing at my very being until I can barely breathe.

If Kyle doesn't kill me first, my own guilt will eat me alive.

The silence is maddening.

Despite my best efforts, I've gotten used to sounds again—to people, to laughing, to basic creature comforts like music and the television. But I've been staring at the ceiling for hours, wishing for sleep, and it was easier when I could hear Ace downstairs on his computer, the faint tapping of the keyboard bringing me a strange sense of comfort. But he went to bed a little while ago, and there's been nothing but me and my thoughts since.

I kick the soft sheets off my legs and slip out of bed. Maybe I just need some water, and then I'll be able to get some rest.

I pad out into the hallway, my bare feet slapping against the hardwood floors as I make my way toward the stairs. The faint glow of a light farther down the hall pulls my attention away from the kitchen, and before I've made a conscious decision to do so, I'm moving toward Ace's room. It's still strange to me to have free rein of the apartment, even though I did when I was with Lombardi to some extent. But it's probably a good thing I'm not quite used to it yet. One less thing to miss when it all goes away.

A groan stops me in my tracks a few feet from the door that's slightly ajar. I listen for a few seconds before taking a step forward. It was probably just Ace making sounds in his sleep. I'll just turn the light off for him and then go get myself a drink and head back to bed.

I'm almost in the doorway when a muttered curse accompanies another moan, and the faint sound of slapping fills my ears. What is he...

I don't get a chance to ask myself the question because a moment later, there's another moan. My name. The sound full of passion and need, and I realize what he's doing.

He's pleasuring himself...to the thought of me.

I take a step back, not wanting to interrupt a private moment, but the next groan pulls me right back to the door like a magnet. I shouldn't want to ever think about sex again after the things I've seen, but of course Ace makes me break all the rules. He always has.

I inch closer until I can see just a sliver of the room through the gap. Ace lies in the middle of the bed, his hand moving slowly over his hard cock. Holy shit, he's huge. His palm glides up and down his hardness, precum gathering at the tip before he drags it down his length in controlled swipes.

An ache pools in my belly, my core throbbing in an unfamiliar way. Have I ever actually wanted sex? Or was it always forced upon me? The question is like a bucket of freezing ice water, but I still can't tear my eyes away from the scene playing out in front of me. My god, is it erotic.

I've seen plenty of men stroke themselves, usually immediately before forcing themselves on me or one of the other girls, but this is different.

This is art.

The movements are graceful, even as his veins bulge from his forearm and his head falls back against the pillows in bliss, it's the most beautiful thing I've ever witnessed.

"Mia, fuck," he groans. My name on his lips is a prayer, but I can't be his salvation. Not when all I'll ever be able to bring him is damnation.

I rub my thighs together, the need for friction too much for me to ignore, despite all the reasons I should. I'm broken. Fucked up. Destroyed from all the men who took what I didn't offer them.

And yet the sight of Ace stroking himself sets a fire to life in my core that I'm desperate to stoke, to watch the flames and feel them lick at my skin.

I want to burn if it means I can accept a man's touch just once and not see the demons of my past.

Twenty-Six

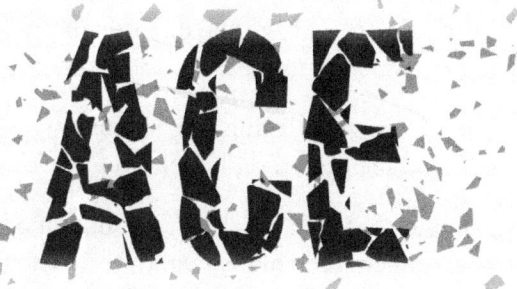

I should have stopped when I heard her soft footsteps on the landing. The sound of her padding toward my room was so quiet most would think they imagined the sound, but not me. I've lived alone for years, and the silence is my home.

The only sounds I'm used to hearing are the tap of the keys beneath my fingers, the soft whir of my computers, and the occasional siren when the cops decide to police in the area where I live. Any other sound is foreign, and therefore it may as well be blaring, no matter how quiet it is. So as soon as my girl stepped foot out of her room, I heard every step she took. I heard the sharp intake of breath when she was in the doorway, the darkness hiding her from me, when she saw what I was doing. I heard her quiet retreat when I blew my load all over myself. Thick ropes of cum covered my stomach and hand from an orgasm made better by knowing she was watching and that she wasn't afraid.

When she first stopped in the doorway, I held my breath, thinking she would run in the opposite direction. She had every right to do exactly that, and I wouldn't have blamed her. But she stayed for the show. She heard me murmur her name. She watched as I choked my cock harder and harder the closer I came to my release, and she stayed through my orgasm that came with her name on my lips.

And she didn't run when I finished, she quietly walked back to her room, and the door didn't click shut.

For long minutes I stayed put, one arm thrown over my face and the other still covered in my cum over my stomach. Fuck. I don't think I've ever come like that. Stars still dance in my vision, leaving me completely immobile.

I should go check on her, make sure she's okay after what she saw, but I need to give her space. After all she's been through, the last thing she needs is for me to push her when it comes to things like this. If it's just me and my hand from here on out, I'll be okay as long as she's there for everything else.

I sleep better than I have in years. Which is ridiculous seeing as I've tugged myself off more times than I care to think about over the years and still slept like shit.

But maybe it was knowing Mia saw me that allowed my body to drift into a slumber so deep I'm pretty sure I would have slept straight through a fucking hurricane.

I throw on a pair of sweatpants and my standard black T-shirt before making my way downstairs barefoot. I like this place. A lot more than I care to admit to anyone. I've lived in my piece of shit apartment for years, and while it had everything I needed, it was still a piece of shit. Every other place I lived before that was almost as scummy, so this penthouse is a world away from everywhere else I've stayed.

I wonder if Snow would sell the place to me.

I'm not hurting for money. My fucking account is bursting at the seams, seeing as I've only spent money to live over the last decade, never splurging on anything other than my car.

I'll have to ask her the next time I see her.

Usually when I come downstairs in the morning, Mia's still sleeping, or at least pretending to sleep, but I stop in my tracks when I notice her sitting at the dining table with a cup of coffee in front of her mid-yawn.

She looks beautiful. Her hair still messy from the pillow, the sleep shirt she's wearing crinkled from a night between the sheets, and the faint marks of the pillowcase still etched into her cheek. Fuck.

Mia hears me too late, her head popping up to meet my gaze as I approach her and a deep blush spreads across her cheeks.

I don't bother to smother the smirk that tugs at my lips, it would only be going backward, and that's the last thing I want right now. "Morning, sugar."

"Good morning," she murmurs, taking a sip of her coffee as an excuse to look away.

"Sleep well?" I make my way to the kitchen and pour my own coffee, all the while keeping my eyes on her. Something has shifted between us the last few days, and I'm certainly not the only one feeling it.

"Not really." She yawns. Up close, I can see the dark circles under her eyes, but the haunted look from when we first saved her isn't there. It wasn't nightmares that kept her awake last night.

I bite the inside of my cheek to keep the smug smirk at bay. "I slept great. Probably the most solid sleep I've had in years."

She looks up at me, her eyes searching for something I'm more than happy for her to find, but just when I think she's going to call me out, she shoves herself up from the table. "I'm going for a shower."

I lean back against the counter and watch her retreat. The sleep shirt she's wearing barely covers the tops of her thighs, her perky ass appearing beneath the soft cotton T-shirt. Fuck, she's beautiful.

I take a sip of my bitter coffee. I've never had cream or sugar, both luxuries I refused to give myself after all my failures. I could always add them now, but I've grown used to the bitterness, and I find solace in it.

There are a few things I could do now.

I could stay down here with my coffee and start work, it's not like I'm low on shit to do and my clients are starting to get real fucking antsy.

I could go upstairs and listen to see if she's getting herself off at the memory of my self-care session last night.

That's where there are some other options. Listening to her pretty moans would likely be enough for me. But what's that saying about an eye for an eye? She watched me, so I could watch her.

The thought has me discarding the steaming caffeine down the sink and striding toward the stairs before I've really made a decision. I want to know how much my girl enjoyed what she saw last night.

I take the steps two at a time, not wanting to miss a second of the show.

The sound of water running hits my ears as soon as I hit the top of the stairs, and I don't bother knocking on her door before barging right in. The bathroom door is slightly ajar, and I can't help but wonder if part of her subconsciously left it open for me to watch her just as she did me last night.

Wishful thinking some might say.

I step up to the door, anticipation building as the thought of seeing my girl getting herself off makes my cock harder than a goddamn rock. Jesus. Mia has always had me tied up in knots, but it's worse now. So much fucking worse.

Steam billows through the luxurious bathroom. Marble tiles and wooden feature pieces match the rest of the apartment, with a huge bathtub on one side and an expansive shower on the back wall. The glass is slightly fogged up, but Mia's frame is still visible on the other side, her head tipped back against the wall and her fingers moving slowly between her legs.

Fuck. Me.

I almost come without even thinking to touch my dick. Jesus, I've never seen anything as erotic as my girl touching herself, made better because I *know* she's thinking about me.

I bite the inside of my cheek to hold back the groan that threatens to blow my cover and squeeze my hardening length through my sweatpants.

Her free hand travels down her body, stopping at her tits, dragging a soft moan from her throat. Water cascades down her body, and more than anything, I wish there was no glass between us. I wish I could see every expression, hear every moan over the shower, watch as she comes apart beneath her own touch.

She's magnificent. Every touch, every sound, every fucking move she makes is like a goddamn work of art.

Right up until she lets out an annoyed huff and shuts off the water.

What the hell just happened?

SHATTERED PROMISES

TWENTY-SEVEN

I didn't know it was possible to be this frustrated.

But then again, I'm not sure I've ever been desperate to release pent-up tension like I am right now.

For hours last night, I tried to get myself off. I tried so fucking hard. I did everything I could think of, right up to watching porn. But nothing worked. No matter how hard I tried, I couldn't reach my release, and every time it faded away was more frustrating than the last.

When Ace walked down the stairs this morning, bright-eyed after the best sleep of his life because of the orgasm I watched him have, it was the end of my tether.

I need to come.

I need the release.

And I'm going to fucking get it.

The warm water falls around me, soothing my sore muscles,

and the rhythmic sound of the droplets hitting the tiles beneath my feet gives me a sense of calm I've often craved.

But release never comes.

And each second that passes is more frustrating than the last.

I shut the water off and press my forehead to the cool tiles.

I always knew I was broken. It shouldn't come as a surprise that I can't do something as simple as get myself off. I'm not destined to feel pleasure, not at anyone else's hand, and apparently not at my own either.

A sob rises up my throat, and I don't bother trying to hide it. There's no one around to hear me. Just Ace downstairs working. I've spent a lot of years masking my pain, forcing myself not to cry, not to show emotion, not to show the men around me how broken I truly was. But at least for a while, I let myself feel it all.

Hot tears fall against my cheeks, mourning all that I could have been. The little girl who dreamed of being a nurse, of helping people. The teenager who studied hard despite how awful her home life was. The sixteen-year-old girl who had everything torn away from her. The woman I've become, shattered into a million pieces after years of a life I didn't ask for and didn't deserve.

For once, I allow myself to feel it all, and each emotion is more soul-destroying than the last until I can't breathe through the rough sobs that force their way up my throat.

Arms wrap around me, and I'm tugged back into a hard body. "It's okay, sugar," Ace whispers, his lips murmuring against the column of my neck.

His touch should startle me. Especially because I didn't hear him come in, and I have no idea how long he's been watching. But as it always has, his touch calms me, it allows me to let go and feel the frustration I would normally bury.

His rough hands on my bare skin makes my heart speed up, the organ that keeps me alive is beating so hard in my chest it borders on pain. The toxic cocktail of fear and lust dance together, frustration only making the tears fall faster.

"I've got you, Mia. I've always got you."

"I'm broken, Ace," I sob, the words barely legible through the crack in my voice.

"You're not." Lips press to the top of my head as he pulls me harder against him. The fact that he's still clothed has butterflies dancing in the pit of my stomach. He didn't bother to undress when he heard I was in distress. He came straight to me, just like he always has.

"I am," I choke out. "They broke me, and I don't think I'm ever going to be whole again."

His hands drop to my hips, and he slowly turns me. Panic claws up my throat. This isn't the body I imagined I would have all those years ago when I dreamed of Ace taking my virginity. The scars from my years in the skin trade aren't just emotional, although I'm not sure which of the two I'm more ashamed of.

But his eyes don't drop to my naked body. They lock with mine, the intensity in the green takes my breath away. He presses me into the cool tiles, one hand on my hip holding me in place while the other moves above my head, effectively trapping me.

I take a stuttered breath, willing down the terror that tries to rise. There's an endless number of people who have forced themselves on me, who have held me in positions against my will, but this is Ace. No matter how cold and ruthless he's become in the years we spent apart, he's still the boy who protected me. He wouldn't hurt me the way other men have.

"Listen to me, Mia, and listen fucking hard. You are not broken. Not to me. As long as you're breathing, as long as air moves through your lungs and your heart beats, you're not broken to me. Maybe the pieces of the girl I once knew have been glued back together, but I'll willingly cut myself on your jagged edges if it means I have you back."

I open my mouth to respond, but there are no words. Ace has always had the ability to render me speechless, even when we were kids, and nothing has changed despite the time we spent apart.

"Do you understand, Mia?" He lifts my hand to his chest, and my fingers wrap around in his damp T-shirt. His heart beats heavily beneath my hand. "This beats for you, Mia. It's yours. It's always been yours. And it will always be yours. So, no, you're not broken. You're every-fucking-thing."

Before I can think to speak, his lips crash down on mine, desperate to taste me. His tongue demands entry, and I'm powerless to deny him. And even if I could, I wouldn't want to. I want to give him everything, even if I'm not the girl I was. I want to be whatever he sees when he looks at me like I'm his entire life.

I wrap my arms around his neck and tug him against me

until I truly am trapped between his body and the wall, and something deep inside me settles. Is it all kinds of fucked up that the first time I've felt truly settled is when I'm caught without an escape? Yep. But I don't fucking care.

He lifts me easily, and I eagerly wrap my legs around his waist before my back hits the cool tiles with more force.

Ace's kiss is rough and untamed. All the passion and pain ravels into one neat package that takes my breath away. But I can think of a million worse ways to die.

Teeth collide, and he nips at my lips, leaving them sore but needy. I need more. I need everything.

Without thought, I find myself grinding on his very hard length through his sweatpants, desperate for any kind of relief from the fire burning in my core. Hours of frustration. Hours of trying to reach my own release only seems to make my desperation worse.

"Mia," he moans, his lips moving over my cheek, kissing every piece of exposed skin he can reach. "We need to slow down." His voice is pained.

I stiffen in his arms, dread washing over me like a cold bucket of water. Of course he doesn't want me like that. Not physically. Because despite what he says, I am broken. Why would he want to be with someone who has been used the way I have? He hasn't seen the scars that litter my body yet, but as soon as he does, he'll only grow more distant.

I unlock my legs from around his waist, carefully dropping myself to the tiles. But he doesn't let me put any distance between us.

Ace drops his forehead to mine, his heavy breath whispering against my cheeks as he struggles to rein himself in.

"It's fine, Ace. I understand." I shove against his chest, but he's too solid, he goes nowhere. In fact, I think he actually presses closer, making sure I couldn't run even if I wanted to.

"Whatever the fuck you think you understand, Mia, I assure you that you don't," he growls.

I open my mouth to argue with him, but his hard stare stops the words before they can fall from between my lips.

"No, sugar. You don't understand how fucking badly I want you. How badly I want to sink into your sweet body and fuck you until you can't tell where my body starts and yours ends. But when I walked in here, you were crying. I'm a lot of things, but I'm not a fucking asshole. Not with you. I won't take advantage of you when you're vulnerable. No matter how much you beg or how sad your eyes get because you think you understand shit you have no idea about. So, until you enlighten me about why you were rubbing that sweet little pussy and then immediately started crying, this is as far as we're going today."

Heat floods my cheeks. He saw me. He watched me try and fail to reach my release.

Somehow that's worse, because there's no way he'll believe any lie I try to tell him.

TWENTY-EIGHT

T ears glisten in the big, beautiful pools I find myself lost in so often.

I was too harsh, but I can't fucking stand it when she says shit about herself. And I won't tolerate it. She needs to see herself the way I see her. Beautiful. Strong as fuck. Incredible in every single way. And until she does, we won't be taking things any further.

The thought makes my cock protest painfully in my pants. When she was rubbing her sweet cunt on me, I really thought I was going to come right there, still fully clothed. The way her hips desperately searched for more, begging for me to fuck her the way we've both craved since we were old enough to understand what sex was. But she's not ready yet. And she might never be.

This time, when she shoves against my chest, I take a step back. As badly as I want to crowd her and force her to tell me what happened to upset her, I'm not that big of an asshole. At least not when it comes to her.

She darts from the shower and wraps a towel around her naked body so quickly I almost miss the silver and pink lines and dots marring her perfect stomach and thighs. Scars. But she flees from the bathroom before I can say another word.

I stand in the shower for a few moments, trying to get control of my raging hard-on and my erratic heart. I'm not convinced the damn organ is ever going to settle down after coming so close to finally having Mia. So goddamn close.

After a few seconds, I follow after her, not wanting to give her too much time to retreat into herself, which is exactly what she's done time and time again in our lives. It's her coping mechanism.

I find her sitting on the edge of the bed, her head dropped into her hands. She's wrapped a towel around her body and another around her hair, but the knowledge that I could have her naked in under a second isn't doing anything to help the painful erection pressing against my pants. I'm just fucking glad I'm not wearing pants with a zipper.

"Mia?" I say gently, but stay near the bathroom. It's a slippery slope I'm walking. Give her enough space that she can breathe, but not so much that she can run.

"I just need some time," she whispers, but I know she's crying even without seeing her face.

"No."

She releases a sobbing breath but doesn't bother arguing. Maybe she knows better, or maybe she just doesn't have the energy.

"Tell me what happened, sugar."

When she doesn't answer, I close the distance between us and drop into a crouch in front of her.

"Talk to me. I can't help you if you don't tell me what's going on." I gently tuck my fingers beneath her chin and pull her face up until she has no choice but to look at me. The blue of her eyes is dull from crying, the rims red and puffy, but she's still so fucking beautiful it hurts.

She shakes her head. "I can't." She hiccups. "It's mortifying."

I give her a soft smile and lean forward, pressing my lips to hers ever so softly. The plush pillows are red from my rough treatment of them, but that only makes me want to take them harder. The sick part of me wants to mark her so no one ever touches her again, but as soon as I find myself thinking that way, I have to remind myself that men have been marking her for years against her will, and I'm not about to join them in that category. No way in hell.

"Did you know I almost came on the spot when I walked up to that door and saw you pleasuring yourself?" I whisper between us. "I was like a teenage boy watching fucking porn for the first time, almost blowing my load without so much as touching myself."

Her eyes widen, and the most beautiful blush spreads across her cheeks and down her neck.

"And last night when you watched me get off, that's the hardest I've ever fucking come in my life. It took like five minutes for the spots to fade from my vision."

"You knew I was there?" she whispers, the pink deepening by

the second.

"Yeah, Sugar, I knew." I chuckle. "It was the fucking hottest thing I'd ever experienced, knowing you were watching me, up until this morning at least."

She opens her mouth to respond, but quickly closes it again. I've rendered her speechless, and I can't help but smirk.

"Tell me why you were crying."

She immediately tries to drop her gaze, but I won't let her. Her first instinct is always to run, but she has to realize I'm not always going to let her do that. There's a time and place for space, but this is not it. She needs to start opening up to me, or she's going to explode.

"Please, Mia."

She releases a breath before searching my eyes for something. I don't know what the hell she's looking for, but she doesn't seem to find it. Her sinfully pink tongue darts out, running over her lips in a nervous gesture. "I can't come." The words rush from her mouth, and she immediately tries to look away again and again, I don't allow it.

"What do you mean you can't come?" I ask, my brows tugging together in confusion. I mean, there are millions of women who can't orgasm with a partner, probably just because he doesn't know what the fuck he's doing or because he doesn't care enough to do it properly, but I'm not sure how common it is for women to not be able to reach a release at all.

"I mean, I tried for hours last night and I couldn't get there. The shower was just another failed attempt, and I'm so frustrated."

Part of me is smug as fuck that my little show was what made her desperate for release, but then the guilt comes. She's crying because of me. She's frustrated because of me.

"Like I said, I'm broken, Ace. They broke me." Her voice cracks and takes my heart right along with it. Her tears have always been my kryptonite, and nothing has changed. Each one that falls is another crack in my armor, and I have no idea how to ease her pain.

I close my eyes for a long moment, gathering myself. My falling apart will only make her feel worse, and that's the last thing I want.

When I open my eyes, I grip her chin tighter and force her to look at me. I search the deep blue for uncertainty, for fear, for anything other than the hopelessness that's taking over. "Lie back," I demand and tear my damp shirt over my head.

She's not fucking broken.

And I'll prove that to her, even if it means crossing all the lines I promised myself I wouldn't cross.

Twenty-Nine

"Lie back."

Two words that don't seem like much. But staring into the fire that's caught alight in Ace's eyes, they're everything.

I open my mouth to argue, but quickly snap it shut again. I don't want to argue. I should. Every single bone in my body reminds me of the trauma I've suffered, of the men who have touched me in the past, but my heart reminds me that this is Ace. It's the boy who gave me his dinner when our foster parents were punishing me. It's the boy I crushed on before I knew what a crush was. It's the man who saved me and hasn't stopped saving me since.

I shimmy my way up the bed, careful not to let go of the towel. I'm not ready for him to see the scars that litter my skin. Some are inevitable, but the worst of them should remain out of sight if the towel stays in place.

A deep rumble fills the room, and when I meet his eyes again, there's a dominance in them I haven't seen since I've been back. My first instinct is to panic, but that feeling fades almost as quickly as it appears.

"Good girl."

The ache in my core deepens at his praise. Men have called me a lot of things, but never that, and it sends butterflies moving through my entire body.

Ace watches me with heavy-lidded eyes, lust pooling in the deep green.

I drag my gaze down his bare chest, taking in every line, every muscle, and every tattoo that covers his skin, and Jesus is the man ripped.

I must stare for too long because a low chuckle fills the room, and I'm forced to turn my attention back to his smug smile.

He crawls up the bed, his sweatpants still covering his legs, and every inch closer he comes, the more apprehensive I feel. My brain screams at me that I shouldn't want this, but my body craves it. It *craves* him.

His hard body hovers above mine, his eyes searching my face for fear, for a reason he should stop, and I realize he's nervous. That makes two of us. No one has ever touched me because I wanted them to, and I don't know what to expect.

"You say stop, and I'll stop." He searches my eyes one last time before dipping his head and pressing a kiss to my neck. And then my shoulder. And then the sensitive piece of skin beneath my ear. Each kiss he trails over my flesh stokes the fire in my core until I'm sure I'll combust if I don't get relief soon.

A frustrated moan escapes my throat, and Ace lets out an amused chuckle. "Patience, sugar."

He presses his lips to mine in a slow kiss, but that doesn't make it any less hot. Lord, this man knows how to kiss. His tongue sweeps over my lips, and I don't hesitate to open for him. Every move he makes is measured and careful, leaving me plenty of room to push him away if I wanted to.

But I don't.

I never want this to end.

For the first time, I'm in control of my own body. There's no one telling me what to do and hurting me if I don't do it right or if I don't do it quickly enough. Ace is focused solely on me, even though the evidence of his own arousal is pressing into my belly despite his best efforts to keep his hips away from me.

He draws back, his eyes lidded and filled with barely contained lust. "Okay?" He runs his tongue over his bottom lip, and I swear I'm going to spontaneously combust.

I nod. "Okay."

"Good." His lips descend on mine again, his kiss growing with need, and I meet him with every swipe of his tongue.

He props himself up on one arm while the other carefully trails down my body, never breaking our kiss. When he comes to the towel wrapped around me, his fingers tease the edge, but he doesn't push it, and for that I'm grateful. I'm not ready for him to see my body. I don't know if I ever will be.

He must see in my eyes that that's not a step I'm comfortable with, and he moves further down. His touch is gentle but deliberate, and I can't help but shift beneath him.

"Stay still, sugar."

I halt immediately, his command causing me to drop my hips back to the mattress. When his fingers reach the bottom of the towel, barely covering the tops of my thighs, he pauses and searches my face again.

I'm nervous, of course I am, but I'm not afraid of his touch. I give him a small nod and tip my lips up into a smile that seems enough for him to continue.

When his hand moves up the towel, I wonder if he can feel the raised scars on my thighs, but he doesn't say anything.

The moment his calloused fingers move over my sensitive folds, my hips leave the bed of their own accord. A needy whine escapes my throat when he draws back, his eyes dark with lust as they stare down at me.

"What did I say?" His brow cocks up, and I can't help but think how fucking sexy he is when he gets bossy like this. A smile tips up the corners of his lips when my hips make it back to the mattress, and a moment later, his fingers are back where I need them, circling the tight bundle of nerves that has caused me so much trouble in the last twelve hours.

Maybe I'm just out of practice. After all, I haven't gotten myself off since I was a teenager.

He dips his fingers lower, teasing my entrance, his eyes locked with mine, constantly searching for discomfort. But if I was going to freak out, I think I would have done it already. He's on top of me, for god's sake. He has me pinned to the bed. Surely if I was going to have a flashback, it would have happened by now.

"You're so wet for me, Mia," he rumbles. "You know, I've always dreamed about what you would taste like. When we were teenagers, I used to get myself off at the thought of sneaking into your room and waking you up with my mouth on your pussy."

A pained moan forces itself from my throat. I may not have been able to get myself off, but if he keeps up with that filthy mouth, he might be able to do it with his words alone.

"Would you have liked that, sugar?"

I nod against the mattress. "Yes," I breathe.

I'm rewarded with a bright smile that makes my heart explode. He pulls his fingers from beneath the towel and brings them to his lips, holding my eyes as he dips them into his mouth and lets out a primal growl so deep it doesn't sound human.

"I knew you'd taste sweet, sugar, but fuck. You just became my favorite snack."

I open my mouth to respond as heat spreads across my cheeks and down my neck, but quickly snap it shut again. Did he just say that? Oh my god.

"I like rendering you speechless." Ace chuckles as his hand disappears again, and this time when he brings his fingers to my aching core, he doesn't hesitate. He presses two into my tight channel, watching me closely as he does, and presses his thumb to my clit.

I scream out, the influx of pleasure taking my breath away.

He's way better at this than I was.

"Fuck, Mia," he groans through clenched teeth, and I notice the tension in his neck and shoulders. He's holding back. He's trying not to scare me.

The love I've always felt for Ace slams into me and tears pool in my eyes, but for the first time in my life, it's not because the man touching me is doing so without permission. It's because he saved me in more ways than he knows.

And even when I inevitably have to leave, it will be him who pulls me through the years ahead.

THIRTY

I t's taking every ounce of self-control I can muster not to grind my aching cock against her thigh. Fuck. I'm ready to dry hump the hell out of her if it means I get a release.

But this isn't about me. Despite my cock's very obvious displeasure with that fact.

Tears gather in Mia's eyes, but there's no fear hiding behind the deepest blue I've ever stared into, just trust. Trust I don't deserve. I never deserved it, even when we were kids, but now I certainly don't.

Everything that happened to her was my fault.

I promised I would save her. And I didn't.

And now I'll spend the rest of my life begging for forgiveness. Praying that she'll one day be able to see past all the ways I've failed her.

"Ace," she moans. Her hips grind against my hand, needing

more than I'm ready to give her.

I shake my head slowly, holding the mask of discipline in place so she won't see how fucking badly I want to ravage her.

"Please." The word falls from her pretty lips, and I swear I almost come on the spot. I want to hear her beg. I want those lips to ask nicely for my cum. I want her to kneel for me and ask me nicely to fuck her. I want it all.

I force out a breath and double my efforts. Part of me begs me to tease her, to deny her until she's so desperate her body can't possibly hold it for another second. But this is about getting her past whatever mental block is stopping her from finding her release.

Mia's pussy tightens around my fingers. We're almost there.

"Are you ready to come for me, sugar?" I croon.

She nods against the mattress, her damp hair fanned out around her.

I press down on her clit and focus my fingers on the spot inside her that should detonate her like a damn bomb. "Come for me, sugar. Come all over my fingers," I demand.

Her body tenses, but the orgasm doesn't come. It's like she's in limbo, stuck right on the edge without a way to fall, and tears of frustration fall against her cheeks.

"I'm sorry," she sobs, bringing both hands up to cover her face. "I'm sorry."

My heart bottoms out, and I'm moving before I consciously make the decision to do so. I pluck her off the mattress and hold her against my chest as tight as I can manage without hurting her.

Mia cries into my shoulder, and each tear that falls is another crack in my heart. I fucking hate this. I have no idea how to help her. No fucking clue what to do to make her believe she's not broken.

I've never felt so lost.

She falls asleep like that in my arms, and it takes an hour of her gentle snores for me to finally put her down.

I watch her from the doorway for a few minutes, committing the rise and fall of her chest to memory, the way her nose twitches every so often in her dreams, before finally dragging myself from her room. She needs to rest, and the longer I spend watching her, the more tempted I'll be to wake her.

I drop into my chair behind my computer and stare at the screens for a beat. I don't know where to start. I've always buried myself in work, but that was when I only slept four hours a night and rarely left my apartment. Now I have another human to look after and spend time with. Not that I'm complaining. Having Mia back is better than anything I ever could have imagined, but I'm still figuring out how to juggle work and everything else.

I rub my face and start working on some shit for one of my harder-to-please clients. Nothing he ever wants is hard to dig up, but he's impatient as hell and doesn't like to be made to wait.

I scroll through pages of dirt I've dug up on one of his

employees, a man he suspects is sleeping with his wife. High-profile men are hard to cheat on, and I don't know what his gold-digging wife was thinking, fooling around behind the back of one of the richest men in the country.

I lose myself in the file, and it allows my thoughts to settle ever so slightly, as well as stopping me from checking on Mia every thirty seconds, which is what my body is screaming at me to do.

I chuckle when I read through the report the private investigator wrote and look over the photos he's taken of the two of them. Oh yeah, this guy is fucked.

The fleeting joy I get from my work comes to an abrupt halt when I see Everett's face light up my phone screen. If the last couple of weeks are anything to go by, nothing he has to say is going to be good.

"Hey." I shove the phone between my shoulder and ear so I can keep working while he talks.

"I just wanted to call and give you an update from the center yesterday. Emerson spoke with the boy's friends this morning, and they haven't heard from him. They said that his dad has had a new friend over recently and that they thought he might be the culprit."

I rub my eyes and sigh. The idea of Kyle anywhere near children makes my blood boil. He's the scum of the earth, the type of man, if you can even call him that, that profits off the misfortune of others. "Any idea what this kid's dad is into?"

"I'm looking into it, but I haven't been able to find much." It's not uncommon for those who don't work within the confines of the law to not have a lot of background. Usually, I love that shit. It's like a puzzle for me to solve. But it's different when it's Mia's safety on the line. "I'll keep looking, but I just wanted to give you an update. How's Mia?"

I open my mouth to respond, but I'm not sure how to answer the question. She's doing okay considering she received a direct threat from the man responsible for years of torture, but the memory of her crying in my arms just a couple of hours ago has a lump building in my chest. "She's doing as well as you could expect."

"I know we're not friends or whatever, but the guys and I have a lot of experience with women and children who have been through the kinds of things Mia has, and from what I saw at the wedding and what Rayne and Emerson told me about her time at the center, I think she's going to be okay. It'll take time, and there will be bumps in the road, but she'll be okay."

I choke on the emotion lodged in my throat and the man I was a few weeks ago would have shied away from this kind of conversation, but from him, I appreciate it. "Thanks, man. And thanks for all your help."

"Of course. I'll call if I find anything else."

I drop the phone on the desk and drag my hands down my face. I hope he's right. Because I don't think I could handle losing her again.

THIRTY-ONE

My eyes are sore and my mouth is dry when I wake up, wrapped in more blankets than were on the bed last night.

I roll over, searching the bed for Ace, but he's nowhere to be found.

Of course.

I wouldn't stay if I were him. He doesn't need me being an unhinged crazy person when he's already done so much for me.

I allow my eyes to drift closed again and tug the covers higher around me. How long can I stay in here and not face whatever I have waiting for me when I step foot outside these four walls?

Even as I ask myself the question, I know it's a stupid thought. Ace won't let me bury my head in the sand, and neither will all the other people that have helped get me this far.

It's strange going from having only those who deemed me their property to having a full support system that wants the best for me.

A mixture of guilt and fear crash into me, and I let out a pained breath. They've done so much for me, they've given me so much, and I'm going to leave them all without a word to go back to the life they saved me from?

But I don't have a choice. Not if I want to keep them safe.

A faint buzzing sound pulls my thoughts from how I'm going to tackle this escape, and I let out a quiet moan. Doesn't whoever's on the other end know I'm having a pity party and I'm the only one invited?

I roll over and pluck my phone from where I left it this morning, answering without bothering to look at the caller ID.

"Hello."

Silence meets me on the other end of the line, and after a few seconds, I pull the phone away from my ear to check if the call is still connected.

No Caller ID

Those three little words make my stomach plummet, and I sit up straight in the bed, suddenly aware I'm still wearing the towel I wrapped around myself after the shower. If I could think through the blinding panic that settles over me, perhaps I would be able to feel relieved that Ace didn't see the scars that litter my body, but I have more pressing issues than him knowing the extent of my torture.

"Hello?" I force through gritted teeth. The last thing I want is for him to know how affected I am by him, but it would be weird if I wasn't afraid of the man who groomed and sold me.

He may never have taken me himself, but he made me into the perfect little whore for his buyers, and in a lot of ways, that makes him worse.

I take a deep, calming breath and wait. If he wants to play a game of cat and mouse, I'm more than happy to wait him out. But his voice never comes. Just silence.

He's trying to unnerve me. He knows that I'd know who's calling. After all, there are only a few select people who should have this phone number. But I'm not going to let him get the best of me, not when he already has so many times in the past, and I'm sure he will in the future too.

The line disconnects, and I let out a stuttered breath.

I'm not sure how much more of this I can handle. But what choice do I have?

THIRTY-TWO

I wish I could say things continued as normal after Mia woke up, but that would be a lie.

It's been three days since I finally touched the woman I've been dreaming about since I hit fucking puberty, and each day she's more withdrawn than the last.

Emerson came over tonight while Rayne had some work to do. Apparently, this apartment and the amount of security they've surrounded it with is safe enough to leave his wife for a few hours.

Mia made an excuse twenty minutes ago about needing to get something from her room, but she hasn't come back, and every time I go to stand, Emerson shakes her head slowly, and I sit my ass back down.

"She's regressing," she finally says from her perch on the couch.

I look up from my screen and meet her green eyes. "Yeah. The last few days."

"She's back to not eating?"

I nod, rubbing my hand down my face. I'm also back to not sleeping, which is doing little for my concentration or patience.

"Was it the note?"

I rub my jaw. I wish I could attribute Mia's complete one-eighty on the note alone, but I'm partially to blame, and there's no denying it. "The day after she received the note, she got it in her head that she was—" I pause, hating the word that's about to roll off my tongue because it's not fucking true. "She thought she was broken because she can't reach climax." It's fucking weird talking to someone about this shit, much less a woman, but if there's anyone that can help, it has to be her. "I tried to help her, but I think it just made it worse."

Shock covers her face, and she doesn't respond immediately, taking a few moments to process what I've just told her. "I'm surprised she would want to try those kinds of things so soon." She tugs her bottom lip between her teeth as she thinks through the issue. "Maybe I shouldn't be though. The two of you were close before she was taken, and she may be wanting to take back the power over her own body." She nods as if she thinks she's onto something, and I hang on to every goddamn word she says. "As for her being unable to get there, without speaking to her and knowing more about her experiences, I can't pinpoint what may be the root of the issue, but from the little bits and pieces I do know, her body may have been reprogrammed, for lack of a better word, to only be able to find release when she's in pain or afraid. I've read about instances of it, and I wouldn't be entirely surprised if that were the case."

"You think she can only come if she's afraid?" I balk at her, but the more I think about it, the more sense it makes. "Fuck."

Emerson's eyes meet mine. "What?"

"She said something last week, but emotions were running high, and I forgot about it until now. Cyrus used to force her to orgasm while he did all kinds of fucked up things." I don't know that I ever want to find out the extent of those things because I already want to tear the motherfucker limb from limb. I can't imagine more information would make my need for blood any less.

Emerson's eyes fall closed for a moment as she takes a deep breath. I guess even in her line of work, it's not any easier to hear. "Without speaking to her about it, I can't give you a one hundred percent sure answer, but if I had to hazard a guess, this would be it."

Before I can respond, the elevator dings, and Rayne strolls in like he owns the place, his suit as immaculate as it was before he left. I can't help but wonder how the guy stays so clean considering the shit he and Tommy get up to, but then I suppose his thirst for blood isn't as strong as my foster brother's is.

Emerson gives me a kind smile as they leave, but her eyes are just as haunted as I feel. Every time I think we're making progress, we take three steps backward.

The idea of scaring Mia both makes me sick to my fucking stomach and makes my cock harder than I think it's ever been. In the years we spent apart, the kind of sex I had was rough, it was brutal, and although it was always consensual, the fear in a woman's eye when you're choking them while your cock slams into them and they're seconds from losing consciousness is fucking intoxicating.

I was more than happy to give all that up for her, but what if I could help her?

I rub my jaw and think through the plan that's brewing in my mind. I'm fucking hesitant to go through with it, but what if it's the only way to make her see that she's not broken?

It only takes a few more seconds for me to make up my mind. This could go terribly wrong, but I have to try.

I won't have my woman walking around thinking she's broken, and there's nothing I won't try if it means helping her.

Shattered Promises

THIRTY-THREE

T he closer I get to having to leave, the less I'm able to sleep.

I went years without a solid night of rest, and I guess my body is preparing for that eventuality again.

But the balcony has become my sanctuary.

Watching the city below me wake up and start their days, the gradual pick up of traffic, and the voices that carry up the high-rise building.

It's calming and something I'm going to miss when I'm gone.

I haven't decided on a day yet, partially because I want to live in blissful ignorance for as long as I can, and partially because I'm not sure when I'll have the opportunity to slip past security and Ace. I can't imagine it's going to be that easy, but Kyle keeps calling, and each time has nausea rolling in my stomach.

Each day he calls but never says anything. It's got to the point now where I don't bother with a greeting. It defeats the purpose. He doesn't want to talk, he wants to scare me into showing myself. I guess he doesn't realize that I've already made up my mind, I'm just biding my time.

I tug the blanket tighter around me and fight against the surge of regret that slams into me whenever I think about how limited my time is.

The thought of leaving Ace breaks my already shattered heart, but I'm not what he needs. He needs someone whole, someone who can give him everything he deserves, because God knows he's given me so much over the years.

I hope that my leaving can set him free.

A tear falls against my cheek, and I quickly wipe it away. I need to shut off my emotions again. They won't do me any good when I'm back in hell. I have no idea what Kyle has planned for me or what he wants from me, but I can't imagine it's good.

The sound of the door opening startles me, but Ace walks through it wearing nothing but a pair of low-rise sweatpants, his abs and tattoos on display. Not that I'm complaining. The man is ripped. But it does remind me of all the things I can't have.

Mainly him.

All I've ever wanted is him. From the moment I walked into that foster home, he was my everything, and I think that's the worst part. I got so close. So fucking close. And now I'm going to walk away.

I watch him out of the corner of my eye, but I try not to turn my attention to him.

He collapses into the seat beside me, rubbing his tired eyes the way I did mine when I first sat down. He's back to not sleeping well, and I can't help but wonder if I'm the reason. If he can feel me withdrawing. It's not like I've been subtle about it.

I hug myself closer and pull the blanket tighter. It is cold out here. I have no idea how he's sitting there with no shirt on. I'm cold just looking at him. But I need something between us. The few inches he's left aren't enough.

The silence is disjointing, given his usual morning greeting. He usually finds any reason to touch me, usually asks me how I slept, if I want coffee. But not this morning.

This morning, he's tense.

Not for the first time, I wonder if he knows I'm planning on leaving. I haven't written it down or made any plans that he could possibly know about, but I've always suspected he could read my mind. When we were kids, he knew when I was hungry even when I didn't make a sound, he knew when I was scared without me saying a word, and he always knew me better than I knew myself.

When I can't handle the silence for another second, I wrap the blanket around my shoulders and stand. I give Ace a wide berth on my way past, holding my breath with each step I take.

But when I reach for the handle, I'm tugged away from the door, and I'm slammed against a hard body. Ace's hard body.

His breath whispers across my neck as his arms band around

my middle, holding me in place. "Where do you think you're going, sugar?" His voice is deep, and if I didn't know who was holding me, I'd likely find his tone terrifying.

But instead, need washes over me like a bucket of ice-cold water, followed closely by disappointment. Because it can't lead anywhere. Not without frustration at least.

"I need to shower," I whisper, not trusting my voice not to show how fucking badly I want him. How badly I wish I could be normal. Even just for one day.

Ace holds me against him with one arm while the other trails up my front, parting the blanket until all that separates me from the cool air is the thin silk nightgown I'm wearing.

My nipples pebble and press against the soft fabric, sending shockwaves straight to my core. He moves back just enough to allow the blanket to drop to the ground, pooling around our bare feet.

"Ace?" I murmur.

He hushes me, slowly stepping us forward until my front is pressed against the glass barrier and I'm staring down at the street below. The high-rise apartment is so high I can barely see the people on the sidewalk, hurrying to their days, and my breath catches in my throat. I'm afraid of a lot of things, but heights always seemed kind of insignificant compared to everything else.

Right now, though? Right now, the wind blowing around us, the moving city below, and the way Ace seems to press me harder and harder into the glass have my heart rate picking up almost to the point of pain.

"Ace, what are you doing?"

His hand trails up my bare thigh, his touch gentle despite how hard he's holding me. He's never been like this with me before, and I can't reconcile the man who has always taken care of me with the one holding me at the edge of a building, with nothing but a pane of glass stopping me from falling.

He doesn't answer me with words. Instead, his foot kicks mine apart, and I follow his silent order without argument.

I suck in a breath when his fingers brush gently along the edge of my nightgown, toying with the sensitive skin there.

I let out a muted moan, my need overpowering my fear. I always knew I was fucked up, but this might be on a whole other level.

Ace presses his lips to my neck in gentle kisses that match his soft touches, and I allow my eyes to drift closed, to be surrounded by nothing but him and the crisp morning air, and everything else melts away.

His fingers creep higher and brush across my panties, a deep groan rumbling from his chest. "So wet for me, sugar."

I nod, chancing a look over the edge of the balcony, and my stomach bottoms out. Jesus is this high up.

As if sensing my renewed fear, Ace pushes me farther forward until my head and shoulders are hanging over the edge, my long hair whipping around my face in the brisk wind.

He moves my panties to the side and slides his fingers through my wetness, dragging a moan from my throat. He draws gentle circles over my clit, driving me crazy with the need for more.

But he doesn't make me wait long.

He presses two fingers into my tight channel, driving them in and out a few times before focusing on the place inside me that will set me off like fireworks on the Fourth of July.

I press back against him, silently begging for more as I stare down at the street below. The rush of adrenaline pounding down on my body makes it hard to breathe through his ministrations, and yet I grind my hips back on his hand, silently begging for more.

"You're needy this morning, sugar," Ace rumbles against my ear, his front pressed to my back as we both hang over the edge.

If I fell to my death right now, it would be worth it to have this moment with him.

Ace's free hand moves from around my waist and wraps around the front of my throat. A moment of panic takes my breath away, but then the fingers moving inside me pull me back to the present.

It's not any of the men who hurt me.

It's Ace.

It's the boy I've loved all my life.

I repeat the words over and over again, forcing my mind to remember that the man touching me has never raised a hand to me, has never hurt me. And he never will.

"You're going to come for me, sugar."

I shake my head. "I can't."

He presses harder into my back, bending us both further over the railing. The wind batters down on us so hard I can barely breathe, but I don't push back. I don't try to escape.

His fingers double their efforts, and I can feel my orgasm right there. So fucking close I can taste it. But it won't come. His hand tightens around my throat, and although I can breathe, I'm well aware he could stop that at any second.

"I swear to God, Mia. Come right fucking now." Ace's growl is so deep I almost don't recognize his voice, but there's something about it that screams danger, and before I've processed what's happening, the telltale signs of my orgasm wash over me. My body tightens as pleasure slams into me so hard stars dance in my vision.

I allow my release to take over because I know Ace won't let me fall.

He never has before, so why would he start now?

Thirty-Four

Her cunt pulsing around my fingers as her body shakes from the power of her orgasm is the best fucking gift I've ever received.

As soon as I saw her sitting out here, I knew what I was going to do. It was risky, especially because we're eighty-odd stories up, and I was only assuming the railing was strong enough to handle both our weights, but I needed her to be scared.

I only wish I could have watched her face as she fell apart. I have no doubt that it would have quickly become my favorite sight on this earth.

But there's time. We have the rest of our lives to work through this shit, and for me to make her come so hard and so many times that she can't fucking breathe through all the pleasure I give her.

"Good girl," I praise against the shell of her ear. "You're such a good fucking girl for me, sugar."

A shiver moves through her body, and this time I know it's from my words, not the freezing cold wind whipping around us. She stopped feeling the cold a few minutes ago, just like I did.

Once I've dragged every ounce of pleasure from her body, I carefully withdraw my fingers and pull us both back from the edge of the balcony, holding her tight against me and then swinging her up into my arms.

I leave her discarded blanket in a pile on the ground and carry her into the warm apartment. Her body trembles in my arms, the cold finally starting to get to her, but it won't be for long.

Before I stepped foot on the balcony, I ran a bath for when we came back inside, knowing she would likely need it.

I carry her up the stairs, taking more care than I normally would to make sure I don't trip with her in my arms, and straight into the room I've been staying in.

The bath salts I poured in the warm water waft through the room as I enter the bathroom and perch her on the basin, but her arms don't release from around my neck when I try to step back, and I can't help the smirk that tugs at the corners of my lips.

"Are you okay, sugar?" I rumble.

She nods against my neck.

"I need to take your nightgown off so I can get you warm. Can you let me do that?"

She turns her face and spots the bath, but that only seems to make her hold on to me tighter. A fucked-up part of me is glad she seeks me out when she needs comfort, because I fucking love being that person for her, but if I don't warm her up, she could get sick, and that's the last thing I want when she's finally starting to look better.

"It'll only be for a couple of seconds, sugar."

"Will you come in with me?" she whispers.

"If you want me to."

She nods and loosens her grip on my neck.

I make quick work of tugging the silk fabric from her skin, shoving her panties down her legs, and shucking my own sweatpants. I lift her back into my arms and step over the edge of the clawfoot tub.

The water sears into my cool skin as I carefully lower us into the water, never allowing any space between me and Mia.

She hisses when the hot water washes over her, but she never pulls away.

Once we're settled in the water, I rearrange her between my legs with her back pressed against my chest.

Perhaps the silence should be jarring, but I've never felt more at peace with my own thoughts, and that's kind of fucked up for a twenty-three-year-old. The beast inside me is sated, the need to dominate Mia is satisfied for the moment.

I don't bother trying to shield her from my hard-on pressing into her back. I'm not going to push her into sex until she's ready, but I'm certainly not going to pretend she doesn't affect me.

I press my hands against her stomach and pull her closer. It doesn't seem to matter that every part of her body is touching mine, I still need her closer.

Her body stiffens against mine when my hands settle over her stomach. A better man would move them, but so far, pushing Mia has worked pretty well for me, and I've never claimed to be good, not to anyone but her, at least.

"Ace," she whispers.

"I've got you, sugar."

She lets out a stuttered breath but leans her head back against my shoulder, and I lap up every second of my time with her in my arms.

The water cools around us, but I'm hesitant to lift us out of the tub because I don't know when she'll open up for me like this again. Or even if she ever will.

It's only when her gentle snores fill the tiled bathroom that I stand with her in my arms and wrap a towel around her naked body. Mia stirs but doesn't wake as I carry her into my bedroom and lay her out on the bed, carefully wiping the droplets from her skin.

Her head falls to the side, and her hair spreads across my sheets like an angel. I've never allowed a woman in my bed, always fucking them at a club or, worst-case scenario, at their place, but seeing Mia on the same sheets I slept on last night makes my cock ache with need.

The dim lighting only allows me to see so much of her silky skin, but I enjoy every piece I can see, pressing gentle kisses in the wake of the towel.

When I reach her stomach, I pause on the marks that catch the light. Small dots. Long scars. A littering of scars I know weren't there when we were kids, and all the air is sucked from my lungs. I saw a glimpse of some last week, but I had no idea they were to this extent.

This is why she didn't want me to remove the towel the other day, and it's why she freaked out when I held her in the bath.

She didn't want me to see what they did to her.

Mia's yawn tears my eyes away from the marks, and I meet her tired eyes. It only takes a few seconds for her to realize what I've seen, the horror in my eyes is probably enough to give me away, but just when I thought we were making progress, I watch as she builds the walls back up right in front of my eyes.

Not this time, sugar.

THIRTY-FIVE

I t was only a matter of time.

I know that.

Part of me hoped I could put it off, that I could leave without him ever truly knowing how broken I am. But that was naive of me.

The disgust is written all over his face, and I flinch just from the sight. I never thought Ace would look at me like this, but I should know by now not to be surprised by anything men do.

I'm off the bed before he can open his mouth, wrapping the sheet around me as I go. I need to get out of here. I need to get away from him.

By the time I make it to the door, Ace is still staring at the spot where I was lying on the bed, and I manage to wrench the door open and make my escape.

Tears I didn't realize I was crying fall against my cheeks as I stumble down the steps, holding on to the railing for dear life as I trip over the sheet over and over again.

I have no fucking idea where I'm going, all I know is I can't be here anymore. I can't see him look at me like that again.

The boy I knew, the boy who loved me when no one else ever had, the boy who gave me my first kiss and was my first love, has turned into a man who is disgusted by what I've been through. And I can't handle it.

A ragged sob escapes from my throat, and I stop to drag in a breath. The toxic cocktail of sadness and fear overwhelms me, and I can't think through my next steps. And yet, I keep moving.

I stumble to the elevator and come face-to-face with one of the security guards who's been here most days. His gray eyes go wide when he sees the state of me, but before he can say anything, strong arms wrap around me and pull me back against a hard chest.

"Is everything okay?" the guard asks. I should know his name, but I think part of me has tried not to get too attached to anyone here, even if I have done a terrible job.

"Turn the fuck around," Ace snaps.

My brows pull together in confusion. Is he talking to me?

The guard opens his mouth to respond, but the sound that rumbles from Ace's chest is barely human. "If you like your eyes in their sockets, I suggest you get them off my woman."

His arms are banded around my middle, stopping me from escaping his hold, but I try anyway. I shove my elbow into his hard stomach with every bit of strength I can muster, but he doesn't even flinch.

Instead, he chuckles against the shell of my ear. "You're already in so much trouble, sugar. But please keep going. Let's see how much deeper you can dig the hole you're in."

I watch as the guard turns his back on us, and Ace's hold on me loosens ever so slightly. What the hell was that about?

He pulls me backward, holding me upright when I stumble on the sheet, until the door slides shut behind us and it's just the two of us standing in the middle of the apartment.

"What the fuck was that about?" I snap, the tears falling against my cheeks now equally about the look on his face when he saw my scars and how much of an asshole he was to one of the men keeping us safe.

"He was looking at what belongs to me," he says simply as if that alone answers my question.

"I don't belong to anyone," I whisper. "Not anymore." The admission deepens the pain in my chest because it's only true for a little while longer.

"Wrong." He turns me so quickly I almost lose my footing before pressing me against the wall. "You've always been mine, sugar, and you always will be."

I squeeze my eyes shut, trying desperately to settle the tears that just don't seem to stop, but my emotions are all over the place.

"Open those pretty eyes for me, Mia," he demands, and I rush to follow his order. "Good girl."

"Just let me go, Ace," I whisper. "Please let me go."

His eyes turn dark, and his hold on me tightens, but not to the point of pain. He seems to know where that line is, and he's dancing on the right side of it. "Never again, Mia," he murmurs, his breath whispering across my cheeks.

I choke on the sobs forcing their way from my throat, desperate to get away but powerless to the man who has always held my heart.

"Every time I let my guard down, you try to run from me."

"The way you looked at my scars—" I choke on the words and squeeze my eyes shut to try to get a handle on my emotions. But it's useless. I'm too far gone. Today has been too much for me, and I should have known as soon as I let myself feel again that years of pent-up emotion would constantly be beating down on me. "I told you I can't see you looking at me like that. I can't."

"You should have told me."

"Why?" I challenge. "So you could save yourself the sight?"

His eyes flare with anger, and he crowds me against the wall, sucking any air that was left right from my lungs. "You know that's not what I meant, Mia," he growls. "I know your automatic reaction to everything is to push me away, but *never* assume that *any* part of you could disgust me." His body is pressed so tightly to mine that I can barely breathe, and for the first time in my life, I think I'm a little afraid of him.

Ace has always been my safe place, my home, but the way he's staring down at me with so much anger…it takes everything in me not to flinch away from him.

I shake my head, but before I can speak, he continues. "If the roles were reversed and I was the one that was missing for eight years, if I was the one who was tortured and hurt repeatedly, beaten, and sold to the highest bidder, and I finally came home to you, and you found me covered in scars and cigarette burns, would you be surprised?"

I squeeze my eyes shut to warn off the tears that threaten to fall. He's right. Of course he is.

"Open your goddamn eyes, Mia. Stop hiding from me." His fingers wrap around my chin in a punishing grip. If it were anyone else holding me like this, I have no doubt that I'd be panicking, but it's not the same with Ace.

He's always been the exception to every single rule.

I follow his command, and my breath catches at the sight of his green eyes on fire, staring at me with reverence and anger, silently begging me to understand.

"Why didn't you tell me about the scars, Mia? You had to have known I would see them eventually. That at some point, it was inevitable living together. So why hide them?" He sounds so angry, angrier than I think he's ever been at me, and his anger only makes me cry harder. I hate that I've disappointed him.

"I...I..." But I'm too far gone. I can barely breathe through the sobs that force their way from my throat.

Something crosses his face, something I can't quite identify. But he doesn't make me wait for long before a deep roar surrounds me. "You thought you'd be gone before I could see them." It's not a question. He knows me better than anyone else ever has and has always been two steps ahead of me.

Emotions flash across his face faster than I can identify them. Anger. Frustration. Sadness. Disappointment.

And each one hurts more than the last.

This is why I can't stay.

This is why I have to go.

Thirty-Six

T he realization hits me like a goddamn freight train.

I thought we were done with this. I thought she was going to stop running from me. I thought we were finally making progress.

But we weren't.

She was just biding her time before she ran again.

I take a deep breath, forcing my hand to release her chin before I hurt her. No matter how angry I am with Mia, I'll never lay a hand on her. I'll never be one of the men who have put the terror in her heart.

"Ace," she whispers.

"Shut up," I snap. I allow myself another second to calm down, but it's no use. The beast is chomping at the bit to escape, and for once, I'm going to let him out to play.

Without a second thought, I throw her over my shoulder with

little regard for the sheet that's wrapped around her and start toward the stairs. She lets out a surprised shriek at the impact but doesn't protest like I expect her to as I take the steps two at a time before walking straight back into my bedroom.

I deposit her in the middle of the bed, and when she moves to wrap the sheet back around herself, I level her with a harsh stare, and she stops in her tracks. Good to know she'll listen to silent commands.

"Stay," I growl.

I walk toward the wardrobe and disappear from her view for a few moments while I find what I'm looking for.

When I return, she's still in the same spot I left her, the sheet barely covering her tits and pussy from my gaze. I allow myself a moment to take in every inch of bare skin before me. She's so fucking beautiful, and all I want is for her to see herself how I see her. I want her to realize she's a fucking warrior, and that no scar or blemish is going to make me see her any differently.

Because I love her.

I'm obsessed with her.

And I'll do anything to prove that to her.

Mia's eyes track down my body, clothed in nothing but a pair of sweatpants, before locking on what I'm holding.

All the color drains from her cheeks, and for a moment, I consider throwing in the towel on this plan. But she needs this. I need this.

I close the distance between us, crawling up the bed until my hips straddle hers, pinning her to the mattress with my body weight. "Grab the headboard, sugar," I command.

She hesitates, her breathing coming in hard and fast as she considers her options. Tears still fall against her cheeks, but some of the panic has diminished despite our current positions. She takes a breath and reaches up, grasping the iron bars behind the pillows.

I barely swallow the groan that claws its way up my throat at the sight and how she obeyed my command with little hesitation.

Once I get control of myself, I make quick work of wrapping my belt around her wrists and securing them to the headboard, taking extra care to make sure they're not too tight.

"Okay?" I ask.

"Yes," she whispers.

"You will do everything I say when I say it from here on out. The only exception to that is if you are afraid or you're in more pain than you can handle. Do you understand?"

She nods against the pillows, her damp hair a wet halo on the pillow.

"Words, Mia. I need your words because I can't risk missing a head movement."

"I understand."

"Good girl." I brush my fingers across her cheek. "Here are the rules, Mia. I suggest you follow them or you will be punished."

She opens her mouth to argue, but I shake my head slowly.

"You will not speak unless I ask you a question or you need to tell me to stop. You will not come without permission. You will not hesitate when I order you to do something. And you will keep your eyes on me at all times."

Her brows tug together in confusion at the last one, and I brush my thumb over her pouty lips. "I don't want to risk you falling into the past, and I think this will help with that."

She captures her lip between her teeth as she takes in a stuttered breath, uncertainty flashing through her blue gaze.

Come on, sugar. Let me in.

"Okay." The word falls from her lips so quietly I barely hear it, but it's all the go-ahead I need.

I shuffle back down the bed and drag the sheet away from her body, uncovering every inch of creamy skin.

I suck in a breath and take my time looking her over. I've spent my whole adult life craving this woman, needing her. I've been desperate to taste her, to devour her, and now that the time is finally here, I'm not sure where to start.

My eyes lock on her stomach and the tops of her thighs, the little silver scars shining in the dim light. Before I can think better of it, I dip my head and press a kiss to the cigarette burn a few inches beneath her breasts. And then the slightly pinker scar beneath it. Over and over again, I press my lips to Mia's stomach, silently reminding her that I will *never* see her as anything other than the woman I've loved for as long as I can remember.

"Ace," she whimpers, and when I look up, tears are falling against her cheeks.

"You're fucking beautiful, Mia." *Kiss*. "Every single inch of you." *Kiss*. "I'll never not find you the most incredible woman on this earth." *Kiss*. "And I will spend the rest of my life." *Kiss*. "Making you see yourself the way I see you." *Kiss*. Her skin beneath my lips is so fucking soft, and even when I run out of scars, I kiss every single piece of skin I can reach as she squirms beneath me.

By the time I allow my gaze to flick back to hers, the tears against her cheeks have dried, and she stares back at me with need.

I can smell her arousal, it's so fucking thick in the air that I'll be smelling her on the sheets long after they're washed.

Slowly, I move down her body until I'm wedged between her thighs. The closer I come to her core, the more desperate I am for her, and although I want to tease her, I can't. Depriving myself of her sweetness would be a cruel and unusual punishment.

The first swipe of my tongue through her soft folds drags a moan from both our chests, but the first taste isn't enough. And neither is the second, or the third. And then I'm a man possessed, a starved man who can't get enough of the woman tied up beneath him.

I waited my whole fucking life for this, and I'm going to savor every single second.

THIRTY-SEVEN

I never thought I'd enjoy a man's touch again.

I thought after the first time a man touched me against my will that I would forever be broken, that I would always dread the touch of the opposite sex.

And yet as soon as Ace touches me, I melt for him.

He eats my pussy like it's his favorite meal, and I thrash against the belt around my wrists, desperate to thread my fingers through his hair and hold him against me.

"Ace," I moan. "Please."

"You taste so fucking good, Mia," he groans against me. "I might just spend the whole day right here, bringing you right to the edge without letting you fall over it. Perhaps that will stop you from running from me in the future," he muses.

He bands one arm over my stomach while the other creeps up my thigh, leaving goosebumps in its wake. Ace focuses his tongue on my clit, circling the tight bud of nerves while he probes my entrance with his free hand, and I can't help but writhe beneath him.

Jesus. I need more. I need it all.

I need him.

He pushes one finger into my tight channel, and if it weren't for his arm across my middle, my hips would come clear off the bed.

A chuckle vibrates over my clit, only exasperating my pleasure. "So receptive to me, sugar."

"I need more, please, Ace. Please don't make me wait," I plead. The words roll off my tongue so naturally, and I try not to overthink the gravity of this moment and the one we shared just a couple of hours ago.

It should feel wrong to enjoy this—to enjoy any pleasure a man gives me after everything I've been through, and how orgasms were used against me—but nothing has ever felt so right.

His eyes flash with a fresh wave of fire as he smirks against my pussy. "Fuck, I love it when you beg for me, sugar."

He doubles his efforts, his fingers massaging my G-spot in focused passes and his mouth alternating between drawing gentle circles over my clit with his tongue and sucking the tight bundle of nerves within an inch of its life.

My pleasure rushes toward me, and I choke on my own breath as I prepare myself for it. This man's mouth is sin.

"Please, Ace," I cry out. I'm so close to the edge, I know I won't be able to hold it for much longer.

"Just a little longer, Mia."

I push my head back into the pillows as my body teeters at the edge, threatening to tumble over without the permission I need. I don't want to disappoint Ace. He's given me so much, and I've already made him so angry today. I need to hold it.

His fingers and mouth disappear from my pussy, and a strangled moan escapes my throat a moment before his rough hand slaps down on my oversensitive clit.

"What the fuck?" I cry.

"Eyes on me, Mia," he reminds me, and I immediately lock my gaze to his. "Your rules are there for a reason, and I expect you to follow them."

I nod against the pillows and hold his eyes, ensuring not to move my gaze from his as he lowers his mouth back to my pussy. He slips his fingers back inside me, filling me so completely as he massages my G-spot with gentle strokes.

"You can come when you need to, sugar."

The words are a beacon for my release, and it's only a few seconds before his ministrations drag me over the edge. Pleasure washes over me in waves I can barely wade through, but I keep my eyes on him through every single second, not risking him stopping if I drop his gaze.

He drags every ounce of release from me, gently lapping at my pussy to not overwhelm my oversensitive skin.

"Good girl," he murmurs.

He kisses up my body, paying close attention to the scars on his way up. He stops at each breast and sucks my nipples into his mouth, kissing and licking the tight buds before biting into them softly and then soothing the sting away with his sinful tongue.

By the time he makes it back up to me, his body pressing mine into the mattress and his lips just a breath from mine, I'm panting, needing more. I always need more when it comes to Ace.

I lift my head and capture his lips, groaning at the taste of myself on him.

He doesn't hesitate, pressing his lips to mine. His tongue demands entry, and I open to him, giving him everything I have left to give. It may not be much. It may not be what I promised him all those years ago, but even if it's for a short time, I'll give him everything.

The hard ridge of his cock presses through his sweatpants, and I can't help but grind against him, desperate to give him the same pleasure he just gave me.

"Sugar," he warns between rough swipes of his tongue.

I tug at the belt around my wrists, relishing in the way the leather digs into my skin. I want to wrap my arms around him, pull him closer, hold him against me, and never let go.

He pulls back just far enough to search my face and make sure I'm still bound. "I should keep you tied to my bed, sugar. At least then you can't run from me again."

His lips descend on mine again before I can respond, and honestly, I don't know what I would say even if I could. Because the reality is that I will run from him again, and I don't have a choice in the matter.

He kisses me for long minutes, alternating between slow, gentle caresses of his tongue and sharp nips of his teeth. But all of it drives me wild.

When he draws back, he rests his forehead on mine and lets out a breath before reaching for the belt around my wrists.

"No," I rush out.

His eyes clash with mine, confusion tugging at his brows. "I need to go have a very fucking cold shower, sugar, and I can't leave you tied to the bed even though it's very tempting." His lips turn up in a smirk.

"I want more," I whisper, not trusting my voice with the admission, one I wasn't sure I'd ever make.

He stares at me for long seconds, his eyes searching mine for hesitation, but he's not going to find any. "Mia..."

"Please, Ace." I catch my bottom lip between my teeth and take a breath to steady myself. "I need more."

His eyes drop closed, and a deep groan escapes his throat. "Jesus, Mia."

I open my mouth to say something, but he shakes his head slowly, and I quickly snap it shut.

"Are you sure about this, sugar?"

"Yes."

He nods and reaches for the belt again.

"No. Leave it." The words fall from my mouth before I can think them through. I shouldn't want to be bound during sex, not after all the times I was when the choice was taken away from me. And yet I'm begging him not to undo my wrists.

"Fuck," he groans, dropping his forehead to mine. "You're killing me, sugar."

He moves his hand away from my wrists to grasp my chin between his fingers. The bite of pain causes a moan to claw up my throat, and that only seems to please him. "You say stop at any time, and everything stops, okay?"

"Yes," I whisper.

Ace climbs from the bed and shucks his sweatpants in one quick movement, and a second later, he's back on me.

His knees press into the mattress between mine as he brings his face back to mine. His naked body presses mine deeper into the bed, and for a split second, my stomach bottoms out and my heart almost leaps from my chest.

What the hell am I doing? I can't do this. I can't allow another man to use me, even if it is consensual. Even if it is the man I always thought would be the only one to ever touch me.

"Mia," Ace rumbles, dragging me out of my panic. "You're okay, sugar. I've got you. I've always got you." His fingers brush down my cheek in a calming motion. "We don't have to do this."

But then they win. All the men who took what didn't belong to them. Kyle. Everyone who has ever worked for The Factory.

They all win. And I don't want that.

I need to do this to remind myself that they didn't win. That I survived. And for a short time, I got to live. I got to make my own decisions. And I got to make love to the man I thought would be the only one to ever touch me.

"I want to," I whisper. "Have you got a condom?"

He shakes his head. "There's no way I'm having anything between us, sugar. I've waited a long fucking time to get inside you. I want to feel all of you."

I open my mouth to argue, to point out all the reasons we should be safe, but then his cock is nudging my entrance, and all protests die on my tongue. The knowledge of the implant in my arm is enough for now.

His eyes stare into mine as he pushes forward, taking the breath from my lungs as he fills me. He's fucking huge, and the stretch is delicious, but there's an element of familiarity that I don't want to relate to Ace.

"Holy fucking shit," he groans, his eyes slipping shut for just a second as he fights to regain control.

My body fights within itself. A war none of my emotions can win.

Every beat of my heart feels steadier than it has in all the time I was away from him, but the stretch in my core, the flood of heat, it's so familiar, too similar to all the times I wish I could forget, and I never want to relate that to Ace.

"Mia?" he murmurs, his lips a breath from mine. "You okay, sugar?"

I nod against the pillows. "Keep going."

He searches my face for hesitation, but he must not find any because he starts moving again. Slow pumps in and out as his cock drags over the place inside me that could set me off, or it could break me.

It's just a matter of time before we find out which one it's going to be.

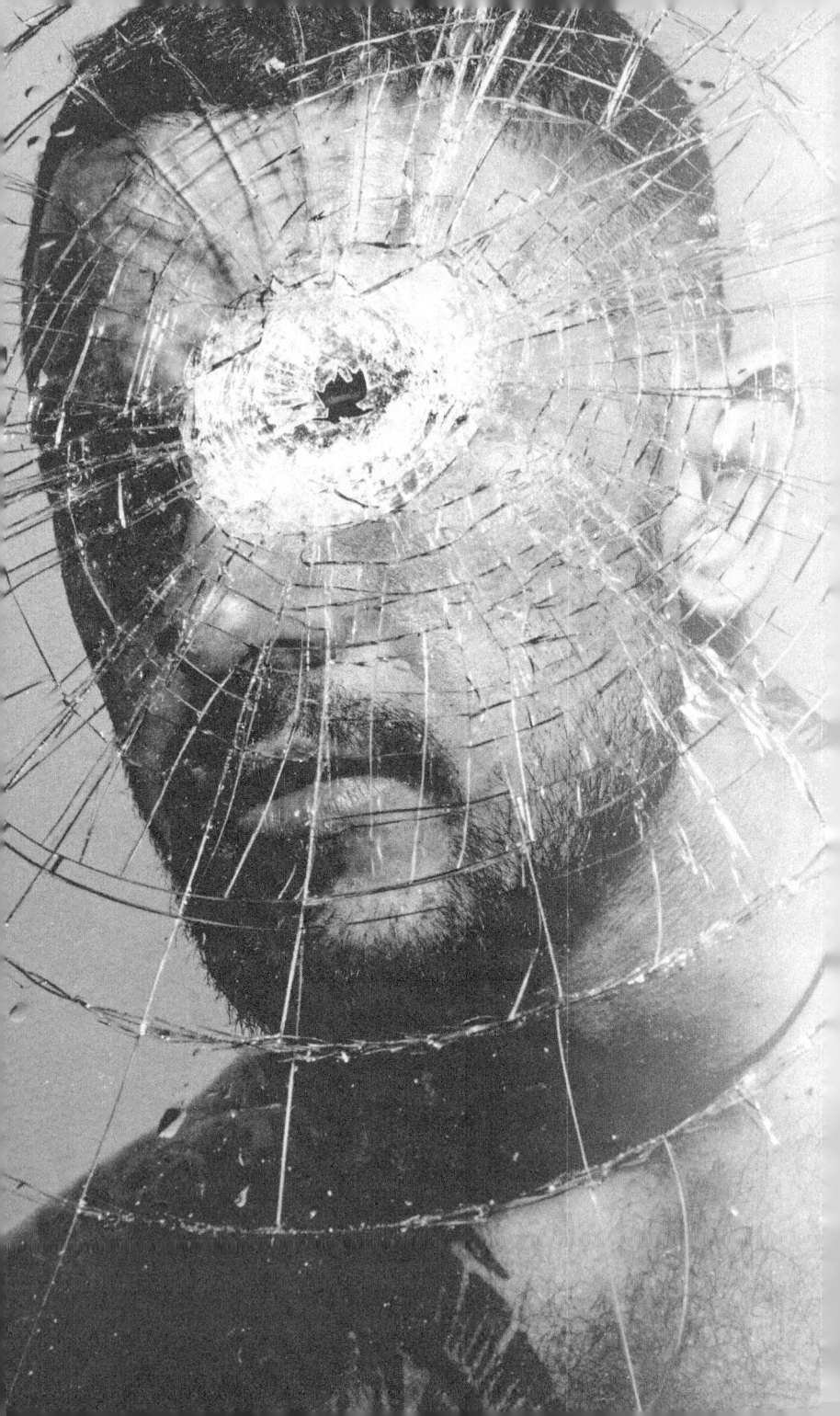

THIRTY-EIGHT

I don't think I've ever felt whole until this moment.

Holding the woman I love in my arms, her trusting me with something of this magnitude, it's like coming home for the first time.

And maybe that's what Mia has always been. Home. And for all the years I was searching for her, it was like being stuck out in the cold, desperate for a place to belong, and it's not until now that I feel it.

Mia's mouth drops open, and a moan escapes her throat. I was fucking hesitant to go through with this because I don't want her to ever compare me to the men who hurt her, but the way she stares up at me is like I hung the fucking moon just for her.

"Doing okay, sugar?"

"I need more, Ace," she whines.

Jesus fucking Christ, this woman is going to be the death of me if she keeps saying shit like that.

I've never been gentle with a woman before. It's always been fucking to fuck. Hell, I don't think I've ever given a fuck about a woman's pleasure before now. Sure, I wanted them to get off, but more so because it felt good for me.

I know that makes me a fucking asshole, but there was only ever one woman I wanted to overwhelm with pleasure, and she's pinned beneath me.

"Please." She catches her bottom lip between her teeth.

I suck in a breath and drag my cock back until just the tip is nestled in her perfect pussy. "Your wish is my command." I stare down at her for a moment longer before driving forward so hard her breath catches in her throat, and she lets out something between a cry and a scream.

I quickly check her face for discomfort or fear, but when I find neither, I let loose. My hips piston back and forth as I ravage her, pressing kisses to her shoulder, nipping her neck, palming her perfect breasts.

"Fuck, Ace," she cries. "Harder. More." Her pants are a fucking symphony, and I oblige her without hesitation.

"You going to come for me, sugar?" I grind out. I've been on the edge of my release since the second I slipped inside her tight heat, but I refuse to come before she does.

"I don't know if I can," she whispers, a hint of dejection creeping into the beautiful blue I've been obsessed with for most of my life.

Without thought, I reach up and wrap my hand around her

throat roughly. She needs this. She needs the fear, and I'm rewarded with her pussy pulsing around my cock. "You will come, Mia. It wasn't a fucking question," I snarl. My own pleasure is rocketing toward me, my balls aching from how long they've been denied their release. But this isn't about me, and they're just going to have to get with the goddamn program.

Her pussy contracts around me, her eyes flashing with fear and arousal the closer she comes to her own release.

"You like that, dirty girl?" I growl. "You like my hand around your throat?"

She nods against the pillow, and I tighten my grip, making her cunt tighten to the point she almost drags me over the edge.

"You're going to come for me, Mia, and you're going to do it right fucking now." The sound of my own voice is foreign, like a man possessed, and maybe I am. Maybe her pussy is like my very own hexing.

Mia's body convulses beneath mine, and her cunt grips me so fucking tight I'm forced over the edge with her.

Stars dance in my vision, the power of my own orgasm taking the air right from my lungs. It's never been like this before. It's never felt like my whole fucking soul was being ripped out. But I'm already fucking addicted to the feeling.

The sound that escapes my throat is barely human as I pump her full of thick ropes of my cum. I've never ridden a woman bareback before, but I want Mia full of my cum at every opportunity. I want to watch it drip down her thighs, to smell it on her.

I collapse on top of her, careful to hold my weight as I press gentle kisses along her shoulder, up her neck, over her cheeks before finally capturing her lips with mine. Slow passes of tongues and gentle nips as we both recover from our releases.

Once I've caught my breath, I brush the hair from her cheeks, my eyes roaming over her face, committing the moment to memory.

It came eight years too late, but I finally claimed her. Finally took what was always mine.

Mia pants beneath me, her face buried in the crook of my neck as I reach up and undo the belt around her wrists.

She wraps her arms around me and holds me close, and there's something so fucking powerful about being needed by her.

A choked sob escapes her throat, and her whole body shakes underneath me. The sound tears my heart clear from my chest.

Did I do that?

Did I hurt her?

Have I just ruined everything?

Shattered Promises

THIRTY-NINE

I've never felt anything so intense in my life.

But then, I've always disassociated during intimate encounters because it was never consensual before. It was rape.

Every single sexual experience I had before Ace saved me was against my will, and I don't know how to reconcile what we just did with all those times and all the horrific things that have been done to me during them.

A tremble racks through my body, followed by a brutal sob that tears through my chest without warning.

An endless battering of emotions slams into me all at once, and I can barely breathe through them. The only thing keeping me grounded is Ace's bare skin pressed to mine.

I'm safe.

I'm okay.

No one can hurt me here. Ace won't let anyone hurt me.

But that thought only makes the tears come in harder and faster because I should leave him. I need to keep him and the people around him safe. But how am I ever meant to live without the other part of my heart?

He's always held it in his hands. Ever since he took my hand when I was six and helped me unpack my things in the house we came to know as hell.

"Mia," he murmurs against my ear. "It's okay, sugar. I've got you." There's a strain in his voice that chips at what's left of my composure. I can only imagine what's going through his head right now. He's still inside me for god's sake. But I can't help it. All I can do is hold on to him like he's the only thing holding me together, and right now, he is. He's the difference between me falling apart and somehow being able to salvage how special the moments we just shared were.

"I'm sorry if I hurt you, Mia," Ace whispers against the shell of my ear. "I'm so fucking sorry."

I shake my head, trying and failing to explain to him that this isn't his fault. That I'm too fucked up, too broken, to be any good for him.

He clings to me almost as tightly as I cling to him, and I know that as soon as he pulls away, I will fall apart. There will be no stopping it because he did exactly as I asked him to.

He replaced all the men that came before, and all the things that were forced upon me. And now all there is, is him. But those emotions, the fear, the terror, the pain, have to go somewhere. It has to escape, and I have no choice but to let it.

Ace rolls to his back with me held close to his chest until

I'm spread out over him and his softening cock is still lodged inside me, like he can't stand to pull out just yet. And I don't think I want him to. I need the extra connection right now.

The tears don't stop for long minutes, and I'm acutely aware of how damp his chest is. I want to apologize. I want to tell him I'm sorry for everything and for ever thinking I could leave him. I want to apologize for always running when things get too hard or I'm scared. But most of all, I want to tell him I'm sorry I can't be the woman he deserves. I'm too fucking broken. And I always will be. It doesn't matter how much time passes, I'll always be the girl who was sold into trafficking by her foster father. I'll be the woman who was passed from man to man, never having anyone respect my body, or any other part of me for that matter. And he deserves so much more.

His hands never stop moving over my back, drawing gentle circles in the soft skin, and eventually, it's focusing on his touch that drags me back to the present and away from the horrors that run on a loop in my own mind.

I lift my head to look him in the eyes, intent on apologizing for ruining what was a long time coming, but when I stare into his gaze, it takes my breath away. The war happening behind the green, his own fear and insecurities right there for me to see where most men would hide them, especially the ones as dangerous as him.

The words catch in my throat, and his fingers toy with a stray piece of hair that's fallen into my eyes. "I'm sorry," I whisper. There are a million things to say, all of which would have been better than the words that just forced their way out, but that's all I can give right now.

His fingers grip my chin, forcing me to stare him in the eyes.

"You have nothing to apologize for, Mia. Never apologize to me for crying. Never apologize to me for healing. If anyone needs to be sorry, it's me. I shouldn't have pushed you like that. I shouldn't have let it go that far."

I stare at him for long seconds, replaying the words he's just said before I sit up suddenly, not giving him a chance to hold me in place, but he does follow me until we're both sitting with me straddling him. "No," I snap. "Don't you get it, Ace? You just gave me exactly what I needed. You gave me everything. I asked you to erase them, and that's what you did." I brace both hands on his cheeks, this time forcing him to stare me in the eyes. "I don't think I'll ever be whole again, but you hold my broken pieces together."

He searches my face for something, and then he leans forward and captures my lips with his in a gentle kiss so unlike the ferocious ones we shared not too long ago. His hands roam my back, and his cock hardens against my belly, dragging a soft mewl from my throat. He breaks the kiss and rests his forehead against mine.

I press my eyes closed, trying desperately to push the tears away. I've already cried enough tears to last a lifetime. "Thank you for saving me. Thank you for always giving me exactly what I need."

This time I'm the one that catches his lips as I shift my hips, desperate to have him back inside me. As soon as his cock slips back inside my aching heat, I sigh with contentment. I missed too many years with him, too many years of normality, and I don't want to waste another moment.

I gently rock back and forth, dragging his hard length against my G-spot.

The tension in Ace's shoulders is obvious. He's not used to not being in control, and honestly, I doubt this will happen often, but right now I want to be in control of my own pleasure. Of both of our releases, even if I'm not sure I can get there without his help.

The slow slide of his cock brings me right to the edge, but no matter how hard I try to focus on the pleasure I can all but taste, I can't quite reach for it.

Without a word, Ace wraps his hand around my throat and squeezes, his huge palm putting enough pressure on my windpipe that my orgasm rushes over me, tearing a strangled scream from my throat.

"That's it, sugar. Come for me. Take what you need from me," he praises, and it only seems to prolong the long waves of pleasure that batter me.

I bury my face in his shoulder and allow him to take over, fucking me as he chases his own release.

It's only another few seconds before he reaches it, his cock swelling inside me, and a roar of pleasure fills the room.

He doesn't pull out. Instead, he lays back against the pillows with me spread out over him. He feels around beside us and tugs a throw blanket over our bodies, his softening cock still inside me. It's comforting being connected like this, but it's when he wraps his arms around me tightly and presses a kiss to my temple that I feel the safest I have since the day my parents died.

"Thank you for trusting me with your heart and with your body."

FORTY

I t's like a switch has flicked in her mind.

All of a sudden, she's smiling more, she flinches less, and the air around her is filled with happiness. Anyone else would probably miss the changes, but they're like beaming lights in my eyes.

I watch from my desk as she moves around the kitchen, baking cookies if the mess she's made is anything to go by. There's flour smeared across her cheek and the way her sinfully pink tongue sticks out as she concentrates on making every cookie the same size, it's like I'm looking at the teenage girl I knew before she was stolen from me.

I can't tear my eyes off her, no matter how much work I should be doing right now. Watching her has become my obsession, and the irony isn't lost on me that a few months ago I was rolling my eyes at Tommy stalking Clara.

I get it now.

I mean, I think deep down, there was a part of me that always understood because my compulsion to watch Mia is hardly a new thing. It started many years ago before I even really knew it was wrong. But now I can barely breathe when my eyes aren't on her.

It's been three days since we fought and ended up in bed together.

She fell asleep on my chest, her body free from the tension she carries with her as gentle snores filled the room. But I stayed awake, protecting her from threats, both external and the ones that beat down on her inside.

The feel of her in my arms, asleep and wrapped around me, it was the calmest I think I've ever felt, and the most peaceful I've seen her since she's been back.

Even on the nights I snuck in to check on her, she looked anything but at peace. Her brow always furrowed, sweat covering her forehead, her head thrashing from side to side as she tried to escape whatever hell she was reliving. But not while she slept on me. And not any night since.

There wasn't a discussion, it just kind of happened. When it came time to go to bed that night, I followed her into her room and tugged her against me knowing I wouldn't be able to sleep without her now that I know what it's like to hold her in my arms.

If it weren't for the fact we can't leave the apartment until we find Kyle, who is harder to track down than any other asshole I've ever investigated, everything would be perfect.

Mia pushes the tray of cookies into the oven and watches

them for a few seconds, like she's worried about leaving them unsupervised for even a minute.

"Sugar?"

Her eyes dart up to meet mine, and her smile grows. "Yeah?"

"Come here."

She doesn't hesitate to follow my command, stepping between my spread legs and dropping her hands to my shoulders.

Without warning, I lift her onto the edge of my desk, tearing a startled yelp from her throat. She tries to push her legs together, but I press her knees apart and rest each of her feet on the arms of the chair.

"Ace?" She worries her lip between her teeth, the nerves obvious as she looks down at me.

We haven't been intimate since that day because I haven't wanted to push her. I wanted to give her some time to process what we did. But I can't wait any longer. I need to taste her.

I shove her black dress up her thighs until I uncover a simple pair of white cotton panties, tearing a growl from my throat. "I need to taste you, sugar," I tell her as I drag her panties down her legs and discard them across the room. If I had it my way, she would never wear underwear again so I would always have easy access to her pussy, but we're not there yet, and I'm not sure if we ever will be.

Before she can protest, I dip my head and take my first taste of her pussy, groaning when I find her already wet for me. Fuck. I will never get enough of her. I could spend every day for the rest of my life with my head buried between her legs, and it still wouldn't be enough.

Mia threads her fingers into my hair and pulls my face closer to her core, her hesitation melting away as I work her clit with my tongue.

I move one hand from her knee up her thigh until my fingers tease her entrance, tearing a needy mewl from her throat. Jesus, she's so receptive to me, and I can't get enough of her.

I dip my finger into her wet heat, and we let out a mutual groan. Her tightness pulses around me as I match the same pressure with my tongue and finger, bringing her to the edge before guiding her back down again.

Over and over, I bring her to the brink of blinding pleasure, but I don't give her enough to fall into the abyss.

Mia's grip on my hair tightens to the point of pain, her need for me making her desperate as she grinds her pretty cunt against my face.

There's something so fucking sexy about her taking her pleasure from me, even if it is just out of reach. When I look up at her, I don't see the broken girl she sees when she looks in the mirror. I see the beautiful woman she's become, who knows exactly what she wants and how to get it, and who survived hell over and over again. I see the girl who has always held my heart in her hands and who I will do anything to protect.

"Ace," she whines as I lighten the pressure on her clit, easing her away from the peak she was just a breath away from. Her whimpers go straight to my cock, the need to be inside her again is stifling, but this isn't about me, it's about her. It's about making sure she knows her pleasure is her own now, even if I drag it out the way I am. "Please. I need more."

I smirk against her pussy. "I know you do, sugar. And you know I'll give you everything you need. On my timeline."

Her eyes roll, but there's the smallest of smiles dancing on her perfect pouty lips, and although bratty behavior would normally only make me drag things out more, the peek at the cheeky girl I left behind, that I let down, is enough to let me overlook the eye roll. Just this once.

I palm my cock through my sweatpants, desperate for relief, but I need to make her come first. "Are you going to come all over my face, sugar?"

She nods her head as her breaths come in sharp pants. Fuck, I love her like this. Free. Wild. Unfiltered. She's not quiet and meek like she so often pretends to be, and she's not nervous or afraid, knowing I'll always give her everything she needs.

I press a second finger inside her along with the first and double my efforts on her clit. She tastes like the sweetest sin you could ever commit. Like temptation and darkness tied up with a pretty red bow.

Her soft moans are a symphony to my ears, better than any music I've ever listened to. Her grip gets more desperate as she holds my face against her. If I suffocated in her sweet cunt, it would be the best way to go.

"Ace. I need more. I can't…"

I dart my gaze up to her, a flash of uncertainty in the ocean blue. This is the turning point, and I have to keep her in the moment with me.

"Come, Mia," I demand. "Fucking come."

Her eyes lock with mine as I push her to the point of no return. Her body is forced to do as I'm instructing, and the scream that escapes her throat fills the otherwise quiet apartment.

I have my sweatpants shoved down just far enough for my cock to pop out when I slam inside her. She chokes on the yelp that escapes her throat, and there's a sick part of me that loves that I caught her off guard.

This time when I slide inside her, I don't hesitate to fuck her the way I crave. I need it hard and fast, and her eyes only seem to heat up as I take what I want from her body.

Every thrust is harder than the last, making the desk beneath her scrape across the hardwood floors with the force of it.

"Ace," she pants against my neck as she wraps her body around mine, holding on for dear life as I slam into her.

"Fuck, Mia," I groan. "Your cunt is a fucking paradise. I could spend the rest of my goddamn life buried inside you and it would never be enough."

I bite into her shoulder so hard the tang of copper touches my tongue, and it makes me rut harder. God, she's so fucking receptive to me. Everything I give her, she takes.

The ding of the elevator drags a growl from my throat as I reposition us, careful to make sure there's no way whoever is about to walk in can see anything they shouldn't.

When I feel her body tense, I slow my thrusts, but I can't bring myself to stop altogether. I'm not sure I'll ever get enough of her sweet pussy.

Footsteps round the corner, and I growl as I look over my shoulder. "Get the fuck out."

Todd, one of the security guys the Saint James family arranged, stands stunned in the entrance, his eyes looking anywhere but at the two of us. "There was a package delivered."

Anger beats down on me, and if it wasn't for the fact my cock is lodged inside Mia, I would have already torn this fucking asshole's head off.

"I don't give a fuck," I snap. "If you're not out of here in the next three seconds, I will tear your fucking eyeballs from their sockets and feed them to you."

It's not until I hear his footsteps retreat that some of the tension starts to fade from my body. I don't want another man to look at my woman ever again, and the possessive need that remains is suffocating.

FORTY-ONE

MIA

I'm frozen in place. Panic rolls over me in ruthless waves, stealing the breath straight from my lungs. The idea of being watched, of having someone see me with Ace, puts me right back to a night I'll never forget. To a night that will star in my nightmares for the rest of my life.

Tonight's different.

I don't know what it is, but the way Cyrus is treating me is almost too nice.

He gave me a full meal and didn't punish me when I ate it.

He allowed me to shower myself, although under his watchful eye, and dress in an expensive-feeling nightgown with a matching robe.

And then when we were done in the bathroom, I wasn't shoved back in the tiny room he keeps me in, barely big enough for the mattress I sleep on. Instead, he leads me through to the formal sitting room. A room I have never been permitted to step foot in.

I'm often allowed into the rest of the house, always supervised, and always for a set amount of time. But each time I've even dared to look at the plush looking couch and soft carpet, Cyrus has snapped at me.

I open my mouth to ask what we're doing in here, but quickly snap it shut. I know better than to question anything he says or does. It never ends well for me, and I don't think I can handle another one of his punishments.

My first owner was bad enough, but he wasn't often violent. He had a perverse need for sweet and innocent, a role I could fill until I turned eighteen and he no longer found me suitable. The one that followed was violent, but nowhere near the level I'm faced with on a daily basis now. It was only when he was angry or drunk that he hurt me, the rest of the time, things weren't so bad. Or at least I've realized it wasn't since my time with Cyrus.

This is hell.

Hell in a fancy mansion with all the things I used to dream of surrounding me, even if I never get to touch or use them. Even if the premium meals that are prepared by the staff Cyrus employs never make it anywhere near my mouth.

Cyrus sits on the couch before nodding toward his feet.

I drop to my knees gracefully, a skill I learned in my first few weeks here. He forced me to practice repeatedly until my knees bled and my muscles ached to the point where I could *barely stand for days.*

I rest my hands on my knees, face up, and keep my eyes trained low. I've made the mistake of making eye contact too many times, and each time has earned me a beating. And that's if I'm lucky.

The soft carpet beneath my knees is such a distinct contrast to the hardwood flooring throughout the rest of the house, and I allow myself to relax into it.

I've lost track of how long I've been here for. The days I don't see a window have blurred into one, and I'm not fed frequently enough to keep track of it that way either.

If I had to guess, I'd say it's been at least a year, but it could have been an eternity for all I know.

His hand rests on the top of my head, but he doesn't say anything. The position we find ourselves in isn't abnormal. This is how he eats most of his meals, with me kneeling at his feet, usually starving. But the rest of the evening is out of the ordinary, and it's making me uneasy.

I don't know how long we sit like this, but it's long enough that I fall deep into my own mind, the blissful silence allowing me to rest for the first time in what feels like days. Sleep doesn't really come to me here because in my first few weeks, Cyrus would wake me every few hours with a new form of torture. But sometimes I get these moments where I'm expecting the worst already, but that expectation is almost comforting to me.

Footsteps in the distance register in my mind, but I don't move. I know better than that.

Cyrus makes a pleased sound in the back of his throat as his fingers glide over my perfectly straightened hair. It's rare for it to be styled these days because I'm not normally given that kind of time to bathe, but it's nice to feel completely clean for once.

"You made it." His cold voice crashes through my calm mind.

"You have her well trained, I see." A man speaks, but I don't think we've met before.

"Aren't Cyrus's whores always?" A woman laughs, and a cold sweat breaks out over the back of my neck.

"I suppose you're right," the man says. They're getting closer, and each step they take toward me has bile climbing higher up my throat.

He's never brought anyone else near me aside from the staff, and even they have strict instructions not to interact with me. So why are these people here?

I swallow heavily, fighting the urge to look up and to remain as still as possible.

Don't embarrass him.

Don't embarrass him.

Don't embarrass him.

The words chant over and over in my own mind. I can't take another punishment, not after the last one. I still can't sit comfortably on the cuts up the backs of my legs where he sliced into me repeatedly before rubbing sea salt into the wounds. My wrists ache from how hard I fought against the binds, and from where the healing process is, I think that was at least a week ago.

I imagine embarrassing him in front of company would result in a much more vicious punishment, seeing as that was the result of me asking for something to eat after being starved for three days beforehand.

"She's a very good girl," Cyrus praises me as he stands.

I remain in my place, knowing that unless I'm instructed to move, I must stay where he put me.

"Up," he commands.

I take a steadying breath and carefully stand, making sure not to hold on to the couch for support. He expects me to be elegant and graceful at all times, especially when there are other people around.

My gaze remains on the pristine cream carpet. If I hadn't seen Cyrus in here some nights with a glass of scotch, I would think no one ever steps foot in this room, and yet right now there are four people in here.

A pair of red heels appear in my vision. The glossy leather is expensive, a pair I could have only ever dreamed of in my old life.

The woman's perfectly manicured finger presses beneath my chin, forcing me to look up into her ice-blue eyes. As expected, her blonde hair is styled to perfection, not a hair out of place, and her makeup is flawless. If I had to guess, I'd say she's in her early forties, not that she looks it, and her knee-length black dress hugs her frame like it was made just for her.

"Pretty eyes," she comments, but not to me. Never to me.

"Yes, they're quite unusual," Cyrus agrees. "It's been quite the treat watching the hope dim from them."

I fight the urge to flinch at his words. I thought I was broken before I came here, that my last owner broke me with all the disgusting things he did to me and forced me to do, but I had no idea how bad it could be until I was dragged through the front door of this mansion.

Cyrus is sadistic.

His tastes are pitch black, and he treats me as nothing more than a toy for him to do whatever he wants with. I used to think once he trained me, things would get better. That once I was a perfect little toy for him, that his sadistic needs would ease. But if anything, they've gotten worse.

"Strip," the woman commands, and for a second, I'm frozen in place. I don't know if I'm allowed to follow her orders or if Cyrus will be upset by that. He's never introduced me to anyone before.

"It's okay, pet, do as Lydia says," Cyrus tells me, and I'm relieved he's not mad at my hesitation.

I shrug the robe from my shoulders and carefully lay it over the arm of the couch before slipping the nightgown from my body. I haven't been given the courtesy of underwear since I arrived, and the only thing that makes that less mortifying is that the implant my last owner forced into my arm the day I was sold to him has completely stopped my periods.

Small blessings, I suppose.

I keep my eyes low, but I feel the way their eyes burn into my naked body. Before The Factory, no one had ever seen me naked, but now it's an almost daily occurrence.

"How is she sucking a cock?" the man asks.

"Excellent. I've trained the gag reflex right out of her so it's just like an extra cunt." His words are so vile my stomach rolls over the food he gave me.

"Back on your knees, pet. Take my cock out and show these nice people what a good slut I've made you."

I do as I'm told, folding myself back onto the soft carpet and unbuckling his pants. At this point, I'm on autopilot. He commands me to do this at least once a day, but usually it's much more than that.

Once I have his dick out, the sight of it forcing me into the numb state I fall into every time he touches me like this, I wrap my arms around my back and link them together as he demands of me.

The other man makes a pleased sound while I see the woman sit at the other end of the couch out of the corner of my eye.

As always, I dissociate the second his cock hits my tongue. That's the real reason I no longer have a gag reflex, because when he touches me, I'm no longer present. I allow him to use my body the way he wishes because it's the only way I can survive each day here.

Not that I haven't wished for death. Because I have.

I wish for death every day. Every night when I go to sleep, I hope I don't wake up, and every morning I curse whatever

God put me in this hell.

Voices carry on around me, but I don't hear what they say. The little bubble that protects me from the vile things Cyrus does to me keeps their words at bay, and for that I'm grateful.

A hand wraps around my hair, but it's not Cyrus, it's the other man. He shoves my face down until my nose rests against Cyrus's crisp white button-down, holding me there for long seconds. Stars dance at the edge of my vision, the promise of blissful quiet just a few moments away before I'm torn backward.

I gasp in a quiet breath, making sure not to make too much noise because I know my owner doesn't like that.

Cyrus sits back on the couch and pats his lap, to which I immediately follow the silent command. Hesitation only gets you beaten and starved.

He tugs me forward until I'm straddling his lap, and his cock is resting at my entrance. "Fuck me, whore."

I swallow the bile that climbs up my throat whenever he forces me on top, because when it's like this, I start to question myself. Is it rape anymore? Is it rape when you're in control? Is it rape when he forces me to come with him inside me? But I do as I'm told, lowering myself onto him and ignoring the bite of pain.

He hasn't been inside my pussy for a few days, opting for my mouth while my wounds from my last punishment have been healing, and as always, he's going in dry.

I grind the way he taught me when I first got here to maximize his pleasure, trying desperately to ignore the two extra sets of eyes on me as I move.

Smoke fills my nose, but when I instinctually turn my head to see where it's coming from, Cyrus grips my chin in his fingers roughly before the palm of his other hand hits my cheek. "Eyes on me, pet. You know the rules."

The ringing in my ears is so intense I can barely force myself to keep going, but my body moves of its own accord, trying to save itself from any more pain.

Another hand touches my back, and I still for just a second, but it's too long, and before I know what's happening, a searing pain burns the top of my thigh.

It takes me too long to realize I'm being burned by a cigarette, but it's the scent of burning flesh that tells me exactly what's being done to me.

Over and over again, the pain is so excruciating I can barely breathe, but I don't let the tears at the edge of my consciousness fall. Not when the cigarette turns to a knife. Not when the woman forces my face down on the other man's cock. Not when I'm thrown to the ground and kicked. And not when they each take turns violating me.

It's not until I'm alone in my room that I finally allow the tears to fall.

I've wished for death so many times since the night I was taken from my bed and forced into a life I wouldn't wish on my worst enemy. But never quite as hard as I pray for it tonight.

FORTY-TWO

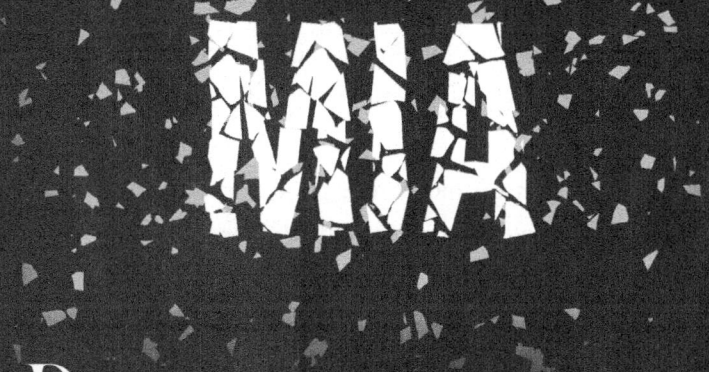

R ealistically, I know it's a flashback, but no matter how hard I try, I can't drag myself away from one of the worst nights of my life.

I wish I could say it didn't get any worse than some cuts and cigarette burns, but I couldn't walk for a week afterward. The things they did to me—the way they laughed at my cries, found my screams of agony amusing—and when I finally succumbed, when my body gave up from exhaustion and pain, they waited until I woke up to keep going.

They made sure I felt *everything* they did to me.

I'm vaguely aware of Ace's gentle touch, his fingers wiping the tears I didn't realize I was crying from my cheeks, but I'm too lost to find my way back to him.

His voice is just out of reach, but I can't hear what he's saying, only the worry in his tone.

Things were so good.

I was doing so well.

But just like I kept telling him, I'm broken. Too fucking broken.

The vision of Cyrus appears in my mind, tearing a ragged sob from my throat. "Please, no," I cry, but I'm not sure if it's out loud or in my own mind.

His cold eyes turn on me before he starts toward me. He's angry. I've disappointed him with my tears.

Stupid. Stupid. Stupid, I chant to myself. I know better than this. I know better than to let my emotions get the best of me.

"I'll do better. Please don't hurt me." Begging only makes him angrier, but I can't help it. I can't take it anymore. It's too much.

"Mia," the soft voice at the edge of my consciousness coaxes, but I can't reach it. It's too far away.

"You know better than to beg, pet." Cyrus's deep voice moves through my mind, so clear and distinct it's like he's right there alongside my own inner monologue.

I cower in on myself, doing what I can to protect myself from any more pain, but there's nothing I can do to stop him. I've tried. Over and over again, I've desperately tried to keep myself safe, to stop him from hitting the parts of my body that are already too broken, but it never works.

I realized a long time ago if Cyrus wants to do something, he's going to do it, and there's no sense in trying to stop him.

Arms hold me close, their warmth holding my own personal

version of hell at bay. "Sugar, come back to me." The voice is faint, but it's there, and I cling to it desperately.

I'm not sure how much time passes, but the body that holds mine doesn't falter.

Soft words are murmured against my temple and eventually drag me back from the darkness.

Ace is cradling me against his chest, his lips against my temple, as he talks to me in hushed tones. It still shocks the hell out of me that he's like this with me, because to everyone else, Ace has always been harsh, unfriendly, and mean even. The only other person who has ever seen the softer side of him is Tommy, and even then, it wasn't often.

"I've got you, sugar," he murmurs, and I find myself burying my face into his chest, holding on to his warmth like my only tether to my own sanity.

I knew I was fucking broken, but this just proves it. This just proves I'll never be normal again and that Ace is better off without a burden like me.

The sooner I hand myself over to Kyle, the better off he'll be.

I force my eyes open and take in the apartment around me. The clean lines. The stark white walls. The wooden features. I use everything I see to remind myself that I'm safe. That I'm not back in that house. That I'm not reliving the single worst night of my life.

There were a lot of bad nights, but that's the one that I'll never run from—the one that will feature in my nightmares until I take my final breath.

"There she is," Ace murmurs, his palm warm against my cheek.

I'm still sitting on the edge of his desk, but at some point he pulled out of me. I can't imagine having the woman that's been nothing but a pain in his ass have a panic attack during sex is doing much for his libido right now.

The tears falling against my cheeks don't seem to have an end, and the rough sobs tearing from my chest are painful. And yet I can't get control of them. Because this is all the proof I needed that everyone is better off without me in their life.

Ace. Tommy. Clara. The Saint James family. I'm nothing but a burden to them, and that's the last thing I want.

"Mia," he whispers. "Look at me, sugar."

I shake my head. I can't see the pity in his eyes. I can't see him look at me like I'm the responsibility he'll never get away from. I just can't do it.

"Mia." The command in his voice almost makes me do as he's said. Almost.

I push against his chest, determined to retreat to my bedroom, but I should know he won't let that fly.

He didn't when we were in the foster home, and he's even less likely to now.

His fingers move to my chin and force my face up until I'm sure I'd be looking him dead in the eye if I wasn't being so stubborn.

"I'm sorry if I hurt you, Mia." His voice is pained, like he can't handle the thought, but he continues. "I imagine all of this is hard on you, and I'm sorry that I've pushed you too hard. I don't know enough about your triggers. I should have taken the time to learn more about what you've been through so I can avoid those things."

That's what has my eyes flying open to meet his, panic flaring to life in my chest. No way is Ace knowing any more about my time away from him than he already knows. It's already way too fucking much, if you ask me. "It's not that," I rasp, my throat sore from the sobs. "It was the guard. When he walked in." I press my eyes closed again, pushing the tears down so I can focus on getting the words out. "Cyrus liked to surprise me with visitors sometimes." I shake my head. "I know you wouldn't do that to me, it's just…"

"A trigger," Ace finishes.

I nod and stare into the deep green of his eyes. The flecks of brown are only visible when you're this close, but I remember trying to count them when we were younger. I'd try to catch sneaky glances at him, but I wasn't always very good at being stealthy, and when he inevitably caught me, he always gave me a knowing look.

"I think I need a few minutes to get myself together." I push carefully against his chest, something I never would have dared to do to any other man who has touched me since I was shoved in that trunk eight years ago.

"No."

My eyes widen at his words, and when I search his gaze, it's clear he's not fucking around. "Ace…"

"No. I'm not giving you space so you can retreat. Because that's exactly what you're going to do. I'm not letting you undo all the progress we've made."

I stare at him, shocked that the boy who never deprived me of anything has grown to be a man so willing to deprive me of my own privacy. He thinks he knows what's best for me, but how could he?

He cups my face in his hands, the warmth allowing me a moment of peace among the chaos. "I don't know how many times I'm going to have to say this before you start believing me, but I'll repeat it over and over again until I lose my voice if I have to. And even then, I'll make sure you know. I'm all in, sugar. There's no hesitation on my part. Nothing you can do to push me away. I didn't spend the last eight years searching under every fucking rock, just for you to talk yourself out of this. You forget that although we spent eight years apart, I still know you better than anyone else on this planet, and I know what it looks like when you're about to run."

I open my mouth to argue, but snap it shut again. What's the point when he'll see through whatever lie that was about to spill from my mouth?

Shattered Promises

FORTY-THREE

ACE

It didn't take Mia long to drift off to sleep once I settled her on the couch, but I didn't leave her side for even a second.

When I carried her to the couch, I bundled her up in blankets in the hope she would fall asleep so I could take care of the asshole who triggered my woman.

Logically, I know it's not his fault, there's no way he could have known what we were doing up here in the middle of the day, but I still want to cut his fucking eyes from their sockets for what they saw.

No one looks at Mia but me, I don't give a fuck what the excuse is.

I take the elevator down to the ground level where three guards are standing, surveying every single person that comes and goes.

One of my favorite things about this apartment is the private elevator. It makes it a lot easier for the guards Everett and

Elijah organized to know if someone is a genuine threat or if they're just trying to get home after a long day at the office.

The guard in question locks eyes with me, and the son of a bitch has the audacity to smirk. Does he not know he's staring into the eyes of his judge, jury, and executioner?

"Sorry, man, I didn't mean to interrupt," he says, his voice even despite the expression on his face.

I advance on him until I'm within arm's reach and wrap my hand around his throat, shoving him against the wall so hard his head thumps against the hardwood. "You ever step foot in that apartment without my express permission, I will fucking end you. Do you understand me?" I growl, my voice so dark I barely recognize it myself.

The color of his face turns deep red as I constrict his airway, but he nods despite it. There's fear in his eyes, which makes me wonder if he should be protecting my woman at all. There's only one thing men like us should be afraid of, and that's losing our queens. Anything else, death included, is completely inconsequential.

"Good." I release his throat, and he immediately wraps his own hands around his neck, dragging in desperate breaths. "Now, you said there was a package?"

He gives me a short nod and reaches behind the small desk they've set up. I get the sense there's always been a security presence here, seeing as this is where Snow lived, but by the way bystanders stare at us, I don't think it's ever been quite this large.

He extends a large envelope toward me, and I quickly snatch

it from his grip.

I flip it over, and the name scrawled across the front makes my stomach drop, and my eyes dart around the lobby as if whoever delivered it is still standing around. But all the wary eyes I meet aren't the culprit, and when my gaze finally drops back to the envelope, I know whatever the contents are will make me fucking homicidal.

Without another word, I step into the elevator and jab the close door button three times, desperate to get the fuck out of the view of other people.

I tear the envelope open and drop the contents into my hand.

It takes me a few moments to recognize what I'm looking at. The simple charm bracelet would look inconspicuous to most. The myriad of standard charms are likely found on thousands of people's wrists around Chicago alone, but there's one I know for a fact has only ever been worn by one person.

The jar of sugar charm I had made for Mia to put on her mother's charm bracelet stares back at me like a fucking homing beacon, and even if I know I'm completely alone in the elevator, I still look around as if there's someone staring right at me.

By the time the elevator stops at the top floor, I've gathered myself enough that I don't think I'm going to lose my shit at any second, but there's always a chance.

I peer over the back of the couch and release a breath when I find Mia still sleeping soundly, her gentle snores bringing me back down from the spiral threatening at the edge of my vision.

Before I can talk myself out of it, I make my way to the balcony and quietly slip into the Chicago afternoon, the sound of the bustling city below assaulting me immediately.

I pull my phone from my pocket and dial Everett's number without thought. Kyle is escalating, and his coming here only proves he not only knows where she is, but that he could get to her at any moment. It's never going to matter to an asshole like him how much security there is in place, he'll find a way, and the daily ads that go up on the noticeboards on the dark web are only proof of that.

The more people that take the job, the more likely we are to be ambushed, and we're just sitting ducks up here in a penthouse apartment, the illusion of safety allowing us to get complacent.

"Yeah?" he answers distractedly.

"You busy?"

"Uh, a little." He curses, and the phone drops, a loud bang filling the line and forcing me to pull my phone from my ear.

"Everett?"

"Yeah, sorry. Changing diapers is a shit ton harder than it looks."

"You answered the phone while dealing with your kid's shit?" I snap.

"That's what being a parent is. Juggling every other responsibility while looking after a small angel that cries and shits a lot."

I scoff. I swear I hated this motherfucker a few weeks ago.

Now I'm finding him amusing? "We have a problem."

He sighs. "What now?"

"We had a package delivered to the penthouse this afternoon. A charm bracelet that would have been on Mia's wrist when she was taken to The Factory but was not with her when we found her in Florida."

"Fuck."

"Exactly my sentiments." I sigh and drop into one of the outdoor chairs, staring across the city skyline like it holds the answers to all my questions.

"Let me take her," I hear Wynter say in the background, and Everett only puts up a small fight.

"Does Mia know yet?" he asks after a few moments.

"No, she's asleep. She's had a rough afternoon."

The sound of him sitting down in his desk chair fills the line, and then the telltale sound of typing follows. "I'm checking the security tapes from the lobby, maybe we can track his movements after he left the building through convenience stores and ATMs?"

"That's assuming Kyle's doing his own dirty work, which doesn't seem likely, seeing as he knows we're looking for him."

There's silence for a few minutes, but while Mia is asleep, I'm not in any rush to move. She needs her rest, and if I start working, I'm likely to wake her.

"It's not him," Everett confirms.

I sigh and rub a hand over my face. Not a surprise, but also not what I wanted to hear. It would be nice if just once, one of these things would go our way.

"I can track the guy that delivered it if you want, but from the outside cameras, it looks like he's a bicycle messenger, so it's probably a dead end."

Like everything else we try.

This motherfucker is way more elusive than I initially gave him credit for.

I guess there's a reason The Factory was able to operate in Chicago for so long before being relocated, but even that we haven't been able to figure out. The assholes are fucking ghosts, and that seems extra fucked up given the size of their operation and how many people they sell each month on the dark web.

From what I've seen, Everett does his best to stop all sales within the city, but there are things not even the best hackers can stop.

I stare down at the bracelet in my hand, looking over each of the charms I'd committed to memory over the years we spent together. Mia never took this fucking thing off. Never. Even when our foster parents tried to tear it from her wrist, she fought tooth and nail to keep it. So I can only imagine what it was like for her to lose it when she was at The Factory. How she lost the only thing she had left of the parents who loved her while she was already in the pits of hell.

One charm in particular catches my eye, and my stomach bottoms out because I know for a fact it wasn't always there, not only because it's not as worn as the others, but because I spent most of my childhood learning everything there was to know about the girl who wore it, right down to what every fucking charm on this bracelet meant.

Nestled between the love heart charm her father gave her mother on their first anniversary, and the cradle he gave her when Mia was born, is a shiny new charm.

The collar stares back at me. Mocking me. And I wonder if perhaps this package wasn't for Mia at all.

FORTY-FOUR

MIA

The mental exhaustion from my meltdown lasts the entire day, long after I've woken from my nap. But what's concerning me more is how Ace is acting.

I can't put my finger on what he's doing that's out of the ordinary, but I know he's been acting weird since I woke up.

Normally, I would put it down to the fact I had a panic attack mid-sex, and there's no way that's winning me any awards for sexiness. But for some reason, I don't think it's that. He's too tightly wound. The way his gaze darts around the room every few minutes, seeking out a danger that doesn't exist, makes me think there's a whole lot more to it.

I move around the kitchen, following a recipe I found online to make rose pasta, my favorite before I was taken. It seems so simple to be able to eat whatever I want again, but my relationship with food is far from cured, and there's still the nagging sentiment at the back of my mind that soon I won't have this luxury. Soon, I'll be back in the arms of men who will hurt me without thought or consideration, and I'll be hungry more often than not.

But for right now, I want to enjoy my favorite food again, even if it means pushing through the mental block I have when it comes to food.

Ace looked shocked when I stepped into the kitchen and started banging around with pots and pans, but he hasn't said anything, and I'm not going to offer any explanation.

Following the steps allows my mind to drift to another place, a safer place, and I allow it to wander without thought or consequence. It's nice to allow myself such a simple luxury, and I try not to consider that this will be one of the last times I have the chance.

My time is running out. Kyle is only going to escalate, and I can't have that touching Ace and the other people who have been so kind to me. I won't.

The pasta comes to a boil, and I quickly drain it, ignoring the questioning stares from behind the wall of screens.

I'm aware of how weird this looks. The fact that I refused to eat for my first few days here and have barely eaten more than a bowl of soup and some toast since. But I can't give him an explanation he's going to accept, so therefore it's better that I don't give him one at all.

"Something smells heavenly in here." A voice comes from the elevator, and I whip around to see Emerson and Rayne strolling through the apartment toward us, the former wearing sweatpants and a matching sweater, while the latter is in his usual dark long-sleeve shirt and black jeans. Does the man have anything other than that exact combination and suits in his wardrobe?

Not that I can say much, seeing as Ace wears pretty much the same outfit every day, with the exception of some gray sweatpants that give the perfect outline of how well-endowed he is.

I flick my gaze to Ace, whose jaw is tight at the intrusion, but he doesn't say anything.

"Sorry for the interruption, I just wanted to pop in and check on you before we head out of town for a few days in the morning." Emerson beams.

"Going anywhere fun?" I ask, busying myself with reading over the recipe three more times to make sure I'm not fucking it up.

"Sadly not. I have a conference in Philadelphia, and someone won't let me go by myself." She side-eyes her husband, but the obvious affection in her eyes discredits any annoyance in her tone.

"There is no way in hell I'm letting you leave the fucking city without me, Emerson. I can barely let you leave the room."

She giggles and moves into the kitchen, peering into the pot to see the sauce simmering. "God, this smells divine. Sadly, I can't cook much. I spent too long living on ramen, and now that's all I know how to cook."

I glance up at her in surprise, the admission catching me off guard because she always seems like she has her shit together. But maybe that wasn't always the case. "This used to be my favorite. Not that I got to eat it much in foster care. But a few times I had families take me out to restaurants to see if I would be a good fit for their family, and I remember this pasta always eased the disappointment of not being good enough." The raw admission falls from my lips before I can catch it, and not for the first time, I'm struck by how easily I open up to Emerson. I'm not sure there's anyone who has ever found their calling the way she has.

She nods, but surprisingly she doesn't look at me with pity in her gaze. It's rare for someone to be able to hear a sob story like that without feeling sorry for the person, and the fact Emerson can hold so much empathy for the people around her, but not judge the worst times in their lives, is a true testament to how good she is at her job.

A phone ringing drags my attention from the sauce I'm stirring, and I realize too late that the ringtone belongs to my phone.

I glance in its direction with panic as I watch Ace reach for it, but there's nothing I can say to stop him from answering it. Not without dragging more questions to the surface.

It was only a matter of time before he found out about Kyle's calls, but I had hoped it wouldn't be until I was long gone. That way I didn't have to see the disappointment in his eyes when he found out I'd been keeping something so significant from him.

"Hello." His voice moves through the apartment, but his eyes are locked on mine, almost as if he knows there's something I haven't been totally honest about.

The wooden spoon in my hand clatters to the ground, sauce flying up my bare legs and cupboards, but there's nothing I can do to stop Ace from learning the truth I should have told him after the very first call.

Too little, too late.

FORTY-FIVE

ACE

The look in Mia's eyes tells me whatever is on the other end of this call isn't good, but I'm too far gone. The phone presses against my ear, and a greeting falls from my lips before I can think better of it.

The only people who should be calling Mia have their number programmed into her phone, so why is this call from a *No Caller ID*?

What isn't she telling me?

I'm met with silence as I watch Mia drop the wooden spoon, and sauce splashes up the fronts of the counter, but I listen intently.

Someone breathes quietly on the other end, and instinctively I know it's not a telemarketer. After the first few days, I stopped monitoring the phone, wanting to give her privacy to speak to Emerson anytime she wanted without me prying, but perhaps I should have known better.

"Hello?" I repeat.

But no one responds, not so much as a heavy sigh or a hitch in breathing, and although I have no way to confirm my suspicions, I know it's Kyle fucking Clark on the other end of the line. How the fuck did he get her number? And how long has he been calling?

I meet Mia's gaze as she rises with the spoon in her hands and sauce all over her. The guilt in the blue pools is clear, and it takes everything I have not to lose my shit.

How could she keep this from me?

How could she keep something so crucial to her safety a secret, knowing this could put her in more danger than she's already in? Is this how they know where she is? Were they tracing the calls? I made sure the phone itself wasn't traceable before Tommy gave it to her, but unless it's a burner, it's hard to make calls untraceable.

"Did you like my gift, Ace?" The voice that comes from the other end of the line is familiar. Too fucking familiar. But I haven't heard it in a long time.

He wasn't introduced to us as Kyle when we were kids though.

Our stepfather called him something else. Something fucking stupid, but I can't quite put my finger on exactly what it was. Men like him don't allow their names to be a matter of public record, which is why I've had such a hard time tracking the motherfucker down.

"No," I growl. "What I would like is for you to fuck off and leave my woman alone." The tone of my voice is so sharp I almost don't recognize that it came from me, but the anger thrumming through my veins won't allow for the calm persona I try so hard to emit.

Rayne moves closer to me, his phone out as he types furiously, and I know he's getting Everett to trace the call. Could we end this tonight? I don't dare to hope often, but right now the idea of nailing this motherfucker is like a shining beacon of light.

He chuckles. "Ah yes, I'm sure you would. You always were obsessed with the little whore. It's part of the reason your foster father gave her to us, you know? To punish you and that piece of shit brother of yours."

It's not easy to render a man like me speechless. And yet this asshole has managed it.

I've been harboring guilt for the last eight years that I didn't get to her in time, that we were *just* too late to save her. But the fact that the reason they ever took her in the first place was because Tommy and I ran and ultimately had The Factory move out of Chicago will eat at me for the rest of my fucking life.

"I suggest you hand over the girl, Ace. She's used goods. Broken. What good is she to you after all she's been through?" He poses the question like he wants what's best for me, but we both know my interests are the last thing he's concerned about.

"Over my dead fucking body." Each word comes out in a harsh growl, but I've never felt rage so deep before. Not when Mia was taken from me. Not each time we've uncovered every fucked-up thing they did to her. And not even when that asshole triggered her earlier today. No. None of that compares to him calling my woman used-up goods. Broken. She's not fucking broken. She's fucking mine.

"That can be arranged, son."

"I'm not your son," I snap.

He chuckles. "Oh, I know. I would never raise a little cunt like you. My own son would be strong and willing to do whatever is required of him to serve the family business. Which we both know you never could. Perhaps once Mia is back where she belongs, I can start working on getting myself an heir. She's not good for much anymore, but she'd still make pretty babies."

I was wrong.

Those are the words that set off the beast I've held at bay for all these years. The one who tore apart my fucking apartment with my bare hands the day Mia was taken. The one who beat my foster father to death with nothing more than my fists. I never wanted Mia to see me like this, but I'm beyond saving right now.

"I'm going to kill you so fucking slowly you'll beg for death. You'll beg for mercy. But when you beg, you'll only prolong it more. More torture. More body parts severed. So much more fucking pain until your heart gives out." I chuckle as the thought brings me too much joy. "But I won't let a little thing like a heart attack stop my fun. I'll have a doctor on standby to bring you back just so we can keep playing. Doesn't that sound like fun?" I snarl.

A gasp from the kitchen drags my attention back to Mia. Her eyes are wide, her mouth agape in surprise, but she's not afraid. Or at least I don't think she is. She's still holding the wooden spoon, and Emerson has moved closer to her, as if expecting her to fall apart hearing my anger. But Mia knows who I'm talking to, and she wouldn't exactly be upset if all the things I've just described actually happened to the man who caused her so much pain.

There's silence on the other end of the line, and I pull the phone away from my ear to check if the call is still connected, watching as Rayne's thumbs fly across his own phone screen.

"You talk a big game, kid. You better hope you can back it up because a man is only as good as his word."

Before I can reply, the line goes dead, and I drop the phone to the table without hesitation. Everett will be working on tracking the motherfucker, and I have other shit to do right now.

I prowl toward Mia, her eyes widening the closer I get, and I notice Emerson looking between us out of the corner of my eye, searching Mia for fear and me for ill intent. But despite only knowing one another for such a short amount of time, she knows I would never hurt Mia. They wouldn't have left her here with me if she did. They would have squirreled her away to the Saint James estate or to the penthouse a few blocks away that she shares with Rayne. They know Mia is in no danger when she's here with me.

"Looks like we should be getting going, sweet girl," Rayne says behind me, the telltale sign of a smirk in his words. Asshole.

Emerson shakes her head with an amused smile and reaches for the stove, turning the dials until the flames beneath the pots disappear. "I think you're in trouble," she whispers to Mia.

"Oh, Mia's in a fucking world of trouble," I confirm, and I don't miss the lust that moves through her eyes. I may be pissed as hell, but I'm searching for uncertainty, for fear. But there's neither in her gaze.

Only need.

I round the bench just as Rayne wraps his arm around Emerson's waist and steers her toward the elevator. "I'll let you know if Everett gets a hit on fuckface's location."

"Thanks," I reply without tearing my eyes off Mia.

"Have fun," Emerson singsongs, taking a second to check Mia for fear once more before they reach the elevator.

The moment I reach her, I dip my head and quickly throw her over my shoulder, not giving her a moment to right herself before I head toward the stairs.

My girl is about to learn that there are to be no secrets between us.

Ever.

SHATTERED PROMISES

FORTY-SIX

I knew he'd be mad when he found out. I just figured I would be long gone and wouldn't have to face the consequences.

I also thought his reaction would be to yell at me, but he hasn't said a word since he threw me over his shoulder.

Each step he takes up the stairs lifts his shoulder into my stomach, but his hold on me is firm but gentle. Two words I didn't think belonged together, and yet here we are.

Rather than turning to the left for my bedroom, he heads to the right, and my stomach flutters with nervous anticipation. After my meltdown this afternoon, I thought it would be a while before he'd touch me again, thinking I'd need time to get back to where we were. But I want to enjoy my time with Ace for as long as I can, and he hasn't scared me with anything he's done. Not in a way I didn't enjoy anyway.

It turns out I enjoy being scared during sex, or perhaps that's what I've been programmed to like, but I don't allow myself too long to think about it, knowing that's the quickest way for me to spiral.

As soon as we enter the room, he deposits me in the middle of the bed and stares down at me with fire in his eyes. He's fucking pissed, and I don't blame him.

I knew I was playing with fire. I knew he was going to find out eventually, and I have to deal with whatever he has planned for me.

"How long, Mia?" he growls, the thickness in his voice taking me off guard.

I drag my bottom lip between my teeth and nibble at the skin there as I consider my answer. I could lie to him, but he'd figure it out. I never bothered to delete the call log, so his answers are sitting on my phone downstairs anyway. "Since we first came here," I whisper.

His head drops back as he stares at the ceiling, blowing out a frustrated breath, but he's not turning his anger on me. He's not like the other men I've known, even if there is a streak of darkness he always tries to hide from me.

I knew it was there, lurking just beneath the surface, but he held it at bay for my sake, even when all I ever wanted was for him to unleash it.

"Why didn't you tell me the second the first call came?" he asks without looking back down at me, and I know it's because he's trusting me to tell him the truth.

"I don't know," I whisper. "I couldn't ever confirm it was Kyle because he never spoke. He would call every day and just sit on the line, waiting for me to speak."

"Bullshit." He turns his green eyes on me, and I see the hurt swirling around in them, the need to protect me, the possessiveness he feels for me. "Once again, it's because you didn't think you'd be around long enough to deal with it." It's not a question, so I don't bother confirming his suspicions. I don't want to lie to him anymore than I already have, so it's better I keep my mouth shut.

He paces back and forth at the base of the bed, his hands running through his hair in rough swipes. I wish there was something I could do to comfort him. I wish I could tell him that I was never planning on leaving, but I don't want to give him false placations.

"Fuck!" Ace growls as he slams his fist into the pristine wall, the drywall giving way beneath the force.

I should be scared. I can acknowledge that. But I find myself rubbing my thighs together as he tugs his hand back, ignoring the blood across his knuckles.

"I'm sorry," I whisper, not trusting my voice not to break. The guilt is threatening to eat me alive.

He turns to me, and his eyes are wild. So fucking wild that it takes my breath away. Because the look he's giving me is full of pure, unadulterated lust, and I'm breathless.

He prowls toward me, each step he takes is full of purpose, and although it occurs to me to run, I'm frozen in place.

His knee hits the mattress as he closes the distance between us. "I feel like I keep saying this, sugar, and yet it seems to go in one ear and straight out the other. Don't mistake my need to care for you as weakness, Mia, because I will not fucking hesitate to tie you to this bed to make sure there's no way you can run from me. I will escort you to the goddamn bathroom if I have to and spend the rest of my days watching every goddamn move you make if it means you're safe."

My breath catches in my throat as he hovers above me, his weight pressing me further into the bed—a feeling that would have had me spiraling into a panic a few weeks ago but feels so fucking right with Ace.

"You are not going back to that life, Mia. I don't care who I have to kill, where I have to hide you, or if you fucking hate me for it. I will do whatever it takes. Always." His breathing is choppy, brushing over my cheeks, and it's clear he's struggling to keep his voice even for my benefit.

He plants one elbow on the bed beside me, leaning most of his weight on it as he brings the other to cup my cheek. "Now I'm going to show you how fucking serious I am, and if you need me to stop at any time, I want you to say 'red.' Understood?"

My own breath catches in my throat as I stare up at him. Fear bites at the edge of my consciousness, but my need for the man above me is so much stronger, and I want him to give me everything.

I nod. "Show me your darkness," I whisper into the space between us, and I don't miss the way his green eyes flare with the challenge I've set him.

I have no idea what to expect from the version of the man I love that he hides away, but I have a feeling I'm in for a wild fucking ride.

FORTY-SEVEN

$\mathbf{A}$nger thrums through my veins, making it almost impossible to be as gentle as I should be with her.

Mia's words repeat themselves over and over in my mind until I can barely fight through the fog of lust to make sense of them.

"Show me your darkness."

Four little words. On their own, they're completely inconsequential. But together? Together, they're like a fucking siren's call. The need to unleash all the desires I've been forcing down on her is so fucking tempting, I don't know how I'm going to stop myself. But I have to, right? I can't show her the darkest parts of my soul because she'll never look at me the same. She'll never forgive me.

"Don't think," she whispers between us, her breath whispering against my cheeks as she leans up until her lips are so close I can taste their sweetness. "Just do."

I'm gone the moment the words leave her mouth. I crash my lips to hers, devouring her mouth with rough swipes of my tongue and bites of her lips. I'm desperate for her. Every single part of her is mine, and if I have to fuck her so hard she can't walk, can't *run*, from me, that's exactly what I'm going to do.

Because Mia is mine.

She's been mine since the moment she walked into our foster home with innocent blue eyes and holding a bear so tight the poor thing looked like it was going to explode under the pressure. The same bear I sewed up every time he grew a new hole, even when I had no fucking clue what I was doing.

My tongue demands entry into her sweet mouth, and she has no choice but to give it to me.

A feral moan tears from my throat as soon as I'm granted entry. Fuck, she tastes like every fucking candy I've ever tasted. Sweet and addictive. Just like I always knew she was going to be long before I took her first kiss.

I grind my hips against her stomach, my hardening cock pressing painfully against the zipper. But I can't stop. Not yet. Not until I've had my fill of her.

I don't think Mia understands what she's asked for, what she's asked me to unleash on her, but I'm too far gone, and unless that single word falls from her pretty swollen lips, nothing is going to stop me from taking her the way I've craved since I first discovered the darker sides of sex.

At first it was a way to escape, to be another person for a little while. Always with a woman I didn't have an attachment to, because after Mia disappeared, there was no one else for me. Just other people desperate to feel a connection to another and not feel ashamed of their desires.

The first time I stepped into a sex club, my eyes were opened to the possibilities, to a whole new world. But I never thought I'd have the chance to explore it with Mia.

I drag her bottom lip between my teeth and bite down. Hard. Until the coppery taste of blood touches my tongue and she lets out a noise somewhere between a moan and a sob, but her hands grip my hair, holding me against her like she's desperate for the pain.

My aching cock feels like it's about to pop straight through the zipper of my pants, and I'm worried if I don't get it out soon that I might do some kind of irreversible damage.

I drag my lips from hers and stare down at her, her blonde hair spread around her like a fucking halo, her eyes wild as she stares up at me with nothing but trust and pure need. I don't deserve her trust. But then I don't deserve her either. And yet I'm going to hold on to both and run with them. Because Mia is mine. She always has been, and she always fucking will be.

Her lips are swollen from my rough treatment, and I long to shove my cock between them, to feel her mouth wrapped around me, to come all over her pretty face and leave it there as my mark on her.

Fuck.

I tear myself from her and force myself to the end of the bed, never breaking eye contact as I watch her take desperate, ragged breaths.

"Take your clothes off," I command, turning away from her for long enough to dig my bag out of the bottom of the wardrobe.

I have no fucking idea what made me pick this up when I dropped past my apartment after killing assholes one and two. But I picked it up nonetheless, sticking it into the bottom of the closet and assuming I'd not need it. But suddenly I'm glad I had the forethought to bring it.

By the time I turn back to Mia, she's unclipping her bra. Her tits fall free, and I barely swallow the groan that climbs up the back of my throat. Fuck, she's perfect. Her pretty rosy pink nipples beg me to clamp them, and I make a note to myself to make that happen.

Her eyes are wide and uncertain as she watches me place the bag on the chair beside the bed, but she's not afraid. She tucks her bottom lip between her teeth and nibbles at the already-abused flesh, and I long to be the one sucking and biting at the soft pillow.

Soon.

I rummage through the bag and pick out what I need to begin before turning back to her as she slips out of her lacy panties.

Fuck, she's perfect.

She catches me watching her and instinctively drops her hands to cover the scars that litter her stomach, but the look I give her seems to force her to drop them.

"You never need to hide from me, sugar. The next time I catch you covering those scars, you will not enjoy the consequences."

She nods, her pupils blown wide with lust. She watches me as I approach the bed, taking my time to enjoy the way she roams my body. I may still be fully clothed, but that doesn't stop her from eye fucking me.

A smirk tugs up the corners of my lips as I place the items I'm holding down on the bedside table and watch as she looks at each one with a mixture of curiosity and uncertainty.

"Is there anything here that scares you?" I ask quietly. I may want to push her, but I never want a repeat of what happened earlier today. I don't think I could handle watching her cry like that again, let alone when we're in the middle of sex.

"No." Mia shakes her head but doesn't drag her eyes away from the things littering the bedside table. Her thighs press together subtly, but I don't miss the move and immediately move toward her.

I dip my head until I'm at the same level as her and grip her chin between my fingers, forcing her to look at me. "You will be given your release when I see fit, Mia, and not a moment sooner. Understand?"

"Yes," she whispers, but makes no move to separate her thighs.

"On your knees on the floor," I command, and she wastes no time following my instructions.

She falls to her knees with such grace and determination before dropping her hands to her thighs, face up.

The sight of her in the submissive pose makes me ache, but it's how flawlessly she executes it that makes my stomach churn.

I'm stuck in place for long seconds, staring at her, my mind running wild with thoughts of all the things that happened to her—the ones I know and the ones she holds close.

"Ace," she whispers, and I drop to my knees in front of her.

"Do you want to stop?"

"What?" Her brows crease as her blue eyes search mine desperately. "No, I don't want to stop. I want this."

I press my eyes closed, and it's the feel of her palms on my cheeks that force them open again.

"You're not them, Ace. You haven't hurt me. Ever. All you've ever done is take care of me, and I know that's not going to change. I know you would rather die than hurt me. And you know that too." Her words filter through my mind, but it's the fact she broke her pose that confirms everything she's said.

I may not know a lot about what happened to her. I may not know how she was trained or what they did to her when she did something wrong.

But I know that simple move to come to me, to comfort me despite the order I had given her, means she trusts me with not only her body but her heart and mind too.

And I won't ever break it.

Shattered Promises

FORTY-EIGHT

His stubble beneath my palms anchors me to this moment, even when my mind threatens to drag me back to a time I wish I could forget.

If I'd even so much as thought about breaking my submissive pose with any of my previous owners, Kyle included, I would have been punished over and over until I knew better.

But I know Ace won't hurt me, and that's what I tell myself repeatedly as I kneel in front of him.

His eyes when he saw me drop to my knees were more haunted than I've ever seen them, and then when he fell to his own in front of me, I knew I had to comfort him. Because I don't want this to end. I want him to take what he needs from me. I want him to show me his darkness and prove to myself I can handle it.

Finally, I'm seeing that although I want to run, to keep the people I've come to care for safe, I can't do it. I can't leave Ace. I can't tear myself from this little bubble he's built for me to heal, only to hand myself to the man who broke me for the first time.

Kyle was never the worst, but he was the one who started the domino effect. Who led the way so the others could continue to shatter me into a million pieces.

And little by little, Ace has been building me up. He's been putting me back together in a way I didn't think was possible.

If you had told me a month ago that I would ever be able to enjoy sex again, I would have laughed in your face. If you'd told me I'd be asking for a man to show me his worst, I'd probably have descended into a panic attack at the very thought.

And yet Ace has proven me wrong at every turn, and I'll never be able to repay him for all he's done for me.

The words are on the tip of my tongue. The ones I never thought I'd have the chance to tell him. The ones I felt in my very soul from the moment I understood what they meant. And the part of me that's still scared, who has been beaten and broken so often that I'm afraid of my own goddamn shadow, begs me to swallow them, to hold them close to my chest to avoid the pain.

But the woman Ace has helped me become in such a short time won't let me. She pushes her way to the front, full of the bravery and bravado I've only ever had in Ace's presence, and I'm powerless to stop her.

"I love you, Ace," I whisper into the space between us. "With every single broken piece of me, I love you. And each day I spend here with you, I become a little more whole."

"Say it again." The green of his eyes darkens, and the wild look he gives me makes it hard not to rub my thighs together.

"I love you."

"Again," he demands.

I laugh, my lips turning up into a smile that feels both natural and foreign. "I love you, Ace. With every single piece of me."

He closes the distance between us so quickly I almost miss the move as his lips descend on mine. The kiss is raw and feral as he pours everything into me, giving me all of him, and I return every nip, every swipe of the tongue, every bit of emotion he gives me.

He drags his lips from mine, his breathing as heavy as mine, as we try to catch our breath. "I love you, Mia. With every beat of the heart that always belonged to you."

I lean forward and catch his lips again, my pose completely forgotten despite it being drilled into me for years that I'm to hold it no matter what.

"We don't have to continue," he tells me between kisses, and it only makes me smile that he thinks either of us could stop after pouring our hearts onto the table like this.

"Show me your darkness," I whisper, reiterating the sentiment from earlier.

He sucks in a breath and presses his eyes closed as he gathers himself, and a small smile tips up the corners of my lips. How did I ever think I was going to leave him? How did I think I was going to walk out the front door and never see him again?

"What's your safe word?"

"Red."

He nods. "If you're scared or need to slow down, I need you to promise me you'll say it." He sounds so conflicted, like my admission of love has made him hesitant to go through with this despite how badly we both clearly need it.

"Ace, I trust you. We both know that if I'm scared, you'll probably realize it before I do." I smile, tears gathering in my eyes. "I promise I will say it if I need to, but I need you not to hold back. I need you to trust that I know where my limits are, and I will tell you if we approach them." It's a plea more than anything, because I don't want him to always see me as broken. I want him to look at me and see the girl he fell in love with all those years ago, not the men who broke her.

He watches me closely for a moment, searching my eyes for any sign of hesitation, but he's not going to find it. "Okay." He takes a deep breath and releases it before he pushes himself to his feet.

I reposition myself into the pose I've held more times than I will ever admit to anyone, myself included, and he gives me a pleased look.

"Good girl," he murmurs, reaching for something on the bedside table.

I keep my gaze on him despite being taught to keep it low and to never make eye contact. I have a feeling that's not what Ace would want from me.

Ace brings the items he's holding in front of me, and I gaze down at the nipple clamps with bated breath. "Have you had these used on you before?" he asks carefully.

I shake my head. "No."

He hums a pleased sound in the back of his throat, as if he's happy he gets to show me something for the first time, or maybe because I have no negative feelings toward what he's about to do to me.

He drops back down in front of me and immediately brings his face to my aching breasts. They're begging for attention, like they know what's about to happen and how fucking good he's going to make it feel.

The moment his tongue flicks across my nipple, I let out a long, needy moan and barely stop myself from pressing my thighs together. Fuck. His mouth feels too freaking good.

He retreats all too soon and blows cool air on the stiff peak, stealing the air from my lungs. His eyes flick up to meet mine, and I give him a nod, telling him I'm ready for whatever he has planned next.

He pinches my nipple between his fingers before bringing the clamp to the peak and allowing it to close over my sensitive bud.

I hiss out a breath as he tightens it, but it doesn't hurt. No. It's more intense than anything else, and it makes me desperate for relief.

He repeats the process on my other nipple, and I squeeze my eyes closed at the overwhelming ache between my thighs. Holy shit. I've never been so turned on in my goddamn life. Fuck.

"Mia?" His worried voice drags my eyes open, but whatever he sees when he looks into my eyes only makes him smirk. "You okay, sugar?"

"Mm-hmm." I breathe through the arousal that floods through me. The insides of my thighs are slick with my need for him, and it's only a matter of time before he discovers just how turned on I am.

"Is my girl feeling needy?" he rumbles, flicking one of the clamps and dragging a strangled moan from my throat. Sweet Jesus, that feels good. I'm starting to wonder if I could come from what he's doing to my nipples alone but decide to keep that little tidbit to myself from fear he might tease me more than he's already planning.

I nod, unable to speak over the thundering of my heart in my chest.

The smile that lights up his face is so fucking breathtaking I wish I could take a photo and frame it. It's the mix of happiness and lust that echoes that of my own heart.

He reaches for the bedside table again, and my eyes widen when I see what he's holding.

Fuck.

FORTY-NINE

ACE

The way her eyes widen as she stares down at the small vibrator in my hand shouldn't bring me as much joy as it does.

And yet here I am.

I'm in fucking agony with my cock pressing into the zipper of my jeans, but I make no move to readjust myself.

Not yet.

If I'm making Mia wait for relief, then I can be patient myself.

"Spread your legs for me, sugar."

She takes a breath and follows the command I've given her. She shuffles her thighs apart, and the first peek at her perfect pussy drags a growl from my throat. Fuck. She's so fucking perfect.

Her inner thighs are covered in her need, and I long to bury my face between them, to feast on the woman who has always been my obsession.

I drag my gaze away from her pussy to the vibrator in my hand. I've never actually used one of these on a woman before, but it's going to be perfect for what I have planned.

I lean forward and press the tip of the silicone vibrator against her clit, her eyes flared with pure lust as she watches my every move. I click the button on the remote, and it flares to life in my hand, tearing a strangled moan from Mia's throat as the vibrations assault the sensitive bundle of nerves.

"Holy fuck!" she cries out.

I hold it there for another few seconds, watching each of Mia's reactions. The hitch in her breath. The tightening of the muscles in her thighs. The way her bottom lip disappears between her teeth. I didn't consider how hard it would be for me to deny her, seeing as making her come has become one of my favorite pastimes, but we both need this, and a little delayed gratification never hurts anyone.

I pull the vibrator away from her clit before she can reach the edge, and her eyes shoot up to meet mine. I chuckle. "Did you think I was going to make you come, sugar?"

"Yes," she breathes.

"You have a ways to go before your pretty little cunt is getting any relief, Mia."

Her mouth drops open in surprise, and it only makes my smile widen.

"This will teach you not to even think about running from me in the future." I press the tip of the vibrator against her entrance and push forward slowly, watching with keen interest as her pussy wraps around the silicone and I long for it to be my cock.

Not yet.

Once it's seated inside her, I press the button to turn it on and watch as her eyes roll back into her head and a moan slips from her perfect lips.

I stand slowly, keeping my eyes locked on her as I reach for the hem of my shirt and tug it over my head.

Mia's bottom lip disappeared between her teeth as she rakes her eyes over my tattooed chest, and I make quick work of the button on my jeans.

I shove the denim out of the way and groan a sigh of relief when my cock pops out of the zipper. When I got dressed earlier, I didn't bother putting boxers on, and Mia seems to like the view as she stares at me with wide eyes.

I increase the speed of the vibrator and relish in the cry that escapes her throat at the added pressure. "How's that pussy feeling, sugar?"

"So good," she whines.

"Are you close, baby?"

She nods, her eyes squeezing closed as she struggles to hold herself still. Such a good girl.

I drop down into the armchair in the corner and watch as her chest heaves and her body tightens, and just when I'm sure she's about to fall, I switch the vibrator off.

Her cry only seems to make my cock harder as I fist it in my hand and give the length a few rough pumps. Her mouth would feel better, but right now I want to watch her reach the edge over and over again, but never allow her to fall over into the abyss of her orgasm.

"Ace," she whines, watching with keen interest as I pump my cock. Her tits look so pretty with the clamps adorning them, and the glimpse of her pussy between her thighs is the perfect view.

"You'll get to come when I see fit, sugar." I flick the vibrator on to the top speed and watch her entire body tighten at the added sensation.

Over and over again, I drag her to the edge, and each time I tear her orgasm away from her just before she can reach it while steadily thrusting my cock into my own hand.

I need to fuck her soon. I won't be able to hold off much longer, and although I would love to fuck her pretty mouth, I don't think I have the restraint right now. I'd blow my load down her throat before I ever got inside her. And that just won't do.

"Ace," she cries as I turn the vibrator off, and her shoulders sag. Her chest rises and falls in heavy pants, only making me squeeze my cock harder.

"Yes, sugar?"

"Please," she breathes. "I need to come. Please."

A smirk tugs at the corners of my lips, and I rise from my seat, releasing my cock before I really do blow all over her pretty face. "You beg so pretty for me, Mia."

The vibrator flares to life inside her again, and she lets out something between a moan and a sob. Her pussy must be really fucking sensitive at this point considering how many times I've stolen her orgasm out from under her, but she can handle one more round of denial before she gets to come.

I stalk toward her and drop down in front of her.

Mia's breathing picks up the closer she gets, and I let her go a little further this time instead of turning it off the second her body begins to tighten.

I watch as her breath stutters in her chest, the taste of her release on her tongue, and then just when her entire body stiffens, preparing for her fall, I turn it off.

Before she can shoot any profanities at me, I grip her chin and drag her face forward until her breath whispers against my cheeks. "If you think you're coming anywhere other than on my cock, you're sorely mistaken, sugar."

"Please," she whispers. "I can't handle it anymore."

Without another word, I reach between her thighs and pull the soaking-wet toy from her pussy. I hold it between us, and Mia's eyes widen at the sight of the object that has brought her to the edge so many times we've both lost count.

I move it until it's resting on her bottom lip, and her eyes flare with uncertainty. "Suck," I command.

She only hesitates for a moment before she closes her lips around the silicone toy and moans as her own taste hits her tongue. "There's my dirty girl," I praise. "Don't you taste sweet, sugar?"

Mia nods as she sucks the vibrator clean, and I pull it from her lips.

Before she can say a word, I crash my lips down on hers, desperate to get a taste of her, even if it is second-hand. We're both too wound up for me to get a taste directly from the source.

Her lips mold to mine, and I groan at the taste of her on her tongue. Fuck, this woman. She's everything. The sun, the moon, the fucking earth. She's my power and poison. She's everything, and I'll never get enough of her.

Without breaking our kiss, I wrap my arms around her and lift us both from the ground. I can't wait any longer. I need to be inside her like I need my next breath.

Mia wraps her legs around me as I carry her to the bed and holds on to my shoulders as she nips and sucks at my lips, just as desperate for me as I am for her.

I crawl across the bed and carefully lay us so her head is against the pillows and I'm hovering above her. Our kiss breaks, and our breaths come in heavy pants as we try to suck in as much air as we can. But she's the only thing I want to breathe right now.

I flick the clamps on her nipples, and she lets out a hiss that brings a smile to my face. I think these are going to have to make a regular appearance, and she looks so fucking pretty with them. "How are these feeling, sugar?"

"They're so sensitive," she moans as I flick the other one, and she jolts beneath me. "Please, Ace. No more teasing. Please fuck me."

"When you ask so nicely, how could I possibly say no?"

I lift her until her calves are resting on my shoulders, and I make quick work of positioning myself at her entrance.

"This is going to be fast and hard, sugar."

She smiles up at me, her blue eyes glistening as they stare me down. "Good."

FIFTY

Ace stares down at me like I'm his entire world, and for the first time, I accept that I am.

This man spent years looking for me, and ever since he found me, he's worked tirelessly to keep me safe, to make me feel like my old self, and to help put me back together again.

Telling him I love him is like lifting a weight off my shoulders, one I didn't even realize was weighing me down, and watching as he processed those words was one of the most peaceful moments of my life.

He presses forward and slips inside me easily. Usually there's a stretch because he's so large, but with how wound up I am, my pussy is soaking, allowing him to bottom out in the first thrust.

"Fuck," he grunts as he holds himself deep for a moment. I'm not sure if it's for my benefit or his own, but I stare up at him, relishing in the grip he has on my thighs.

Once he seems to have himself under control, he pulls back and surges forward again, and this time he doesn't pause.

He pumps in and out of me with wild abandon, dragging screams and cries from my throat and pulling me right back to the edge he had me teetering on for what felt like hours.

"Ace," I moan.

"Fuck, Mia." He presses his eyes closed for a moment before his gaze meets mine. "You're so fucking perfect, sugar."

Tears gather in my eyes, but not because I'm sad, or scared, or unsure. No. These tears are happy. They're accepting of the life I've fought for. The one I dreamed of. The one I almost gave up on. They fall against my cheeks, and Ace watches as they slip down across my cheek and into my hair fanned out beneath me.

He reaches forward and swipes a tear from my cheek before bringing it to his lips, and I watch with bated breath. Why is that so hot? But then again, everything Ace does is hot as fuck. I don't even think he's trying at this point.

"What's got these pretty tears falling, sugar?" he asks with more softness than his voice has had since we came up here, but his thrusts don't slow, and for that, I'm glad. I need him to keep fucking me. I need the release that's barreling toward me.

"How perfect I feel when I'm with you." I choke on the lump in my throat. "Scars and all."

He smiles down at me and cups my cheek in his palm. "I told you, Mia. I love every single part of you, and there's nothing that's going to change that."

I nod against the pillows, but my words are caught in my throat as he overwhelms my senses.

"Are you going to come for me?"

"Yes," I whisper, because there's no way I can force my voice any louder with the way my heart is hammering in my chest.

He smiles down at me, the softness he showed me a few moments ago melts away and is replaced with the unhinged version of him. His hand closes around my throat, and my breath stutters in my chest. How does he always know exactly what I need?

"Fuck, you look good with my hand around your throat," he rumbles as he thrusts into me so hard it borders on pain. But the good kind. The kind only he can give me.

"Please," I choke out. "Please Ace."

He growls, and his hand tightens to the point I can barely pull in a breath, and that's what brings me right to the edge of what I know is an orgasm that will fucking wreck me. He brought me to the edge so many times with that vibrator that this release is going to be a whole new level of intense.

"Come for me, sugar. Soak me with your come," he commands as he reaches toward me with his other hand. I stare up at him for a moment, unsure what he's doing, but when he reaches the clamps on my nipples, my eyes widen. So quickly, I barely catch the movement. He pulls both clamps off, and the sensation is so fucking intense, it throws me right into the abyss. My vision blurs as my body clenches, and my breath stutters in my lungs. The combination of my release and Ace constricting my airway has my entire body shaking, and everything blurs at the edges.

I'm vaguely aware of Ace's roar of release, and then hot ropes of cum fill me, but I'm too far gone, too sated.

I fall limp against the mattress and allow my eyes to slip closed. Ace releases his hold on my throat, and it takes a few moments for me to right my breathing.

Holy shit.

Ace carefully moves my legs to either side of him and collapses on top of me, careful not to give me too much of his weight. He presses a kiss to my neck, my jaw, my cheek, before finally coming to my lips and planting the sweetest of kisses on the abused pillows.

My entire body is like a live wire, every touch like a million volts of lightning bursting through me.

"Are you okay, sugar?" he asks, concern lacing his voice as he wipes at my cheeks, and I realize I'm crying. But not just a few tears.

No, my cheeks are wet with my tears, and a sob releases from my throat without me even realizing it.

So quickly, I almost miss the move, he rolls us so he's on his back and I'm sprawled out on top of him, his softening cock still lodged inside me, and I find comfort in the connection.

"Mia, talk to me. Did I hurt you?" His brows pull together at the thought.

"No." I shake my head. "No, you didn't hurt me." I press my eyes closed for a moment, trying desperately to get ahold of my emotions long enough to tell him what's going on. "I just...I feel whole. Or at least my version of whole. I feel like you've glued all my broken pieces back together, and for the first time in as long as I can remember, I'm not scared. Because you, and therefore I, have everything."

Ace stares up at me with a smile on his lips. He reaches up and wipes the tears from my cheeks and presses a kiss to my forehead in a gesture that makes my fucking heart explode. "I would have spent the rest of my life searching for you. Even if it meant we only had one perfect moment like this, it would have been worth it."

I lay my head on his chest, the steady thump of his heart lulling me into a dreamless state where only he and I exist, and it's the most peaceful I can ever remember being.

Fifty-One

A loud crash downstairs tears me from my sleep, and it takes me a moment to figure out where I am. I'm so used to sleeping in my shitty apartment downtown that some nights when I wake up here in the penthouse, I forget where I am.

Mia's sprawled out beside me, her ass pressed snuggly against my cock, and that fact almost distracts me from what woke me up in the first place.

I slip from between the sheets before I can reconsider and stay curled up with Mia, and make quick work of tugging up a pair of sweatpants. Whoever the hell is making all that racket better have a good reason because I've killed people for less, and I would take great pleasure in killing the fucker who tore me away from my woman at an ungodly hour of the morning.

I reach into the nightstand and pull my gun out, slipping it into the back of my sweatpants. I doubt I'll need it, because it's probably just one of the asshole guards or a member of the

Saint James family who have decided three in the morning is the perfect time to pop in for a coffee and a chat.

The entire apartment is engulfed in darkness as I slowly move downstairs, but I don't see anyone hiding in the shadows.

Did I imagine the sound? Maybe it was part of my dream?

I shake my head. No. I don't dream. I never have, and for that I'm fucking grateful. I would hate to think of the nightmares I would have if I did.

My bare feet hit the bottom step, and I move into the shadows, just in case there is someone here who shouldn't be.

I'm almost ready to assume it's not someone we know, because they would have this place lit up like a goddamn Christmas tree.

The realization that it's not a member of the Saint James family makes me reach for my gun, but before my hand can wrap around the handle, it's torn from my sweatpants, and the cool metal presses against my temple.

My eyes widen, and panic sets in for the briefest of moments. Not for me. But for Mia. This isn't random. This building isn't the type that a random thief might choose to rob.

No, the only way you're getting in here is with knowledge and research, meaning not only is it premeditated, it's most likely someone here to hurt my woman.

"Mr. Weber. It's been a long time." The voice is so familiar, it's like I've heard it every day of my fucking life. But I haven't. I haven't heard it in a decade, and for that I'm fucking grateful.

Kyle Clark is the last person I want to speak to. Ever.

"Cat got your tongue, son?" He presses the barrel harder against my temple as if proving to me he has the upper hand like it's not fucking obvious. "You're probably trying to work out how we got up here, but I can easily answer that for you if you'd like."

"Does it matter how you got here?" I snap.

"No, probably not. But I'd like to tell you regardless." He nudges me forward until I'm standing in the middle of the apartment, staring at the stairs that lead to Mia. A very naked Mia.

My stomach sinks at the thought, at the idea that they could see her body and I wouldn't be able to do anything to stop it. I just have to fucking hope she wakes up quickly enough to hit the panic button beside the bed.

This place is riddled with them, but by putting me in the center of the room like this, he's cutting off my access to them and therefore rendering me more useless than I already feel.

I glance around the room as inconspicuously as I can manage, looking for anything I can use to wake Mia without drawing attention to her, but there's nothing within reach, and that's likely by design. Kyle isn't an idiot, sadly. There's a reason he got to where he did with The Factory, and a reason it still operates outside the city.

Another man comes into view, and I blink a few times to make sure the darkness isn't playing tricks on me. It's the asshole security guard I almost killed with my bare hands earlier for walking in on Mia and me. Fuck.

"Surprised to see me?" He smirks.

"No. I already figured out you're a fucking moron, so this kind of tracks."

He glares at me but makes no move to come closer, choosing instead to remain by the stairs. Exactly where I don't want him.

"Let me guess. The package you delivered to us today was more than just a gift to fuck with us. It was a guise to allow this asshole to test how long it takes for the elevator to reach this floor and how long you would have to cut the cameras so the rest of the security team wouldn't notice the two of you coming up here in the middle of the night?"

His face falls as I detail exactly what played out today. This idiot seems to forget I do this shit for a living. I find the holes in security so I can watch a target, survey them, and when necessary, either myself or someone I work with can sneak in and kill someone.

This isn't exactly my first rodeo.

"How the fuck did you know that?" he snaps, and before I can make a move, the gun is pressed harder against me, as if reminding me I'm being held at gunpoint and I should watch what I say next.

"Mr. Weber here seems to think he's smarter than us. But he seems to forget we kept Mia from him for eight years, and no matter how hard he looked, he couldn't find her."

The dig is a direct hit, and I'm too fucking tempted to throw him to the ground and kill him with my bare hands. But right now, I'm the only thing standing between them and my woman, meaning I need to be on my best behavior.

The guard, Todd, I think, laughs, his head falling back as if it's the most hilarious thing he's ever heard in his life. This motherfucker clearly hasn't seen *The Other Guys* if he thinks that's funny.

"What do you want, Kyle?" I ask through gritted teeth.

"I've come to retrieve what belongs to me."

"Nothing in this apartment is yours, so you can see yourself out."

He chuckles, his rancid breath moving across my cheek. "Mia is mine. She always has been, and she always will be."

I blow out a calming breath, trying desperately to hold on to some semblance of composure. "See, that's where I'm confused. I would never let another man put his hands on my woman. Definitely not willingly. And yet, you *sold* Mia, more than once. And most recently to a man who was intending to marry her and pump her full of his kids. So either she's yours or she's not. You can't have it both ways."

Hands in my back are the only warning I get before I'm shoved to the ground, but I manage to catch myself and roll to my back before my face can hit the hard floor. I've clearly struck a nerve.

I catch sight of one of the panic buttons beneath the side table that runs along the back of the couch. It's not far away, only a few feet, but I need a reason to go in that direction, or it will be too obvious.

I shove myself to my feet, suddenly wishing I had bothered to put a shirt on, but I didn't expect to have these two assholes to contend with the moment I opened my eyes.

"So why would you do that, Kyle?" I sneer. "Why would you sell someone who was allegedly so important to you? Not just once, but four times?"

He advances on me like I knew he would, and I back up until I crash into the side table hard enough that the lamp balancing on the edge hits the floor in an almighty smash.

Come on, Mia. Wake up.

I slide my fingers beneath the wood as if I'm catching myself, but quickly activate the security system before either of them can notice what I'm doing.

"And you." I turn my attention to the guard. "Do you think it's a good idea crossing the Saint James family? I hear they pay well and offer protection to family members as part of the employee benefits."

At this point, I'm just trying to piss them off. The angrier they are, the more noise they're going to make, which gives me the best chance of being able to wake up Mia and get her to the panic room.

When Elijah gave us the tour on the day we moved in, I thought it was crazy to have a panic room at all in a building with so much security, but right now I'm grateful for it. Or at least I will be once Mia is tucked up inside where she's safe.

"You don't know what the fuck you're talking about!" Todd shouts.

I turn to Kyle, the gun at his side as he stares me down, and for a moment I worry he's cottoned on to what I'm doing, but then he turns to the guard and laughs.

"Why don't you answer him?" He raises a brow at the guard expectantly.

"Even if they pay well, they don't pay as well as The Factory."

My stomach recoils at the thought. The Saint James family may not have been my favorite people in the world prior to finding Mia, but they're certainly not a fucking human trafficking ring.

"Plus, the perks are better." He shrugs, and I stare at him in surprise for a moment. You'd think after all these years I'd be numb to the disgusting parts of humanity. But somehow this motherfucker has rendered me speechless. "And after I saw that tight little piece of ass you were fucking today, I asked if I could have a round before Kyle here marries her."

Red clouds my vision, and before I'm conscious of the decision, I tackle him to the ground, my fists finding his face immediately. "You will not touch her," I roar as I slam my fist into him over and over again. It won't be long before Kyle tears me off him, so I need to get in all the hits I can.

"Enough!" Kyle yells, and a moment later, something heavy slams into the back of my head.

Darkness clouds my vision, and no matter how hard I fight it, I slip into the abyss.

FIFTY-TWO

Someone shouting drags me from my sex-induced sleep, and I blink my eyes open slowly.

A yawn forces its way from my chest, and when I turn my head, I realize Ace is no longer lying beside me.

My brows crease as I look around the dark room for him, but he's nowhere to be found, and I immediately reach for my phone, only to realize his is charging right beside mine.

Where the hell is he?

Raised voices downstairs remind me of what woke me in the first place, and my stomach recoils at the sound. I slip from between the sheets just in time to hear something crash to the ground, and I immediately duck as if it's been thrown at me.

Get a grip, I reprimand myself.

I take a deep, steadying breath and reach for one of Ace's shirts, immediately finding comfort in how much it smells like him.

I clutch my phone to my chest and move toward the door, my stomach churning uncomfortably as reality sets in. Something is wrong. No one who has regular access to this apartment would be shouting at three in the morning, which means it's someone else entirely.

I gulp and search my contacts for someone to call, but the only person I'm close with is Emerson. Tommy whisked Clara away for their honeymoon a couple of days ago, so neither of them are going to be much help right now.

I tug my bottom lip between my teeth as I consider my options, but the voices downstairs drag my attention back to whatever the hell is going on downstairs.

"You don't know what the fuck you're talking about!" someone shouts, but I don't recognize their voice.

I'm about to quietly pull the door open to see if I can see from the doorway, but then another voice comes. One I do recognize. One that makes my stomach recoil painfully.

"Why don't you answer him?" Kyle's voice carries through the apartment and immediately has me clicking the door shut as quietly as I possibly can. I don't want to know the answer to whatever the hell the question was.

I fumble with my phone, dialing the first number I see and hold it to my ear, not daring to breathe in case someone downstairs realizes I'm awake.

"Mia?" Everett's voice comes across the line, but he doesn't sound half asleep. Fuck, he was probably up with baby Summer, I shouldn't be bothering him. "Is everything okay over there? One of the panic buttons was activated. We're deploying a team right now."

"Kyle's here," I whisper so quietly I'm not sure he'll hear me.

He curses, and I'm pretty sure he pulls the phone away from his face for a moment to say something to whoever he's with, but I'm too distracted by my own fear. Is this it? The end of my freedom? The last moments of the life I never thought I'd have the chance to live?

Will the next time I see Ace be the last?

Will I ever hear Emerson's kind voice again?

Or be in the room with the woman who helped me escape?

Silent tears fall against my cheeks, and I desperately try to swallow them down. There will be time to fall apart later, but I don't want them to see my weakness.

"Mia?" Everett's voice comes through the line, and I startle at the sound, almost forgetting I was waiting for him. "I need you to get into the panic room. Do you remember where it is and how to open it?"

I swallow heavily and nod to myself. "Yeah, I remember."

"Are you in the main bedroom?"

"No, in the other room."

"Okay, I have a visual of the downstairs area. They're distracted right now, so if you open the door and crawl across the landing toward the main bedroom, I don't think they'll notice you."

I take a deep breath to steady my erratic heart and breathing, but it does little to settle the panic that's taken root inside me. "I don't know if I can."

"Yes, you can, Mia. You can do this." His words are soft, but there's an urgency to them that makes it even harder to breathe.

"Is Ace okay?" I ask as I push myself to the door and carefully open it.

"He's distracting them. If I had to hazard a guess, I'd say he's trying to wake you up and alert you to the danger."

The tears against my cheeks are hot and coming in way too fast for me to wipe away as I crawl out onto the landing that overlooks the living areas.

I stay as close to the wall as I can, trying desperately to keep out of their view, and even though I long to check on Ace, I force myself not to. I hate the idea of him being hurt because of me, it makes me sick to my stomach, but I know in my fucking soul he would never forgive me if I went down there to save him, and I can't do that to him again. I won't.

"You're doing great, Mia," Everett says through the phone I have balanced awkwardly between my shoulder and ear.

"Enough!" Kyle yells, and a moment later, there's a loud thump that stops me in my tracks.

"Keep going, Mia. Don't stop. Ace will be okay. Our team is a few minutes away. Just get yourself into the panic room now." The urgency in his tone makes me think everything is not okay, but I keep moving.

My breaths are choppy from the effort it's taking to keep moving despite the panic, but I reach the bedroom I've been sleeping in without pausing to check on Ace, even though my heart aches for me to do exactly that.

I quietly push the door open and crawl inside, closing it with a quiet click.

"You're out of my sight now, Mia. There are no cameras in the bedrooms, but you remember where the panic room is?"

I gulp. "In the closet."

"Exactly. Close the door behind you as soon as you get inside and pull the dresser in front of the door. It will slow them down if they come upstairs."

"Are they coming upstairs?" I choke.

He pauses and lets out a breath. "I think they're about to, which is why I need you to keep moving for me. I know you're scared, but we will keep you safe, I promise."

I force a deep, steadying breath into my lungs before standing and moving toward the closet. I don't have that many items of clothing, so it's pretty sparse in here, but at least it makes it easy to move around.

I close the closet door with another quiet click, the sound of footsteps on the stairs making me move a little faster.

"You okay, Mia?"

"Yeah," I whisper. "I'm just putting the phone down for a second to move the dresser."

"Okay. I'm going to open the panic room for you while you

do that."

I let out a breath I didn't realize I was holding because, although the memory of them showing me how to use the thing is in the back of my mind somewhere, it's currently lost in the panic swirling around, so I didn't love my chances.

I place the phone down on top of the dresser, and as quietly as I can manage, I shuffle it in front of the door. The sound of the panic room door sliding open drags my attention from the task at hand for just a second, still mind-blown that there are people who have things like this in their homes. The dresser is solid wood and heavy as hell, and as someone who has only just started eating more than once every day or two, my strength is lacking.

"Everett, I don't think I can do this," I say as I pick up the phone.

"That's okay, Mia. I need you to get inside the panic room for me." He's trying to keep his voice calm, but all that does is confirm they're getting closer.

"Everett?" I whisper as I move closer to the small room that is nestled between the master bedroom and the gym.

"Mia, now."

I don't waste another second, quickly ducking down before crawling through the small door. I'm just as struck by the space as I was the first time I came in here. It's much roomier than you would think, with a full-size bed and a couch. There's a television on one wall, while another has several screens showing the downstairs area.

I shuffle further in, stopping to lean against the wall as soon as

I'm clear of the door. "I'm in."

"Good work, Mia. I'm closing the door now. The only way to get in will be for either you or me to press the override button. Do not do that unless you're sure you're safe. I would prefer you stay in there until I say it's clear."

"Okay," I whisper, watching as the door slowly slides shut.

The sound of the bedroom door slamming open makes my breath stop in my lungs, and I'm frozen as the footsteps grow closer.

"Everett."

"What is it, Mia? What's going on?"

"They're in the bedroom."

The closet door meets a similar fate, and before I can take my next breath, I'm face-to-face with the man who started it all.

"There you are. I've been searching for you."

FIFTY-THREE

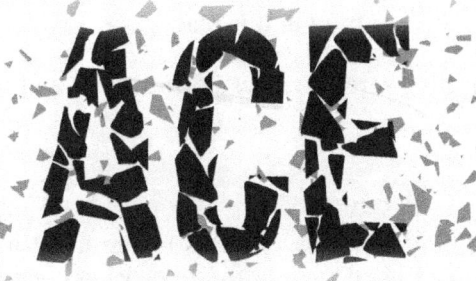

Like before, it takes me a moment to figure out where the fuck I am when I wake up, except this time I have a piercing pain shooting through my head, and I'm immediately aware of the fact I'm not laying down.

I pry my eyes open and look around the dark apartment. What the hell happened?

I move my gaze over the room until I pause on the broken lamp by the side table, and it all comes crashing back.

Waking up. Kyle and the idiot security guard. Being pistol-whipped. It's like a movie playing in front of my eyes, but it feels more like a nightmare.

My eyes move to the stairs and flick between the two bedrooms. Please be in the panic room, Mia. God, I hope she woke up and called for help. Any of the Saint James family would have coached her to get her into that panic room, and I don't care about anything except making sure she's safe.

I look down at the chair I'm in and sigh. I'm tied to one of the expensive dining chairs, and the only way I'm getting out of this damn thing is to break it. Hopefully Snow's not too attached to the furniture in this place.

A bloodcurdling scream rattles off the walls, and my stomach sinks.

Mia.

Panic flares to life in my chest as I stare up at her bedroom door. She went for the panic room, that much I'm certain of, but she didn't make it. Not if her scream is anything to go by.

I tug at the rope around my wrists, trying to remember how the fuck the Doms at the club I used to attend taught the subs to break a knot. Of course that was with Shibari rope and not whatever hardware store shit they've tied me up with, but desperate times call for desperate measures.

The rope cuts into my wrists, but the pain doesn't register. The only thing I can think about, the only thing I can feel, is making sure they don't leave this apartment with Mia.

Another scream comes moments after the first, followed by a string of profanities that would make a fucking sailor blush.

There's my girl.

I consider tipping the chair over to try to break it, but this thing is sturdy as hell, and even with my height and build, I don't like my chances at getting it to splinter.

I catch sight of movement upstairs and pause, considering my next move. Do I pretend I'm still knocked out? If they know I'm awake, they might knock me out again. But then they may want me to watch them take her from me. That's the type of assholes they are, and at least if I'm awake, I have a better chance of being able to catch up to them.

I watch as Todd carries Mia across the landing, kicking and screaming like her life depends on it. A month ago, she never would have fought like this, but she has something to live for now. She has friends, a life, me. And she's going to fight tooth and nail to keep the life she worked so fucking hard to get.

"Get your hands off me!" she screams, beating her fists against his back with every step he takes, but the move only has me holding my breath. One wrong step, and he could drop her. If she moves the wrong way, she could go straight off the edge, and I would be forced to watch her die in front of me.

The thought has bile climbing up the back of my throat. No. I won't let that happen. And they're sure as hell not taking her from me. Over my dead body.

"Oh good, you're awake." Kyle grins like the fucking Cheshire Cat as he leads the way down the stairs. "I wouldn't want you to miss us taking her from you…again."

A growl escapes my throat before I can swallow it, my body fighting against the binds with every ounce of strength I have.

He's not taking her.

Not again.

Not when we're both starting to live again.

I won't be able to live with the guilt of her slipping through my fingers, that much I know for a fact. They'll never give me another chance to save her. Kyle will keep her hidden away for the rest of her life, which if his previous wives are anything to go by, won't be very long.

The idea of Mia no longer breathing makes me feel physically ill, but I can't focus on that right now. Not when there's still a chance.

They reach the bottom of the stairs, and Todd drops Mia in front of me, her body crumbling to the floor with a pained yelp.

Kyle crouches beside her, his fingers wrapping around her chin and forcing her eyes up to meet his. "It seems you've forgotten your training during your little holiday," he muses, his voice light despite the darkness swirling in his eyes. "But we'll get you back on track." He moves so quickly I almost miss his other hand raising and his fist coming at Mia's face. But there's nothing either of us can do to stop it.

The heavy thump makes my stomach revolt against me, and I almost lose the contents, but I refuse to appear weak.

Mia doesn't make a sound, despite the tears falling down her cheeks.

My brave girl.

"You don't want to do this, Kyle," I growl. "You don't want to start this war with the Saint James family."

"I couldn't give a shit about those assholes." He laughs, his attention pulling from Mia and allowing me to breathe for a moment. "The Factory is moving its headquarters, so any business we may have had in Chicago is over."

I open my mouth to reply, but I'm quickly cut off by the

asshole himself.

"You may be wondering why we would choose to do such a thing considering our long-standing tenancy in Illinois, but this is something we put into the works soon after the Saint James family took out our connection at the Loudner Cartel. It's just a happy accident that I'm getting Mia back at the same time and can squirrel her away somewhere that none of you can find her."

Blood drips from the corner of her mouth as she stares down at the floor, but it's her silent tears that break my fucking heart.

I've let her down again and this time she knows what's in store for her. Perhaps that's better than whatever her imagination conjured the first time she was taken, or maybe it's worse. But either way I won't blame her for whatever resentment she's bound to feel toward me. I promised to keep her safe, and I've failed. That's all there is to it.

"I'm sure you know they're on their way," I tell them, forcing as much confidence into my voice as I can manage. "They would have known you were on your way up here the second you stepped foot into the elevator."

Todd laughs. "You think we're that stupid? We cut off the camera feed inside the elevator right after we killed the other guards."

I smirk at him, the cockiness I wish I actually felt coming to the surface. I've played this part my whole fucking life, and this might be the most important time, so I need to make it count. "This entire apartment is full of cameras, panic buttons—you name a security measure, and it's in this place. You think Rayne and Storm Saint James would have let their baby sister live in a place without a state-of-the-art security system with every fail-safe possible? If so, yes, I do think you're stupid."

Todd's eyes flick to Kyle, who shrugs it off as if it's nothing. I need to keep them here. Even if that means antagonizing them. The longer I can keep them in this apartment, the better chance we have of someone coming to help.

"That may be so, but they won't be getting up here. We have men in the stairwell and stationed around all exits of the building. There's no way they're getting in here without tarnishing their reputation, which we both know they won't do for two people that have no connection to them."

I force my body to remain still, my gaze to remain locked on his, but there's an element of truth to what he's saying. They don't owe me or Mia anything. We're not family. We don't work for them. And up until a month ago, they probably would have considered me their enemy.

So why the hell would they sacrifice everything to save Mia?

Shattered Promises

FIFTY-FOUR

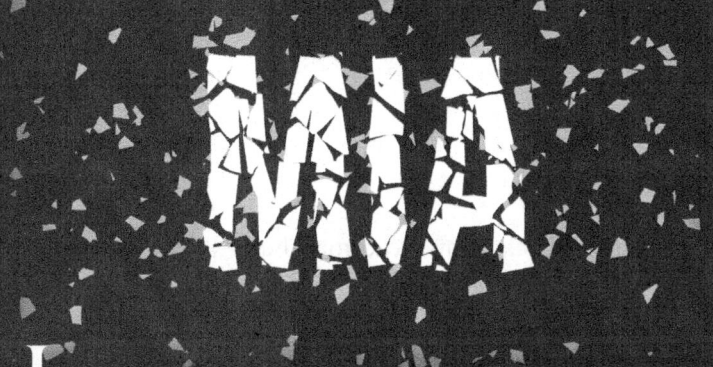

I know what Ace is doing.

He's trying to buy us time.

The longer he keeps Kyle here bragging about how he's won, the more likely it is that the Saint James family will come to our rescue.

But Kyle is right.

Why would they?

Everyone in Chicago knows what they're involved in. The police are in their pocket, and they own most of the media companies in the city, so they control a lot of what is said about them, but that doesn't mean they're willing to risk it all on Ace and me.

I take a deep breath and chance a look up at Ace, where he's tied to one of the dining chairs. He looks okay, but the way his eyes droop closed every so often and the blood dripping from his hands tell me that's probably not the case.

I drink in his features, knowing this is probably the last time I'm ever going to see him outside my dreams, and I'm desperate to remember every little detail.

Every tattoo.

Every freckle.

Every toned muscle.

I store it in the back of my head for when I'll inevitably need it, because even when we've been apart, Ace has always been my guiding light.

I swallow the sob that rises up the back of my throat, as if by not showing weakness it will make this easier on Ace somehow, but just as I know I'm not going to be okay, I know he won't be either. Because he's the other half of me, just the same way I'm the other half of him, and the only thing I can find solace in right now is the fact we had time together that I never thought we would.

His eyes meet mine, the determination behind the green proving just how far he'll go for me. He'd go to the end of the earth if it meant he could save me. Too bad I'm beyond salvation.

"Pick her up, it's time to get out of here. The jet will be waiting."

My entire body stiffens at the idea of being put on a plane to an unknown location, but I force it to relax. It will only hurt me more if I'm tense, and considering this time I know what I'm in for, I'd like to limit any unnecessary pain.

The guard that triggered my panic attack earlier today throws me over his shoulder like I weigh nothing at all, but I still wince on impact. I need to get used to people manhandling me again, to them not treating me like I'm human, but instead an object for them to throw around.

I lift my head and meet Ace's panicked gaze, but it's not his eyes that have my heart in my throat. It's the tears falling against his cheeks. I've never seen Ace cry. Not when our foster parents would hurt him, or the night he said goodbye like we weren't sure we would see one another again, or even when I've repeatedly tried to leave since he found me.

But the idea of losing me again is too much for him.

I squeeze my eyes shut to warn off my own tears before meeting his gaze once more. There are a million things I want to say, but none of it feels like enough, not when he's done everything for me. Not when he saved me in more ways than one. Not when I know losing me is going to kill him. But I force out the only words that feel right, and the ones I wish I'd said more in our time together. "I love you." They come out on a choked whisper, but I don't care if Kyle and his goon hear it. It would do him some good to know I'll never feel this way about him, no matter what he does to me in the time between now and when he ultimately kills me. "Don't look for me, Ace. Live. I want you to live. For me."

Each step we take away from him is another crack to my already shattered heart. It's like I'm being torn apart from the outside in, and the tears I tried so hard to hold back fall.

Ace struggles against the chair so hard the legs slam against the hardwood floors over and over again, but there's no point. It's too late. "Mia," he calls out, but we're almost at the elevator, which means our time is up.

"I mean it, Ace. Don't come for me. I need one of us to live. To really live. Please." I'm begging now, pleading with him for one of us to have the life we dreamed of when we were kids. But it won't be me. It was never destined to be me.

"I can't," he chokes. "Not without you."

I hear the moment doors slide open and my heart lodges itself in my throat as I look Ace over one last time. One final look to last me the rest of my life.

We step into the elevator but I hold Ace's gaze until the final second as the doors slide shut.

And then he's gone. Just a memory for me to hold on to until my dying breath.

Shattered Promises

FIFTY-FIVE

ACE

Watching the elevator doors close and Mia fade from view is more painful than anything I've ever felt in my life. I thought it hurt the first time she slipped through my fingers, but I was wrong.

Nothing could ever hurt as much as failing her for a second time.

I tip my weight, desperate to chase them, to follow close behind and make sure they don't disappear into the night, but first I have to get the fuck out of these binds.

The chair clatters to the hard floors and my shoulder aches from the contact, but I don't care. I don't give a fuck about anything but making sure Mia doesn't have to live a life of misery.

I tug at the ropes, hoping the wood at my back would have given way between the ground and my heavy weight, but I should be so lucky.

Fucking Saint James family having good quality shit. Almost any other chair would have broken, but of course not this one.

And where the hell are those assholes? Surely, they should be here by now.

I try to shuffle toward my desk. Maybe if I can just get to my computer, I can track them. It won't be easy without the use of my hands, but I've worked with less.

By the time I get to the desk, I'm out of breath and sweat drips down my bare chest. Why does this chair have to be so fucking heavy?

But I'm running out of time. They have too much of a head start, and it's making the panic in my veins that much more prominent.

The elevator dings, but I can't see who's walking through the apartment from the way I'm facing. It might be one of Kyle's men coming to finish off the job, although he seems like the kind of guy who would get sick satisfaction out of forcing me to live with my failure, knowing there's no way I'm ever going to stop looking for Mia.

Footsteps grow closer, and I hold my breath despite myself. I'm not afraid of dying. There's nothing I'm afraid of except for losing Mia again. Everything pales in comparison to that, and honestly, if it came down to me living and Mia dying, I would follow her every single fucking day of the week.

"Fuck," Elijah grumbles as he slices through the ropes at my wrists. "Are you hurt anywhere else?"

I roll onto my back, staring up at the tattooed asshole I've come to not despise over the last few weeks. "Took you long enough."

He rolls his eyes. "Don't get your knickers in a twist. Rayne and Storm are pursuing the car Mia was shoved into with Everett running point. The assholes disabled the elevator, and it took Everett a minute to get it back online remotely."

I breathe a sigh of relief as I shove myself to my feet. "They have eyes on her?"

He nods. "We have from the second they walked out the front door." He hands me a towel he's pulled from God knows where. "Clean up. I don't want your blood in my car."

I scoff and carefully pat some of the blood from my wrists. Those ropes really did a number on me, but any pain I've felt today pales in comparison to what Mia will feel if we don't get her back.

By the time I've finished wiping the blood from my face and wrists, Elijah is handing me two bandages he seems to have pulled out of thin air and an earpiece that I assume he had in his pocket before he turns on his heel toward the elevator.

I follow after him, and by the time we reach the parking garage, I've wrapped both wrists up and have the earpiece settled in position.

"You got him?" Everett asks.

"Yep, he's about to bleed all over my car." Elijah stops next to a black sports car, and I round the hood to climb inside.

"I am not," I snap. "Can someone give me an update on Mia?"

"Rayne and Storm are in pursuit. They haven't let the car out of their sight, and I've confirmed several times through traffic cams that she is in fact still in the car."

I let out a breath. They've done this more than once. They know how to follow someone, but I won't feel better until the car Mia is in is within my own sights.

"Where are they headed?" Elijah asks.

"We think the airfield, but we can't be sure just yet," Everett tells us. "They hit some roadwork, which we think made them have to reroute and that slowed them down."

"Thank God," I breathe as Elijah turns the car on and tears out of the parking garage like he's a fucking race car driver. Hopefully I'm still alive by the time we get Mia back if this is how this asshole is going to drive.

"We have a team at the airfield just in case. As soon as you triggered that panic button, we fanned out across the exit points of the city to make sure there was no way they were getting her out," Everett explains, and I swear to fucking god I've never been more grateful to other people as I am right now.

They didn't have to help us. Hell, I'm not even sure I would have if our roles were reversed, but I definitely misjudged these assholes all those years ago, something I'll never be able to take back.

"We're on our way," Elijah says, his eyes darting around the street before he takes off down the road, and if it wouldn't make me look like a pussy, I'd be tempted to hold on for dear life.

We're coming, Mia. Hold on for me.

Shattered Promises

Fifty-Six

I sit quietly in the back seat, my hands bound with zip ties that dig painfully into my flesh, but I'm numb to the physical pain because what I feel inside is so much more excruciating.

No amount of time with Ace would have been enough. Even if we lived to be one hundred and one and died in each other's arms, it wouldn't have been enough. We could live a thousand lifetimes side by side, but the moment we were torn apart at the end would still hurt more than any physical pain I'm capable of feeling.

Silent tears fall against my cheeks, but Kyle and the asshole guard aren't paying attention. They're too busy barking orders into the phone and cursing every time they get rerouted. If I didn't know any better, I would think this was planned. That somehow the Saint James family have enough sway within the city that they can set up roadblocks anywhere they please, and hell, that may be the case, but not in this instance. I'm not lucky enough for that.

We come to a stop, and I chance a look around at where we are. We're still in the heart of the city, and the longer we remain on these streets, the better chance I have to escape.

I watched as they put the fucking child lock on the doors, so I know for a fact I'm not going to be able to slip out of the car while we're stopped, but maybe someone will see me bound through the tinted windshield.

There are men in bright vests, and I notice a huge hole in the road ahead of us. Okay, the Saint James may have pull, but I don't think anyone has this much pull.

"For fuck's sake," Kyle growls. "We need to get the hell out of this city."

"I'm trying," the guard snaps. Why the hell don't I know this guy's name? "We should have killed him so he couldn't come after us."

"There's no fun in that. The fun is in making him live without his precious sugar. Isn't that right, Mia?" He peers over his shoulder at me, but I'm already looking down at my bound hands like the good girl he taught me to be all those years ago.

"Yes, sir," I say quietly, falling back into the role I played for so many years as if I haven't missed a beat.

He makes a pleased sound at the sight of my obedience before turning back to the front of the car. "Turn around, let's go another way."

The guard sighs but does as he's told, and my glimpse of freedom is left behind. I got lucky once, and I know more than most that I will never get that lucky again. I imagine I'll be punished for running from the Lombardi family, but there's a chance they don't think I was involved in the escape, in which case I may be safe. We'll just have to see how things play out from here.

"You know, Mia. You should have been mine long before now." Kyle turns around, and I immediately drop my gaze again. It will take a bit of time to get used to keeping my head down, but I'm sure after the first few hits I'll learn pretty quick. "You may look at me."

I let out a breath and do as I'm told, meeting his dark eyes, and a chill moves through my body. How many nights were these the eyes that watched me fall asleep? How many days did they watch as my body was beaten and hurt? I almost wish I could disobey him and look away and look anywhere but into his soulless eyes.

"You never should have been sold to those idiots in Florida." He shakes his head with annoyance, and my brows pinch together in confusion. "I didn't broker the deal, you see. It was a man we have been training at The Factory so some of us can take a bit more time to ourselves. You can't imagine how hard it is always having to be on like that."

I stare at him for a long moment, my head spinning with the idea that he's talking to me, his victim, about how hard his job is, training women, just like me. But he's serious, and I snap my mouth shut before a snarky response can fall from my lips.

"Anyway, I left you in the care of some of our trusted men in order to take some time off and get my home ready for you. After Cyrus, you were always meant to be mine. I wanted to give you some time to get over the things that sick fuck did to you, so you would be good as new by the time I brought you home."

This man is fucking delusional. That's the only conclusion I can come to as he continues to sprout bullshit like he truly believes it.

"By the time I came back to work, our men had betrayed us by touching you, and you'd been sold to Lombardi. And I'm sure you understand he's not the kind of man you break a contract with."

I nod, even though the idea of selling human beings is still wild to me. It shouldn't be, seeing as I've been sold multiple times in my life, but that doesn't make it okay or make it make sense.

"The best thing that ever could have happened is that you were extracted at the same time as the woman that psycho Tommy is in love with. I didn't think the boy was capable of love, men like us aren't. But I suppose it could be infatuation. Perhaps she just has a golden cunt."

"Tommy is nothing like you," I snap before I can stop myself. I know better than to backchat, and yet I can't stop the words before the escape.

His eyes turn dark, and before I can think to flinch, his fist flies toward me, but I manage to duck out of the way before he can make contact with my face.

"Come here, you little bitch," he growls, shoving his large body between the seats to reach for me.

"What the fuck, Kyle?" The guard swerves the car, and I realize, although the SUV is large, it's not big enough for him to be chasing me around the car without causing an accident.

Kyle continues his advance on me, and I quickly dive to the

other side of the car, holding myself against the window as best I can to avoid him from reaching me. If this works, I'll have much bigger problems than just a fist to the face, but it'll be worth it.

The car swerves again as Kyle's knee hits the guard, and I catch sight of a red light ahead that we're careening toward. It's the middle of the night, but there's a chance there are police out at this time. In a city this large, there has to be at least one patrol around here. I hope.

"You know you're going to be punished for running," he growls.

I kick out at him, shoving him further into the guard in the hope of keeping them both distracted, but he gets hold of my ankle and drags me toward him.

"You know better than this, Mia. You know the more you resist, the more it's going to hurt."

"I don't fucking care," I snap as I use my other foot to shove myself back toward the window. The red light is getting closer, and the more the car swerves over the road, the more I wish I had a seat belt on, but death would be a far kinder fate than marrying Kyle just to inevitably be killed. A man like him could never keep the same woman around for long.

The anger in his cold, dead eyes should scare me, but it doesn't. Not anymore. After surviving Cyrus, there isn't much he could do to me that would be worse than him.

I flick my gaze to the windscreen and see the red light just as we pass through it, but what I don't notice is the car speeding through the same intersection.

The impact is immediate—the feel of my body being jolted as I desperately try to find something to hold on to with my bound hands. The sound of screeching metal and cursing, quickly followed by the car spinning out of control.

I watch with wide eyes as Kyle is thrown into the back seat, his body making a crunching sound that is far from natural, but I keep myself as far away from him as I can. Just in case.

Glass breaks around us, and it takes me a moment to realize the pain in my skull is a direct result of the broken glass.

I reach up with both hands and wince as I touch the spot that hurts most, and when I bring my hands back in front of myself, I see blood coating my fingers.

The car finally comes to a stop, and I hold my breath. If the window is broken, I might be able to reach out and open the door, or even crawl out of the window. I might be able to escape.

When I turn my attention back to the men in front of me, I'm staring into Kyle's furious gaze, and my breath stutters in my chest.

"You're going to regret that."

FIFTY-SEVEN

E lijah drives like he has a fucking death wish.

Every corner he takes is sharper than the last, and I'm beginning to wonder if we're going to make it to Mia alive.

Everett has been giving us regular updates, which is giving me some semblance of calm, but I won't feel settled until I have my woman back in my arms. After all this is said and done, I don't know how I'm ever going to be able to let her out of my sight. I was struggling before. But now? Now that she's been taken from me while I was there, while I was tied up and rendered useless? I don't know how I'm going to recover from that.

"What the hell are they doing?" Rayne says and startles me from my thoughts.

"What's going on?" I ask.

"As soon as they turned around at the last road closure, they started swerving all over the road."

My stomach gurgles with uncertainty. "Can you get any closer?"

"Not without drawing suspicion to ourselves," Storm tells us.

I nod despite them not being able to see me. I get it. I've done my fair share of surveillance when my computers couldn't give me the answers I needed, but it does nothing to settle my anxiety about Mia and her safety.

"Everett, can you change this light up here to green?" Rayne's voice is nervous. There's something he's not saying.

"Don't we want to slow them down?" Elijah asks.

"We do. But they're not slowing down. Whatever is going on in that car is distracting the driver, and I think they're going to run straight through," Storm explains.

"Fuck," Everett mutters, and I hear the comforting tapping of a keyboard. I'm not cut out for being in the field. I do much better behind a screen where I have eyes on the whole situation. But right now, there's nowhere else I'd rather be.

"Everett?" Storm asks with more urgency, and my stomach bottoms out with panic.

"Change the goddamn light," Elijah snaps. "We're a few blocks away, and I can see the fucking green light from here."

"I'm trying. But funnily enough, hacking into the city's servers isn't a fucking walk in the park."

I rub my hands over my face and spot the blood seeping through the bandages around my wrists. Better not let Elijah see it, or he'll be angry about something else.

"They're speeding up. I don't know what the fuck is happening in the car, but I don't think it's good," Rayne says.

Fuck. I almost wish they would stop giving updates because each one is dragging me closer and closer to the edge of my temper.

"Okay, it's changing now." Everett breathes out a sigh of relief, and I let one out right alongside him.

I haven't taken a fucking holiday in my life, but after this, I think I'm going to need one.

I watch with bated breath as the light two intersections ahead of us turns yellow, and I almost allow my body to relax, but then I see the car speeding toward the intersection. The one who is definitely not going the speed limit in order to avoid the red light.

Everything moves in slow motion as I watch the SUV Mia's in speed through the intersection at the same time the car ahead of us does, and then it's spinning out of control, and my heart leaps straight from my chest.

Please don't let all of this be for nothing.

Please let her be okay.

Please don't make me lose her after all we've been through.

I'm praying to a god I don't believe in for a miracle, because I know I won't survive losing her.

Fifty-Eight

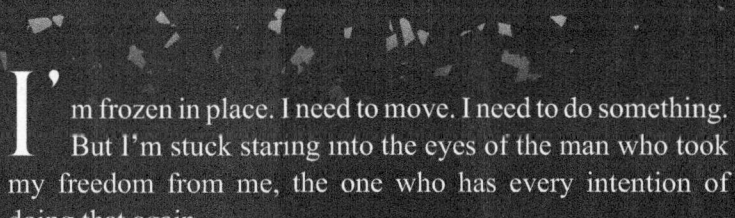

I'm frozen in place. I need to move. I need to do something. But I'm stuck staring into the eyes of the man who took my freedom from me, the one who has every intention of doing that again.

The guard groans in the front seat, but out of all of us, he's the only one that was wearing a seat belt, so I can't imagine he's as hurt as Kyle is.

Kyle's shoulder is out of place, his head is bleeding from where he must have hit it during the accident, and his eyes are heavy, like he's struggling to keep them open despite the anger staring back at me.

He's in no position to hurt me, and that allows me a moment to breathe.

"Get us the fuck out of here," Kyle demands, and my breath stutters in my chest.

The words take a moment to sink in, as if it never occurred to me that the crash wouldn't total the car and they'd still be able to get me out of the city.

"The steering column is shot, we're not going anywhere in this car."

As calmly as I can manage, I reach for a piece of broken glass on the seat beside me. If he catches me, I'll be in for a world of hurt I'm sure not even I can imagine, but I have to try. I have to do something to stop this from happening.

I refuse to remain a bystander in my own life.

I refuse to let men who wish me harm to rule my life.

And I refuse to go back to being the perfect little doll they trained me to be.

I take a deep breath, forcing my hands to steady around the glass. It bites into my palm, and the pain allows me to ground myself. To remind myself why I have to do this. After all I've been through, I deserve to choose my path, and I have no qualms killing the asshole who started this journey for me. I'll never miss a wink of sleep.

I swallow past the lump in my throat, and then I force my aching body to move. I'm going to be feeling that accident for a while, but at least I won't be recovering from it in a tiny room on a mattress on the floor, not if I have anything to say about it.

Kyle notices my movement and turns his attention to me, but it's too late. I slam the glass shard into his throat before I can think better of it, before he can stop me, and before my body can protest against the movement.

The shard slices through his skin with ease, almost so much so that I question my own strength, and his eyes turn wide as he stares at me like he can't believe I've done it.

I reach for another piece of glass and slam it into the other side of his neck, watching as blood drips from the wounds I've inflicted, and there's a sick sense of satisfaction knowing I'll be the last person he sees as he takes his final breaths.

The guard is too busy trying to free himself from his seat belt to pay us any mind, and although Kyle is sputtering as he tries to breathe through the blood that drips from the corners of his mouth, he seems oblivious to it.

I lean forward, my wrists still bound by the zip ties that slice into me painfully, but the pain only fuels me. "You will never hurt another woman," I say quietly, my voice coming out even and clear despite how hard my heart beats in my chest. "You're going to die for your sins, for every woman you hurt, for every human being you sold like fucking cattle. You're going to drown in your own blood, and I'm going to watch every second of it to make sure you never have the chance to hurt anyone else."

He tries to speak, but he can't force the words out, and that only makes my smile grow. Maybe I am just as crazy as Tommy and Ace turned out to be, but I don't care. I only wish I could drag out his pain, that I could make him feel an ounce of what he's inflicted on others during his miserable existence.

"Hey, what the fuck?" The guard finally notices us, and I lift my gaze to meet his, not bothering to wipe the smile from my face.

I swipe another piece of glass from the seat beside me, not

even flinching as it digs into my palm and blood weeps from the wound. "There's no saving him, the glass is lodged in his carotid artery, and I intend to let him die slowly and painfully. But you don't have to meet the same fate." Even as the words leave my mouth, I know Ace won't let him live for the part he's played in this, but at least I won't have his blood on my hands. I feel no guilt for killing Kyle, just the same way I wouldn't care if I killed every single man that ever touched me without my permission, but I'd rather not have the death of a man who only threw me over his shoulder and carted me out of an apartment on my conscience.

He glances between me and Kyle, weighing up his options, before he reaches for the door handle, exactly as I suspected he would.

I tear my eyes from his retreating form and look down at my blood-stained hands. The crimson is a stark contrast on my skin, but I don't allow myself to lose myself in it, not when I have to make sure Kyle dies.

I look up at him, and a smile tips up the corners of my lips at the blood staining the front of his shirt. It's really flowing now, and the life is beginning to drain from his eyes.

"Did you ever think one of the girls you trained would be the one to end your life?" I muse as I reach forward and tear his shirt open. The buttons fly across the wrecked car, but I'm too focused on the task at hand to care.

His bare chest comes into view, and he watches me carefully as he tries to work out what I'm about to do next.

A laugh claws its way up my throat, and for a moment I pause to consider the idea that I've finally lost my mind, and hell, that may very well be the case, but I really don't care.

"Part of me wishes you would be forced to live with these scars, but I'm glad after tonight you'll never breathe the same air as another woman again. You don't deserve to live. You don't deserve to take another breath."

I force air into my lungs and for my hands to steady around the shard of glass. My own blood drips onto his bare chest, and I make a mental note to be careful I don't get his blood on any of my wounds because I don't want to catch anything from this asshole.

I bring the glass toward his chest and don't hesitate to carve into his skin. I relish in the way he thrashes and how it makes him bleed more. I bask in the knowledge his life will end any moment now at my hands. But I don't allow any of it to distract me from what I'm doing.

I slice into his skin over and over again. It's surprisingly easy to write a word in someone's flesh, so I decide, why stop at one?

Rapist.

Sick fuck.

Cunt.

Kidnapper.

Trafficker.

Word after word, I write, and there's a part of me that feels infinitely lighter as each one appears on his chest.

His screams come out as gurgles, but I pay him no mind. I'm

surprised he's even lasted this long between the blood loss and the pain, but I'm glad he has.

I want him to be dragged to hell, kicking and screaming in agony because he deserves no peace. Not after all he's done.

I sit back and look at my handy work. I'm impressed with what I've been able to achieve with my hands bound in front of me, but now it's time to end this.

"As fun as this has been, Kyle, I have places to be. A busy man like you understands, I'm sure." I parrot his sentiment from earlier. "Enjoy your trip to the pits of hell."

His eyes widen as I reach for the glass in his neck and drag them both from his throat, watching as blood gushes down his bare chest and over the words I carved into his flesh.

The life fades from his eyes, but I don't move until I'm sure he's dead. Until I know for a fact he's dead and there's nothing that can bring him back, closing a chapter of my life I wish I could forget, and opening the one I've longed for my whole life.

Shattered Promises

FIFTY-NINE

ACE

The car has barely stopped when I throw myself out of it, the need to get to Mia stronger than my own sense of safety. I hear Elijah scoff as I slam the door shut behind me and move toward the spun-out car in the middle of the intersection.

Rayne and Storm climb out of their SUV as I run toward the scene of the crash, completely ignoring the other driver. He's mostly in the right, apart from the fact he was speeding and may have killed my reason for breathing, but I don't have the time to give a fuck about him.

The closer I get to the car Mia was in, the more dread moves over my body, grasping me around the throat until I can barely breathe.

What if she's hurt? Or worse?

What if I didn't get to her quickly enough?

What if she's not in the car?

There are a million what-ifs filtering through my mind, and all of them have an uneasiness settling over me.

The driver's side door swings open, and Rayne draws his gun with a trained precision I'm sure he's used repeatedly in his line of work, but right now I'm grateful for it.

There's only one seat I'm certain Mia's not in, and it's the door that's just opened.

Todd climbs from the car, his hands up in a sign of surrender. "I'm not armed."

Rayne chuckles. "I wouldn't give a fuck if you were." He's barely through his sentence when he fires two quick shots into his chest.

Normally I would have wanted him tortured for the part he played in all this, but right now all I care about is getting to Mia. Everything else is a waste of my time.

I reach for the backseat door at the same time it swings open. and I immediately step back, ready to draw the gun I pulled from Elijah's glove box, only to watch Mia step out of the car, covered from head to toe in blood.

Her hands are bound with a zip tie in front of her, and it looks way too fucking tight, but I can deal with that once I find the source of the blood.

I rush toward her, wrapping her up in my arms before I can consider that the hug may hurt her. I just need to be reminded she's okay and that I'm never going to ever let anything happen to her.

A quiet sob breaks from her throat and it only makes me hold her against me tighter. I should free her wrists. I should check her for injuries, but I can't. I can't fucking move, not when I have my whole fucking world in my arms again.

Out of the corner of my eyes, I notice Rayne and Storm walk around the car, their own guns drawn as they prepare themselves to be face-to-face with Kyle and whatever he's planning to use to escape, but I'm too focused on my girl.

"Are you hurt?" I ask quietly.

"No. Not really. I hit my head in the accident, and I have a cut on my palm," she whispers.

"Then where's all this blood from, sugar?"

I peer down at her as she opens her mouth to respond, but then Rayne's laugh distracts us both. His head pops up on the other side of the car, and he nods toward the cab. "You gotta see this. Your girl has a sadistic streak you're going to want to see."

My brows tug together as I look between her and the car, but it's the smirk playing at the corners of her lips that has me dragging us both toward the car.

The moment my eyes lock on Kyle spread out across the back seat, his neck punctured in two places, and his chest and stomach carved up like a fucking jack-o'-lantern, I'm stunned.

It takes long moments to process what I'm looking at, and the fact that the meek woman who has been terrified of her shadow her entire life, not only killed a man, but enjoyed doing it.

I glance down at Mia and find a small smile on her lips as she looks over her handy work.

I've loved this woman for as long as I've known love existed, but right now, as I stare down into her blue eyes with the splatter of our enemy's blood coating her skin, I've never fucking loved her more. She took her power back. She killed the man who caused her unimaginable pain. She ended a life to allow her to live hers. And I've never been so fucking proud of her.

Rayne rounds the car, slowing his approach so he doesn't spook Mia. I swear she flinched once when he was walking toward her, and he's known ever since to slow down. Before I realize what's happening, he plucks her out of my arms and wraps her up in his own. "I'm so proud of you, kid. I can't wait to show Emerson your handiwork. She's going to be proud too."

"That I killed a man?" She half laughs.

"That you killed your tormentor and set yourself free."

I shake my head and steal her back. If it were anyone else apart from someone I've watched stalk their own wife around constantly, perhaps I could find it in me to be jealous, but Rayne has no interest in Mia, not in that way at least.

Mia shakes her head, but her eyes flicker to the dead body in the backseat without an ounce of remorse.

Elijah peers into the back seat and lets out a whistle. "Girl's got skills. Might have to send her to work with Tommy."

"Not fucking likely," I snap.

He chuckles. "Is Doc still off work this week?"

Storm nods and taps something out on his phone. "I'm organizing for our backup doctor to meet you at the penthouse." He pauses and looks up at us. "Are you okay to go back there?"

The question isn't for me, and I look down at Mia, waiting for her response. "I'm fine, honestly."

I pull her against me and hold her tight, relishing in the feel of her in my arms. I don't know how I'm going to let her out of my embrace anytime soon, even if that means I'm working with her sitting in my lap. I could live with that, hopefully I can get her on board.

"Let's go, sugar." I steer her toward Elijah's car, and I hear him curse about her being covered in blood. But the man has more money than God, he can afford to have his fucking car detailed. I'm sure as hell it won't be the first, or the last, drop of blood to get on the interior.

All I care about is getting my woman home and washing that asshole's blood from her skin, even if she does look so pretty covered in the evidence of her revenge.

SIXTY

MIA

A ce hasn't let me even an arm's length away since we left the site of the accident, with Rayne and Storm telling us they'd deal with the bodies and the car.

I'm still not entirely sure if I'm numb to the situation I'm in, or if I actually feel no remorse for killing someone, but either way, my mind feels quieter than it has in years.

The constant fear I've felt, the horrors that have continued to haunt me for all these years, the sadness and dread I had when I thought I would be forced to go back to that life.

It's all gone, and the peace is better than I ever could have hoped for.

Ace leads me into the bathroom off my bedroom and turns the shower on, testing the water until he's happy with the temperature before turning his attention back to me.

He reaches for me, and I don't stop him as he drags his blood-stained shirt from my body. I wish I at least had more clothing on during this ordeal, but I guess I've been in worse situations wearing less.

He doesn't pause as he drops into a crouch and carefully pushes my panties down my legs and carefully helps me out of them. The tenderness he's showing me is so at odds with the man he shows the rest of the world, and it makes my heart burst with love for him.

I've always been grateful for Ace and the care he's shown me, but right now, it feels like so much more.

He makes quick work of his own clothes, shoving his sweatpants down his legs and reaching behind him to tug his shirt off in one fluid movement, leaving his perfect, tattooed body on display for me.

"Don't look at me like that, sugar." He smirks.

"Like what?" I ask innocently, my voice hoarse from the tears I've shed.

"Like you're thinking of all the ways you want to fuck me."

I shake my head, but the smile playing on my lips gives me away. That's exactly what I was thinking.

Ace guides me into the warm spray, and I immediately sigh as the water washes Kyle's blood from my body. The white tiles at our feet turn crimson, and I watch as it drains away, searching for the guilt that doesn't seem to come.

"The first person I ever killed was a guard at The Factory," Ace tells me as he reaches for the sponge and shower gel, his eyes focused on the task at hand. "It wasn't long after we left, and Tommy and I had a plan to take out the low-level guys first and work our way up, dismantling the organization piece by piece. Tommy had recently started working for the Saint James family, and they'd just taken down my business in Chicago, so I wasn't talking to him at the time. We grew apart after we left, but we never lost sight of our goals.

"I hunted this guy for days, but it took so long for me to get him alone so I could end his miserable existence. But I remember when the time came, I hesitated. I'd never get that piece of my soul back, you know?" His eyes flit up to meet mine, and I nod my understanding. There's a part of you that changes when you kill someone, even when they deserve it. "He begged for his life, swore he would turn over a new leaf, you know, the usual bullshit that cowards spew when they're about to meet their maker. But then I remembered why I was doing it, and the hesitation melted away.

"At first, I wondered how long it would take for me to feel guilt for what I'd done. I'd left a mother to plan her son's funeral when she had no idea why he had to die, but how could I feel guilt when it was the right thing to do? When I was taking down an organization that had hurt so many people. That would end up hurting you, even if I didn't know it at the time." He pauses as he gently moves the sponge over my body, showing more care than most would think a man his size could. But he's always been a gentle giant to me, even if the rest of the world has always been shown his brutal side.

"I've killed a lot of people, Mia, and I won't lie to you and tell you that it didn't change me, because it did. But every single death at my hand had a purpose."

I nod, a small smile tugging at the corners of my lips. It seems ridiculous to be smiling right now, after I was dragged out of this apartment kicking and screaming only a few hours ago. After I was abducted and could have died in that accident. After I sliced a man open and carved into him like he was a pumpkin at Halloween. But the fact that Ace knew what was on my mind, that he knows me so well that he knew where my head was at, just proves how perfect we are together. I always knew we would be, but apparently his brand of fucked up and mine play nicely together.

"I don't feel anything about killing him other than relief," I say quietly, voicing it out loud for the first time.

Ace nods as he drags the sponge down my arm and pays extra attention to my wrists and palms to wash away any dirt from the wounds. "I'm sure Emerson would know more about this, but I would imagine that's the case for most people that kill their abusers. You set yourself free, sugar, and you never have to feel guilty or apologize for that."

"It feels like I can breathe again," I whisper. "I don't know how to explain it any better than that. Even when I knew I was safe with you, he was hanging over my shoulder, telling me my time was limited, that it wouldn't be long before I was back to being starved and beaten and used. And now...now it's like the life I always dreamed of, the one with you by my side. It's a reality, and there's no one waiting at the sidelines to steal it away from me."

Ace smiles down at me as he brings one of his hands up to cup my cheek. "I know exactly what you mean, sugar, because that's how I felt the day I found you in Florida."

Tears gather at the corners of my eyes, and I do nothing to stop them from falling. They're happy tears. Tears of relief, and I don't have to hide them anymore.

Ace tosses the sponge to the corner and wraps me up in his arms, enveloping me with his huge body as if he's reminding me I'm safe here, with him, in his arms. "I don't know what our future looks like, sugar, but I know we're happy. I know that every morning I'm going to wake up with you in my arms, and every night I'm going to fall asleep knowing how fucking lucky I am to have you."

I smile against his bare chest because, for the first time in eight years, I can allow myself to dream. "Even if we could see the future, I wouldn't want to," I say quietly. "I just want to live in the moment with you."

SIXTY-ONE

The doctor comes and goes, and I like him even less than I like Doc, which is really saying something. I hope that asshole comes back to work soon, because he's the only person I seem to trust with my woman.

Mia's hands are wrapped in bandages after being thoroughly washed and disinfected, and both our wrists have been tended to, as well as our head injuries. Neither serious, thankfully.

I watch Mia from the kitchen, a blanket pulled over her lap as she chats excitedly with Emerson and Snow, while Rayne and Elijah hover in various parts of the apartment.

They came over with the guise of making sure the security system was up to speed after Kyle and the guard hacked it and killed the guard in the security room, but they're really here to keep an eye on their women.

Emerson's watches Mia closely—the whole reason I asked her to come over in the first place. I like to think I can read her better than anyone else, but what she's been through today has been traumatic, and although she's nothing but smiles and laughs, I want to make sure she's not burying her emotions because they always have the tendency to crop up later.

Elijah approaches me, his gaze flicking to where Snow is curled up beside Mia with a cup of tea resting on her knee. "Security is back up and running. Everett is putting an extra fail-safe in just in case, but I can't see anyone else coming after the two of you."

"Thanks." I push a glass of whiskey toward him even though it's nine in the morning. It already feels like the longest day of my life. "I wanted to talk to you and Snow about buying this place. Mia seems settled here, at least for the moment, and I would rather not uproot her again. Plus, the state-of-the-art security system definitely allows me to sleep better at night."

He nods. "Snow and I were talking about that on the way here. We'll get it all sorted once the dust has settled."

I let out a breath that at least one part of our future is settled for the moment. I like the idea of not knowing what's coming at us next, but I also want to make sure Mia has somewhere safe to find herself again.

"Everett wanted me to let you know that we may have a location on Cyrus. He's got a couple of our men traveling to Greece to check it out. What would you like us to do if it is him?" he asks.

I flick my gaze to Mia on the couch and smile. "Bring him back to Chicago. I have plans for him, seeing as I got to play no part in Kyle's death."

"I thought as much. I'll keep you updated."

"Thank you for all your help," I say, and although I expect to resent the words as they fall from my lips, I find they come easily. They've done so much for us, and maybe some of my dislike for the family as a whole has bled away.

He shoots me a look as he downs his drink in one hit. "I don't do this mushy shit, so I will say this once, and then we never talk about it again." He pauses to reach for the bottle, and I push it closer to him. "The Saint James family is a close unit. They choose people to become their family, and they protect them fiercely. You saw how they came together when Clara was in danger. When we rescued Mia, the two of you got into that club, even if you have never seen eye to eye with them before." He downs another shot of whiskey. "Which is why they're going to offer you a job. You can take it or not, whatever the hell you want to do, but Everett needs help now that he's got Summer and isn't available twenty-four-seven, and they're generally better to work for than the scum of the earth you're used to."

"You know I used to do a lot of work for your family, right?" I quirk up a brow.

"Like I said, scum of the fucking earth."

"I'll think about it."

He nods. "I thought you'd want to consider your options, which is why I'm giving you the heads up before they ask."

"Thanks, man, for everything."

"Don't mention it." He claps a hand on my back and gravitates toward Snow. I think to the outside world, watching these men interact with their wives may seem overbearing, but maybe they've just never felt a love so deep they can't breathe without the other person.

I've felt that kind of love, and I've lost it, so I'll spend every single day for the rest of our lives making sure Mia knows there's nothing I wouldn't do for her.

Shattered Promises

SIXTY-TWO

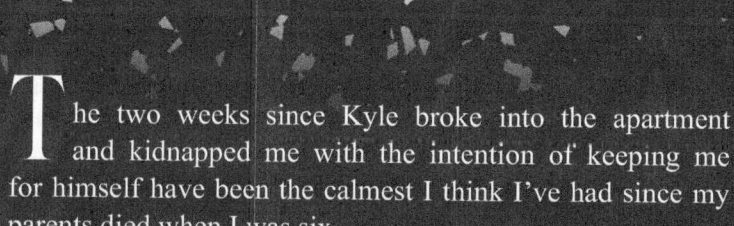

T he two weeks since Kyle broke into the apartment and kidnapped me with the intention of keeping me for himself have been the calmest I think I've had since my parents died when I was six.

There's no one looking for me, no one intending to hurt me, no reason to look over my shoulder, and it's nice. Really fucking nice.

My hands and wrists have healed, with the scars beginning to fade with the crazy moisturizing routine Snow insisted would help them fade. But from what she told me, she knows from experience, and I'm willing to believe whatever she says.

Ace has been giddy since we woke up this morning, which is not a word I would often use to describe him. He insisted we get up and go out, which was my first sign of something weird happening because he usually dreads me stepping foot into the elevator, something that has been evident during the two therapy sessions I've attended since I killed Kyle.

It was time to speak to someone, time to get some help so I can go on to live a normal life, and so far, it's doing wonders for me, even in such a short amount of time.

Ace sits across from me at the diner down the road from the apartment building. Apparently this place has the best pancakes in Chicago, and from the first bite, I can confirm that's definitely the case.

But the whole time I'm eating, Ace's leg is jiggling, his eyes darting out the window like he's waiting for something.

A week ago, I would have thought it was because he was looking for a threat, but he's calmed down a little since Everett reminded him that I still have two guards with me every time I step foot out of the house. It's an unnecessary precaution, but one that will be in place until they've been able to eradicate every person involved in my captivity.

I tried to tell Ace it was unnecessary to do that, that it's unlikely any of them will be coming after me now that Kyle is dead, but he was insistent that he couldn't allow people who hurt me to live. And who am I to argue with a man who wants to kill for me?

"Ace, what's got into you?" I ask as I shove the last piece of pancake between my lips. My relationship with food began to improve almost as soon as the threat of going back was taken off the table. I'm not saying it's good every day, because that's certainly not the case, but so far this week I've been able to eat two meals a day.

"I have a surprise," he beams, as if he's been holding in those words ever since we left the apartment.

A smile tugs at the corners of my lips, and I look down at the yoga pants and sweater I pulled on as I was being shuffled out of the apartment. I pull my bottom lip between my teeth and nibble at it as I try to tell myself Ace would have told me to change if I wasn't dressed appropriately for whatever the surprise is.

"You look perfect, Mia," he tells me, and when I look up, I'm staring into his eyes.

He throws some bills onto the table and takes my hand as he drags me out of the diner so quickly I can barely say a thank you to our waitress. Once we're on the cold street, he pulls me under his arm and walks us back toward the apartment building.

"The surprise isn't sex, is it?" I scoff as we step into the private elevator to the penthouse.

"Would it be so bad if it was?" He stares down at me with mischief in his eyes.

"I mean, no. But if that were the case, you've woken me up with a surprise three nights this week." I laugh, and the sound almost feels foreign to my own ears. I went so long without hearing it, and I never realized just how much I missed it.

He winks at me as the doors to the elevator slide open, and I spot the group of people standing in the middle of the apartment with bright smiles and a drink in their hands. Above them is a banner that has my brows pulling together in confusion.

Welcome Home.

I look up at Ace as he ushers me out of the lift and toward everyone standing in the living room. I find Tommy and Clara

441

standing at the front, his arm wrapped possessively around her waist and her smile so huge it could almost blind someone.

Emerson and Rayne are beside them in a similar position, and behind them, Snow and Wynter are fussing over baby Summer, while Everett and Elijah flick their gazes between us and them. The only Saint James missing is Storm, but that doesn't totally surprise me. Or at least until he and Ayvah appear from the kitchen with two glasses of champagne each, handing one to Ace and me.

"What's going on?" I ask quietly as I take the glass from Ayvah and thank her quietly.

"We're having a housewarming party," Storm answers for him, and my brows pull together in confusion. I'm missing something here.

Ace pulls me into him and presses a kiss to my temple. "I bought the apartment from Snow for us. This is officially our home."

I stare up at him with wide eyes as I consider the words he's just spoken before looking around at the people who have come to celebrate. "You bought an apartment for us?"

He nods, doubt creeping into the moss green. "I thought, seeing as you already feel safe here, that this was a good place to start our lives together, if you don't—"

Before he can finish his sentence, I'm throwing my arms around him. He bought me an apartment. We needed a home, and he made it happen.

"Thank you, Ace," I whisper against him. "Thank you for constantly making my dreams come true."

He holds me tightly against him, his arm banded around my lower back as he presses another kiss to the top of my head. "I have a lot of years to make up for, but this is just the beginning."

Doesn't he get it? He's already given me everything I ever could have hoped for.

Sixty-Three

This surprise is much more unhinged than the housewarming party was, but I think she's going to enjoy it just as much.

Mia's gaze bounces around as she wraps her arms tighter around herself. The tunnels that run beneath the city are always cold and damp, but I imagine seeing them for the first time is daunting.

"You're not bringing me down here to kill me, are you?" she asks with a nervous giggle, but surely she should know by now I would never do anything to hurt her.

I shake my head and tug her closer to me. I don't love having her down here. It's a fucking cesspool, and that's why Tommy has used it as his killing field for all these years.

I lead her through the tunnels, keeping a close eye on every corner we take. There aren't many people who know this place even exists, let alone how to access the tunnels, but I'm not willing to risk Mia.

There's a scream from somewhere deeper, and Mia stops in

place, fear taking hold in her gaze. "Ace, I don't think I should be down here."

I turn to her and cup her face in my hands. "You know you're safe with me, sugar. I'll never let anything hurt you."

She lets out a breath and nods, but the terror is still in her eyes as they dart over the damp bricks around us. This is the first and last time I'm ever bringing her down here.

I take her hand and lead her deeper into the tunnels. That scream was probably from Tommy's torture room, but that's not where we're going today.

We're going to one of the spare rooms the Saint James brothers use when they do their own dirty work.

I'm vibrating with barely contained energy. I have no idea how Mia is going to react to this surprise or if she's going to want to leave the second we walk through the door, but regardless, I'm giving her the option.

Her hand tightens in mine each time she hears a scream, but she doesn't pause again, allowing me to guide her closer to where the sound is coming from.

"Is this some kind of weird sex thing?" she asks, the nervousness in her voice making the joke fall flat, but I chuckle nonetheless.

"It can be if you want it to be." I smirk down at her, and a smile tips up the corners of her lips. When I told her to dress like she would for a workout, I was not prepared for her to step out of the bedroom in the tightest fucking yoga pants I've ever seen, paired with a long black shirt and a puffer vest that I want to tear from her body almost as badly as I want to take my next breath.

I tried before we left, and she batted my hands away as she walked to the elevator, ready for whatever surprise I was taking her for.

We reach the door and I stop us, turning her to face me and planting my hands on her hips to hold her in place. "If you get in there and don't want to do this, you can say so. You don't have to do anything you don't want to."

Her mouth pops open, and her brows tug together in confusion. "I don't understand—"

I shake my head and reach behind me for the door, opening it slowly and carefully watching her expression as her gaze bounces off the small room, and then her eyes land on him and they darken.

There's my girl.

Sixty-Four

C yrus fucking Kemp.

He spent years tormenting me. Years dragging me closer and closer to my own death. I don't think he ever would have killed me, he had too much fun breaking me for that, but I likely would have ended it eventually. There's only so much one person can handle before they can't take anymore, and every day I spent with him was a step closer that I got to that limit.

Seeing him tied to a chair, his face bleeding, and his eyes downcast shouldn't bring me this much comfort, and yet the idea that he's not hurting anyone else the way he hurt me allows me to breathe a little easier.

I look up at Ace and find him staring down at me with concern, but I step around him into the room in the hope it will give him some peace.

I have to admit, when Ace led me into a weird stairwell in the middle of a vacant lot, I was a little concerned about where we were going and why. But this makes sense. You can't exactly leave one of the world's richest men tied up in the middle of the city and not expect his people to be looking for him.

My eyes move over the table set up a few feet from Cyrus, an array of tools laid out neatly. Rows of knives, screwdrivers, and even something that looks a little like a kitchen blowtorch. It's quite the collection of implements, and I find myself looking over my shoulder at Ace.

He's standing by the door, his eyes watching my every move like he always does, but there's an extra sense of urgency, and I find myself wanting to give him comfort.

"How long has he been down here?" I ask evenly. I feel nothing but hatred for the man bound beside me, and I certainly don't feel bad for him being tied up like the scum he is.

"Elijah and Tommy brought him down here last night and roughed him up just enough to shut the asshole up," Ace tells me, and I nod, my fingers moving over the instruments in front of me.

I'm so distracted by the shiny shiver knives that I completely miss Ace moving across the room until he spins me to face him, a look of concern tugging at his brow. "I wanted to give you the option to kill him to give you the power back, but if you don't want to, you don't have to. I'd be more than happy to end this fucker's miserable existence for everything he did to you."

I shake my head. I don't know that I've ever been an especially bloodthirsty person, and I'm certain I would never have been at the hands of killing someone before I was taken by The Factory, but now? Now I want to be the last person the assholes who hurt me see as they take their final breaths. "Thank you," I whisper.

His shoulders fall slightly, the relief obvious on his face as he flicks his gaze to Cyrus. He's awake, but only barely. I'm sure that will change once I start slicing him up the way he used to do to me. I want him to feel every bit of pain he inflicted on me. "Do you want me to leave?"

"No. Please stay."

He nods and turns the chair in the corner around, ready for him to take a seat, but before he does, he picks up a bucket I hadn't noticed and dumps it over Cyrus's head, the asshole squealing like a pig as the ice water washes over him. I mean, that's one way to wake him up.

"That's better," Ace murmurs as he moves over to the seat in the corner and swings his leg over it so his front is pressed against the backrest, his chin leaning on his arms across the top of the chair.

He looks too fucking hot doing that, his tattooed arms making me lose myself for just a moment until he gives me a knowing look. "Keep looking at me like that, sugar, and we might have to give Cyrus here a show."

My breath stutters in my chest as I expect panic to wash over me. But it never comes. Ace is joking. Or at least I think he is, and even if he isn't, I know he's never going to let anyone hurt me the way Cyrus let his friends hurt me.

I shake my head and turn back to the table, giving myself a few moments to steady myself. I dreamed of this moment so many times as I lay awake at night, waiting for him to come for me. I thought about taking his knife off the table when I was kneeling at his feet as he ate and shoving it through his chest.

I thought about stealing his gun as he forced me to go down on him and shooting him in the dick as punishment for all the things he did to me. If there's a way to kill someone, I've probably thought about killing Cyrus like that. But now that the choice is upon me, I can't decide which one will cause him the most pain.

I turn to the man who caused me unspeakable pain. His blonde hair is slicked back with sweat, his dark eyes just as cold as I remember them. Even tied up and at my mercy, he looks fucking cruel. "It's been a long time," I muse, leaning back against the table casually.

"You don't have to do this, pet. You know I'll have people looking for me. Do you want to cause problems for your new friends?" His voice is hoarse, and I imagine he spent a good amount of time overnight screaming for help.

"If I don't kill you, they will." I shrug. "And they're far more practiced at making it hurt than I am…kinda like you were with me."

His eyes flash with something akin to fear, but I know better than to think a man like him could feel such an emotion. He's heartless. Dead inside. He has to be to have done the things he has as he made the world believe he's an upstanding citizen.

I swipe a small knife off the table and turn to face him, taking in his naked body. He's not an unattractive man by any stretch of the imagination, but having a soul as black as his could make anyone ugly. His washboard abs are as I remember them, and memories of being forced to kneel in the corner on hard concrete while he did his workouts wash over me.

Fuck.

I close my eyes and breathe in a steadying breath.

I'm safe.

Nothing can hurt me.

Not with Ace just a few feet away.

"You know, I used to imagine killing you all the time. Probably the same amount I considered ending myself. I wished for death more times than I can count." I half laugh and shake my head. "And I'm going to make you wish for death now."

The first slice across his chest is almost too satisfying. I didn't get to take my time with Kyle. It was rushed. Messy. Desperate. But I have all day. Hell, I'm sure if I wanted to keep him alive, Ace could have Doc come in once a day to clean up whatever mess I've made and make sure it doesn't get infected, just so I can do it all again the following day.

I glance over at Ace, who watches me closely, his brows tugging together with a mix of concern and something else I can't quite put a finger on.

I don't want to drag this out.

I want to go home with Ace and show him how grateful I am for this gift. A gift I didn't even know I needed until I walked into this room and saw my tormentor bound and at my mercy.

The knife moves through his skin easily, and I watch as blood drips from each of the wounds I inflict. It's fucking addictive, and for a moment I wonder if Tommy needs any help in his role with Frost Industries.

Then I consider whether it would give Ace a heart attack knowing I was surrounded by criminals all day every day and decide against it.

Cyrus tries not to react, and he does a decent job at it, if I'm honest. Perhaps this is an instance of him practicing what he preaches because he used to expect me to take every single beating without flinching, just accepting what he was doing to my body.

A smile tugs at the corners of my lips as I carve his chest up the same way I did Kyle, but the words are different. I want his body found. I want the whole fucking world to know what the leader of the world's most prestigious chain of banks was doing in his spare time.

Rapist.

Abuser.

Captor.

Owner.

Cunt.

It's only when I approach his lower stomach that his body begins trembling. Either the pain is getting the better of him, or he's worried I'm going to hurt his precious penis. And it's not completely off the cards, but I don't think Ace would want me touching another man's dick, and I'd rather never have that vile appendage near me ever again.

Cyrus pants as he watches my every move, and I can't help but enjoy the fear in his eyes. Does that make me as sick as he is? Or is this part of taking back my power?

"Having fun, sugar?" Ace's voice is amused, and when I turn back to him, his eyes match as they roam over me hungrily. I look down at my hands and arms, the blood of my victim coating them. "Fuck, you look hot as hell right now, baby. I can't wait to get you home."

A small moan escapes from my throat, and a blush hits my cheeks. Maybe Ace is just as fucked up as I am.

I let out a steadying breath and reach across the table for a tool I recognize too well. One that was used on me time and time again during my training. A cattle prod. And I fucking relish in the way Cyrus's eyes flare with fear.

Fuck. It's intoxicating.

"I bet you think you broke me," I muse as I turn the device on as high as it will go and immediately jab it into his side.

The scream that fills the chamber brings a smile to my lips, and I don't even try to analyze how fucked up that makes me.

"I thought I'd never be able to enjoy sex because of all the things you did to me." I shake my head and zap him again. "But all it took was a man who loves me, and I have my body and mind back."

"You're fucking crazy!" he yells.

I laugh, my head falling back. "That's rich coming from you. So far, I haven't done anything you didn't do to me. So which one of us is crazy?" I raise a brow in challenge. "You used to get off on my pain. Used to fucking thrive on it. And how many women were there before I came along?" I question. If there were others and they're still alive, I need to know. I need to help them the same way Ace and the others have helped me.

"Does it matter?" he challenges. "They're all broken beyond repair."

I force the prod into his ribs and hold it there for long seconds as bolts of electricity force their way through his body and his screams bounce off the walls. "Like I was broken beyond repair?" I snap. "The thing is, that sure, I was broken. Fucking obliterated after what you did to me. But all it took was the right person to piece me back together."

Arms wrap around my waist and tug me back against their hard body. The tension in my body releases the second I'm in his arms, and I drop the cattle prod onto the table where it was before. "You don't know how fucking sexy you are right now, sugar," Ace growls against the shell of my ear, and I feel the evidence of his arousal against my ass.

I watch as Cyrus stares at us, his eyes so fucking cold it looks like he's already dead. Soon enough he will be, and then that's one less scumbag to hurt innocent women.

"How's the used-up pussy?" Cyrus challenges Ace, and I feel him stiffen behind me. He's trying to provoke him to take over because he thinks death will come quicker. But he doesn't need to know that he's going to take his last breath sooner rather than later. "She was never much of a fuck when I had her, but she could give a mean fucking blow job."

A laugh bubbles in my throat before I can swallow it down because he's grasping at straws. He's doing everything in his power to make us kill him quickly, but he's only going to make things worse for himself.

Ace's body relaxes slightly behind mine, the sound of my amusement must be giving him an ounce of comfort.

"The world will be a better place once you're not in it, Cyrus." I reach for a knife on the table and bring it to his throat, watching in delight as fear flares behind his cold dead eyes. "Enjoy hell."

Before he can say another word, I slice across his throat, watching with bated breath as blood falls from the wound and his eyes flare with panic. I don't know why I remember the time he told me this was the most effective way to kill someone after he caught one of his guards looking at me a little too long, but the irony isn't lost on me.

"Bend forward, sugar," Ace murmurs against my ear.

I look over my shoulder at him and meet his heated gaze. Oh fuck. "Ace…"

"Do as you're told, Mia. Don't make me ask again."

SIXTY-FIVE

I have to have her.

There's something so fucking sexy about watching my woman torture the man who held her captive, who kept her away from me for so many years, and I've been rocking a hard-on since she picked up the first knife.

I truly thought neither of us could be as fucked up as Tommy is, but it's pretty clear the insanity didn't miss us.

There's a hint of trepidation in Mia's eyes as she looks over her shoulder, but I refuse to go another moment without being balls deep in my woman, and I want this asshole's last moments on earth to be filled with how much he didn't break her.

I want him to see her pleasure as the life fades from his eyes.

Mia complies slowly, leaning forward until her back is arched and she's a few feet from Cyrus. Without hesitation, I tug her yoga pants and panties down before making quick work of my belt. I never fuck her without foreplay, and it's not something

I plan to make a habit out of, but right now I can't wait. Not when my cock is aching for her and Cyrus is bleeding out before our eyes.

As soon as my jeans and boxers are down, I press my aching length to her entrance and groan. "You're so fucking wet, sugar. Did hurting him make your pussy ache for me?"

"Yes," she moans, pushing herself back against me, almost as desperate for me as I am for her.

I rest one hand on her hip as the other guides my cock until I'm notched just inside her, her pussy pulsing around me before I can even push inside. Fuck, she's perfect. So fucking perfect.

Without hesitating, I push forward and bottom out inside her, dragging a cry from her pretty lips, and I watch as Cyrus's eyes widen. He's gasping for air as his throat fills with his own blood, and the sight of the life fading from his eyes only makes me fuck Mia harder.

"Ace!" she cries out as her pussy clenches around me, and I groan at the feeling. Her perfect fucking cunt is about to pull me over the edge well before my time.

I hold her hips in a punishing grip that I'm sure will leave bruises. Good. I'm never going to get sick of seeing my marks all over her skin.

Mia gives me all her trust as she allows me to fuck her without her being able to hold on to anything, and that only makes me take her harder.

"Such a perfect fucking pussy," I grunt.

"Ace, please, I need to come, please."

I smirk and drop one of my hands from her hip, making quick work of pulling her up until her back is against my chest and my hand is wrapped around her throat. "Is that better?"

"Yes," she moans. "Fuck, Ace."

"I've got you, Mia," I croon against her ear and tighten my grip on her throat, making her pussy tighten impossibly around me. "Mm, my girl sure does love being choked."

She nods against me, and I drop my face to the sliver of her shoulder that peeks out from where her vest has fallen during my manhandling. I bite into the flesh so hard, the taste of copper touches my taste buds, but that's also what brings her right to the edge, her pussy fluttering around me as she struggles to hold her orgasm back, knowing she's not to come without permission.

My perfect girl.

"You ready to show this asshole how pretty you come for me as he chokes on his own blood?"

"Yes, fuck, Ace. Please let me come." Her plea falls from her lips, and I watch as the light begins to fade from his eyes.

I press my lips against her ear. "Come for me, sugar. I want it to be the last thing he ever sees."

Her body tenses in my arms and her pussy pulses around me, dragging me right over the edge with her as I fuck us both through our releases. Her wetness drips down my balls and the tops of my thighs, but I don't care. I'll wear her cum like a badge of honor.

The roar that escapes my throat is barely human as I pump her full of thick ropes of cum. There's a part of me that hopes it takes root, that it beats the implant in her arm, and I'll see her swell with my baby, but we're not ready for that yet. We might never be. And if we're not, that's okay. Mia spent eight years not getting to enjoy life, and if she chooses she would rather not have kids, that's a decision I'll be happy with, as long as she's content with the life I give her.

We both drag in heavy breaths, but I make no attempt to withdraw. I never do. I would live with my cock inside her tight pussy if I could, but sadly, I don't think that's something she would get behind.

Neither of us says a word as we watch Cyrus lose his battle and his eyes slip closed at the same time his body goes completely still, and I feel as Mia relaxes against me as she realizes her tormentor is gone, that he's dead, and he'll never get to hurt her again.

"Let's go home, sugar," I whisper against the shell of her ear before pressing a kiss to the sensitive skin just below.

She nods and flinches slightly as I withdraw. She'll be sore for the rest of the day from being taken so roughly without a warm-up, and that brings me a weird kind of satisfaction.

I help her pull her yoga pants up her legs before I tuck myself back into my pants and make quick work of doing up my belt.

When she turns around, her eyes are filled with tears as she stares down at the blood coating her hands and arms. Before she can say a word, I tug her over to the spare bucket of water in the corner and use a piece of cloth Tommy keeps in here for waterboarding to wipe the evidence of that asshole from her skin.

"You okay, sugar?" I ask quietly as I cup her cheek in my hand.

She nods and leans against my hand, a few stray tears escaping down her cheeks. "Thank you for giving me the world."

A smile tugs at the corners of my lips, and I wrap her in my arms, holding her so tight I'm surprised she can breathe. "Don't you know you're the one who gave me everything I never dared to hope for?"

EPILOGUE

MIA

FOUR YEARS LATER

I dump my handbag on the side table beside the elevator and move into the apartment, kicking my high heels off as I do.

It was a long day.

A really fucking long day.

When I decided to go into trauma counseling, I knew it would be challenging. I knew it would break my heart more often than not. But I did it because I wanted to be what Emerson was for me when they first brought me home to others in need, and every day is just as rewarding as it is challenging.

I finished my degree a few months ago, and I've been working at the Chicago Center for Women and Children, the second location Emerson and her father opened.

The smell of my favorite meal hits my nose before I can reach the kitchen, and I find Ace by the stove with Fergus, our cat, under his arm as he stirs the pasta sauce.

He learned to make it for me not long after I killed Cyrus and I finally decided what my future was going to look like. He said he wanted to be able to have dinner ready for me after a long day, and most days he makes good on that.

Who would have thought the wall of a man was capable of cooking after all the years he spent eating nothing but takeout?

"You're home late," he comments, but when he turns to me, there's only concern etched in his brow. He lets Fergus down, and the gray rag doll runs straight to me.

I scoop him up and breathe him in. The day Ace came home with this cat, I swear I fell in love with him all over again. He said Emerson had told him that animals can be good for emotional support, and the next day I had a kitten.

By the time I look up, Ace is wrapping me up in his arms, sandwiching Fergus between us, but he's used to it at this point. This is a pretty normal afternoon for us.

"I missed you today, sugar," he murmurs.

"You miss me every day," I point out. "And I always miss you."

Ace started working for Frost Industries not long after I was taken and he bought the apartment for us. But the problem is that he works from home more often than not, and he still struggles to let me out of his sight, but he loves what he's doing. It's all the shit he loves without the added pressure of working for people that might kill him for what he knows.

He pulls back and gives Fergus a quick scratch on the head, and I catch sight of the gray titanium around his left ring finger, bringing a smile to my lips.

We got married on a spring afternoon. Just the two of us and Tommy and Clara. Part of me wanted to have everyone with us, but another part longed for the little family I found all those years ago, with the addition of Clara, of course.

It was the happiest day of my life.

"Emerson brought Gale in this afternoon. He's getting so big!" I tell him as I take a seat on the other side of the kitchen island.

Ace's gaze flashes with something that he quickly masks and that I was oblivious to until a few months ago. I don't know if I was just so busy with school that I didn't realize there was something missing in our lives, or if I just wasn't ready to admit it was something I wanted after everything I'd been through. "That's because he eats as much as Rayne does." He chuckles at his own joke, and I shake my head.

"Do you want to know why I was late home?"

"Because you were cuddling a baby?" he guesses.

I shake my head slowly, my bottom lip disappearing between my teeth. "I had Doc come to the center this afternoon—"

He doesn't let me finish before he's back around the island, his hand falling straight to my forehead. "Are you okay? Are you sick? You should have told me you weren't feeling well."

I slap his hand away and laugh. This man is as overprotective as they come, but I wouldn't have him any other way. "I'm not sick, stop that."

"Then why did the giant asshole come visit?"

"He's not an asshole." I sigh.

"Not to you, maybe," he grumbles.

I carefully push my cardigan off my shoulder, wincing at the pain in my arm. The anesthetic didn't last anywhere near as long as I was hoping.

Ace spots the bandage immediately. "What the hell happened? Did someone hurt you? Why the hell didn't you call me?"

"Will you let me finish?" I snap. "I had Doc come to the center to take the implant out of my arm."

He stares at me for long seconds, his mind working overtime, and I watch with amusement. This is way more fun than I thought it was going to be. "It wasn't due to be changed for another year."

"I know."

"Then why would you…" He trails off, and then a smile so bright I swear it almost blinds me takes over his handsome face.

"I want to try for a baby," I say quietly. I haven't felt nervous or anxious about this decision at all since I made it last week, but right now, I feel vulnerable. What if I've misread Ace? What if that's not what he wants?

Before I can take my next breath, he scoops me up and starts toward the stairs.

"Where are we going?"

"To start trying for a baby."

I laugh, tears filling my eyes. "It'll take a couple of months for my body to right itself from the implant."

"That doesn't mean we can't practice." He winks.

"What about dinner?"

"Fuck dinner." He turns back only for long enough to turn the stove off, and then we're on our way back up the stairs.

By the time we reach the master bedroom, I'm desperate for him, like I am most days, and his eyes roam over my body hungrily.

He prowls up the bed until he's hovering over me, his hardness pressing into my lower belly. "I can't wait to see you carry my babies, sugar."

"Babies? I said baby," I point out, trying to keep the smile from my face.

"We'll see about that." He chuckles darkly.

I wrap my arms around his shoulders and tug him down until his lips are just an inch from mine. "I love you, Ace. Thank you for making all my dreams come true."

"I promised I would spend my whole life making you happy, sugar, and I meant it." His lips crash down on mine, and I lose myself in his kisses, desperate for him to make good on his promise, but he pulls back abruptly. "We have to move."

"What? Why?"

"This place is a death trap for a baby."

The laugh that tumbles from my throat is light and free of the weight of the world I used to carry on my shoulders. There was a time I thought I'd never laugh again, when my life was so dark, so miserable that I wished for death, and more than anything, I wish I could tell that version of myself just how good life can be.

I wish I could tell her that if she just holds on a little while longer, every single one of her dreams will come true. That she'll feel love and warmth, that she'll finally belong somewhere.

But seeing as I can't go back and tell her all of that, instead, I thank her for being brave enough to fight.

Thank you for reading Shattered Promises. I hope you loved this story of survival, and the final book in the Tainted Love series.

If you enjoyed Shattered Promises, it would mean the world to me if you could review it on Amazon, Goodreads, Social Media, carrier pigeon, I'm not fussy.

You can follow me on Facebook and Instagram or my reader group, for sneak peaks of future projects, including release dates and secret snippets!

My next release is the first book in the Syndicate of the Legion series, In the Shadows, is now available for preorder.

Want more dark romance by Montana Fyre? Start Frost Industries, A Bestselling Dark Mafia Series, with When it Raynes!

ALSO BY MONTANA FYRE

Frost Industries (Dark Mafia Romance)

When it Raynes

Dead of Wynter

Fall of Snow

Before the Storm

Tainted Love (Dark Romance)

Severed Ties

Fractured Vows

Shattered Promises

Syndicate of the Legion (Dark Why Choose Romance)

In the Shadows (Coming 31 May 2024)

Forbidden Pleasures (Dark Romance)

Trust in the Fallen

Pray for the Damned (Coming Late 2024)

Forest Falls (College Hockey Romance)

Wager

Flight

Fight

Betray

Made in the USA
Las Vegas, NV
16 June 2024